To Dan

Thanks so much

for your support.

All the best to

you,

Love,

[signature]

7-18-15

Bibsy

Brenda Ross

AuthorHouse™
1663 Liberty Drive
Bloomington, IN 47403
www.authorhouse.com
Phone: 1 (800) 839-8640

Published by AuthorHouse 05/05/2015

ISBN: 978-1-4969-6589-9 (sc)
ISBN: 978-1-4969-6590-5 (e)

Library of Congress Control Number: 2015901168

Print information available on the last page.

This book is printed on acid-free paper.

Acknowledgements:

Honoring the Memory of:

Elizabeth "Bibsy" Barnes

Eleanor Barnes, Kenneth Archibald Risien Sr. and Sarah Barnes Risien, Mary Barnes James and James Barnes

Letitia Grierson

Heartfelt appreciation for the encouragement, support, critique and guidance along the path to completion:

Mayra Bloom, Patricia Dunn, Jimin Han, Susan James and Carol Clarke.

To those who provided invaluable assistance along the journey:

Jacqueline Cherry, Ellen B. Holtzman,
Venita Whidbee-Jordan, Steven Edwards,
Dolores Remsen and Gayle T. Williams.

To Aunt Cora, at 95-years-young, a family treasure who continues to bequeath her gift of love and laughter daily.

Special Acknowledgements to:

Tasha M. Ross, for a lifetime of being a part of, believing in, and supporting *Bibsy.*

Evelyn Risien Taylor for suggesting I self-publish *Bibsy.*

To Nicole, Tasha and Nekiera

with all my love.

Chapter One

Langston County is tucked into the southern tip of New York State, wedged between the Hudson River and the New Jersey state line. And it was home to Jake Tucker. Fishing, hunting, drinking and being independent were what he cared most about in life, and Jake always said he could do none of those things living in the city. Except drinking. When he did go to New York, he'd raise enough hell in that town to make the thirty-mile trip more than worth it. He'd drive down in his rickety Ford pickup with about fifty dollars burning the insides of his back pocket and try his best to overthrow Harlem single-handedly. When Jake drank, his light-skinned complexion took on a deep red overcast and he became loud and boisterous. His larger than average size made bartenders think twice about trying to throw him out, and besides, he was free enough with his money that they just let him drink himself into a stupor and sleep it off in a back room somewhere. That was how he met Bibsy. She was in the upstairs room of the Big Top Club on One hundred forty-first Street and Lenox Avenue when he came to one spring morning.

"'Bout time you woke up," she said when his eyes first opened.

He was flat on his back and staring at the ceiling. He turned his head to focus on the female figure whose voice he'd just heard. As his blurred vision began to clear, he saw a dark-skinned woman seated at a small table against the wall, her legs crossed. She was wearing just a slip and one of the prettiest smiles he'd seen in a real long time. The smile jolted his memory, and he not only recalled the previous night but the exact moment a certain woman walked into the Big Top and caught his attention. His facial expression relaxed with the memory of them closing down the bar in a corner booth. He had a weakness for pretty dark-skinned women, and the fond remembrance of the night before prompted him to make an effort to pull himself together. She had a tooth missing on the side, and he liked that too. Although he wasn't a religious man, Jake believed that God didn't make nothing or nobody perfect. To him, that missing tooth made her more like real folk. She had a paper coffee cup in one hand and a lit cigarette dangling from the other. Instinctively, Jake's eyes scanned the room for his pants where he had his money.

"Your pants are right here on the floor where you left em," she said pointing with her toe.

Her sassy style combined a rare self-confidence and courage, qualities he took an instant liking to. He hated playing guessing games with people. Especially women. Bibsy reached for her garter belt and stockings and slipped them on while she talked. "Your money's still there. What's left of it. I took out five dollars to give to the barkeep for the fifth of whiskey you asked for and this room." She picked up the half-empty bottle from the floor and placed it on the table, then wiggled her petite frame into her dress and sat down again.

Jake leaned over and snatched his pants from the floor beside the bed and thrust his hand in each pocket. Finding he still had fifteen dollars surprised him; usually these slick New York women left him high and dry the next morning. Sometimes he'd have to borrow two quarters for the toll back across the George Washington Bridge. He got out of bed, pulled on his pants, grabbed the fifth of Jack Daniels and brought it to his lips.

"Gotta take a hair from the dog that bit ya." Jake wiped his mouth with the back of his hand. "Come on. Let's find someplace ta eat. You know of any good places to eat around here?"

Bibsy was about to tell him as she stood, when Jake suddenly lifted her into the air grinning at her. Then just as unexpectedly, yet tenderly, brought her down close to him and hugged her. Though initially puzzled by his impulsive embrace, she returned the gesture. Squeezing harder, he swayed from side to side saying, "Why, you're jus a lil bit of a thing. What's your name?"

"I got a lotta different names, you can take your pick. My mother named me Elizabeth, but most people call me Tiny. My family calls me Bibsy though."

Jake put her down and the top of her head reached no further than the middle of his upper arm, yet she had the kind of figure that would provoke a man's comment.

"Bibsy! What kind of a name is that?" He laughed.

"Look," she said, "Don't you go makin fun of my name or we won't never get along. That name was given to me by my sister's kids and I'm proud as hell of it."

"Well, if that's the name you're proud of that's what I'm gonna call you if you don't mind…even though I'm not family. It's different, and I like it…Bibsy, hmm…I like that."

Jake asked the waitress behind the counter for three orders of sausage, home fries, eggs, biscuits and coffee; one order for Bibsy and two for himself. Neither of them talked much while they were eating. After their meal Jake belched loudly. A few patrons turned to look but that didn't faze him. Bibsy just smiled. She thought he was a real character and found herself falling for this man. His rough ways seemed to endear him to her. She thought it took a lot of courage not to care what people think about you. She felt really big that morning; being around Jake made her feel as though her small size swelled to as big as his. She felt important too. Folks took notice of them when they walked down the street and she liked that a lot. They took a stroll through the neighborhood, laughing and talking like old friends. He told her about his two boys, Jake Jr. and Robert, and how he'd been raising them by himself since their mother died seven years ago. He went on about life on The Beach in upstate Haverton, an inlet on the Hudson. "I guess to some it jus looks like a buncha rundown shacks. No 'lectricity. No inside plumbing. But I'll take it over this," Jake's gaze swept the brownstones on either side of the avenue, "any day. People up there, Cousin Gus, Aunt Carrie and all the rest, are jus plain hard-workin honest folk. I got my own chickens, a coupla pigs and vegetable garden. The garden's doin kinda poor cause the boys don't take care of it like they should. We live off the land too, eatin wild turkey, coon, rabbit, squirrel and sometimes even pheasant and deer if we're lucky."

He had a shepherd named Rain who went with him everywhere, except when he came to New York because all the noise and people made her too jittery.

"There's lots of hard work but we all chip in and help one another and make a nice life for ourselves."

"It's hard work walkin around in these high heels too." Bibsy pulled off her shoes and continued in her stocking feet. "My feet been killin me."

"What you wear em for if they hurt your feet?"

"That's the style."

"Goin round with hurtin feet is the latest New York style! Lawd, what they gonna come up with next?"

Bibsy playfully hit Jake on the arm and started laughing.

"You live around here?" Jake asked. "You don't act or talk like you from round here."

"I been up here four months now. Got a job in a dress factory downtown. Folks around here call it the Garment District. I was born in Maryland. Ellicott City. That's right outside Baltimore."

"Guess you like it better back home, huh?"

"No indeed. Me and two of my sisters were brought up by nuns in a Catholic home. My mother visited us regular but she was too busy workin to raise us. My sister Martha, she's the oldest and the one I'm livin with now, was brought up by my father and his family. Seemed like nobody wanted us three after Mom and Pop split up," she continued, "Pop took the oldest cause they was old enough to help out doing chores. Guess we was too small to be of any use to him." Bibsy took a deep breath, stopped in the middle of the sidewalk and stared at Jake. "Look at me goin on and on about all the sores in my past. People who've known me for years don't know as much of my life as what I've already told you. You sure are easy to talk to, Jake. If I'm borin you jus say so. Won't hurt my feelings one bit."

"Unh, unh. You ain't borin me none. If you was, I'da changed the subject a long ways back. To tell you the truth, it's kinda interestin. Never met nobody who grew up wit nuns like that. I see em in town every once in a while. Dressed in all that black and lookin real spooky. But I don't believe I ever seen no colored tend they church. Seen them Puerto Ricans that's new in town go there, but not colored."

"Oh, there's a good amount here in New York. Seems a lot more in Baltimore though. My older sister Ruth even joined the convent to be a nun herself."

"No foolin?"

"Yep. Right after school was finished she stayed with em and joined the all-colored order, the Oblate Sisters of Providence. It's right there in Baltimore."

Jake smiled. "Now that must be a sight. A colored nun."

"She swears things is changin in the church, but I'd had enough when I was growin up with em. Boy, I wouldn't care if I never did no housework again in life. We kept that place so clean you could eat off the floor. They didn't have no janitors or handymen at St. Cecelia's. Didn't need none with the way they worked us." She took a deep last drag from her cigarette before flicking it into a puddle in the gutter. "Never did understand how Mom could belong to a church that didn't even allow colored folks to sit past the last three pews. Never will understand that."

"Hey," Jake said spotting an ice cream parlor across the street, "Let's stop for some ice cream, then head over to the truck." Afterwards, they walked down the street licking double scoops of cherry vanilla ice cream, in silence. When they finally got to the pickup, before he let her in Jake stopped and looked down into Bibsy's face, his expression suddenly very serious. "You comin home with me."

"Oh, I don't have nothin to say about it one way or another, huh?" Bibsy retorted in her usual sassy tone. She climbed into the pickup and he slammed the door.

Jake went around and got in on the driver's side. "Damn, damn, damn," he shook his head slowly, still gripping the steering wheel until the knuckles on his huge hands whitened.

"I don't like bein told what to do. I can make up my own mind about things."

"Never said you couldn't," Jake snapped back. "I wasn't tryin to tell you what to do. Look, I ain't gonna ask you no better'n that. That's me. What'd you think I was gonna do, tie you up and shove you in the back of the truck?" His nostrils flared when he talked. For a long while, only quiet and warm sun filled the cab of the truck.

"You know I can't cook a lick. Never could. They tried to teach me at school but I just couldn't get the hang of it. Really wanted to learn too, cause I like to eat. But I burnt up food so bad they kept me outta the kitchen and gave me other chores to do, like sewing and stuff."

Bibsy could see Jake's chest heave as he stared through his side window. But it was hard to tell whether he was listening at all, he appeared so distant at that moment. When he did speak his voice didn't sound the same, the mindful way he picked his words.

"That's why you think I want you ta come live with me...so you can cook and clean and look after my boys? That's what you think?"

"Well, I don't know. It's just that I guess most men expect for a woman to know how to cook at least a little." She hesitated before adding, "And I ain't much on housekeeping neither. I told you that already."

"Look," he said, with his voice becoming more serious, "You don't wanna go? Say so right out. Don't try ta be all slick about it."

"No, Jake. I wanna go, I really do. I jus don't want you thinkin you're getting somebody you're not."

"Huh!" A slight trace of a smile played at his right cheek. "I can cook. Cook damn good if I do say so myself. And I'll teach you, cause I ain't gonna have you burnin up food I spent half the day huntin for." He grabbed Bibsy closer. "And as for that house, it ain't useta bein kept up no how, and that's fine wit me. I want you. Not what you can do. Don't forget that."

Bibsy's whole body broke out in a grin.

"You ready now?" Jake put the key into the ignition.

"Yeah, Jake. I been ready."

Chapter Two

Bibsy directed Jake the several blocks to her sister Martha's apartment. She and her husband, Kalvin introduced Bibsy to the classier cliques within New York's colored society. Champagne and supper clubs were their signature style. The two were regulars at the Savoy and Renaissance ballrooms where they often drew crowds as they took the fox trot and waltz to ever greater heights each weekend.

Although the glitz and glamour was nice in the beginning, Bibsy found most of their crowd too stuck on themselves to enjoy her company, or she theirs. But that didn't stop Kalvin and Martha from steadily trying to fix her up with their friends from the minute she hit town.

Bibsy left Baltimore after she broke up with her last boyfriend who she discovered was married and had a family after going out with him a few months. Coming on the heels of several failed relationships, she thought it was time for new scenery altogether, then called her sister in New York.

Because Martha hadn't grown up at St. Cecelia's, Bibsy and her eldest sister had only now gotten to know each other. A friendly outgoing type, Martha easily made Bibsy feel comfortable in her home where laughter was natural and easy. At the orphanage, or "The Home" as their mother preferred to call it, just waking up in a good mood was reason enough to attract unwanted attention from the nuns. Being around Martha's feisty children though, made her long for her own. Cheryl, the only girl and the oldest, tried saying, "Aunt Elizabeth," when she was a toddler, but it came out as "Bibbat" and pretty quickly shortened to "Bibsy", where it eventually stuck for everybody.

It only now dawned on her that leaving to go off with Jake meant she wouldn't be seeing Martha and her family every day; and she knew she'd miss them something awful, especially since it was the first real family life she'd been a part of. In the numerous times retelling the story of how they arrived at St. Cecelia's, her sister Mary always blamed their father, because she remembered him bringing them there without their mother present. Bibsy and Cora followed her lead, knowing her recollection was more reliable since she was the only one old enough to have any memory of it. Mary said she and Cora were laughing and giggling all the way because they'd never been on a trolley before. Their father carried six-month-old Bibsy in his arms. Once he dropped them off, she said he left right away without so much as a glance back, in spite of Mary screaming her head off for him to not leave them there alone.

As Bibsy got older, at each of those strictly enforced third-Sunday family visits at St. Cecelia's, she regularly asked their mother, Letty, why they had to be there and her answer was always the same – she had to work as a live-in cook because it paid more money. But Bibsy never understood the connection between money and being with your children and resented the answer just as much as their circumstance. Bibsy often wondered if their mother even missed them at all and felt she should have done whatever it took for them to be together.

Their father died when Bibsy was in high school and she remembered only a few people attended his service. With his children lined up like wooden soldiers in front of his casket, Bibsy was disoriented by the emotional battle she experienced seeing her father for the first time while he lay in a casket.

They got out of Jake's truck and he said, "I forgot to ask you…I ain't steppin on nobody's toes, am I? Let me know if I gotta go into my Joe Louis act to get you outta here."

"Humph! Ain't nobody got no claim on me."

"Uh, huh. I heard that before too."

"Will you stop that! Ain't nobody gonna...." as they reached the median dividing Lenox Avenue, Bibsy's gaze casually traveled from the cobble-stoned street upwards and she came to a dead halt. "Oh no."

"See. Lookathat. Couldn't even get it out your mouth good fore you run up on somebody. Where is he? And it's such a nice day to be knockin somebody out."

She couldn't help laughing. "Jake, you're crazy."

"Sure, you think it's funny. It's my neck in a noose and you're laughin. You could at least point the man out so I can size im up."

"I ain't talkin about no man. I'm talkin about Mrs. Tilson. Looks like she's gonna fall outta that first floor window from stretchin to see who you are. Over there." Bibsy nodded in the direction ahead. "She'd be alright if she didn't mind everybody's business so much."

"Oh shoot. Is that all?" Jake tucked Bibsy's hand under his arm and they marched across the second half of the avenue.

When they got to the stoop, Bibsy said good morning and introduced Jake to Mrs. Tilson.

"Last night's party lettin out kinda late ain't it, Tiny?" Poised to register any juicy gossip, Mrs. Tilson's eyes widened with expectation.

“It sure did turn out to be one fine lookin day, didn’t it m’am?” The power in Jake’s voice snatched some of the brilliance from Mrs. Tilson’s eyes.

“Uh, yes, it did.” The woman managed before saying, “That’s why this is my favorite spot. Right here. Every day. Ain’t that right Tiny?”

“It sure is. If your face ain’t at that window, things just ain’t the same around here.” Bibsy pinched Jake’s arm.

“I kinda look forward to Sundays though. Things is so much quieter round here. Folks ain’t hangin round waitin for the number to come out. The children even plays quiet, so not to get they nice clothes messed up. Your sister’s kids just got home from Mass a little while ago. She keeps them kids so nice. I think it’s wonderful how they go to church every Sunday. You know....”

Jake nudged Bibsy toward the steps. “Nice meetin you, m’am. Enjoy the rest of this fine day.”

“Same here, Jake. And, Tiny, you tell Martha hello for me and to please remember me when she bakes bread again.”

“I will.” Bibsy shouted from the hallway.

Bibsy found herself chuckling as she climbed the first two flights of stairs bringing them to her sister’s fourth floor apartment. When she and Jake reached the third landing, a faint aroma of greens loitered in the air.

"Sister's already cooking supper."

"How you know that's comin from her place?"

"I know it is. You wanna bet?"

"Unh, unh. You sound too sure."

When they got to apartment 4B, Bibsy pulled out her key and opened the door. The humid air was deliciously heavy from the pot of smoked ham hocks and collard greens in the kitchen. Early Sunday dinner was law in Martha and Kalvin's home. The children were used to Bibsy staying out all night on weekends. Even all weekend. But she'd never brought her company home and they were curious about the tall stranger.

Eight-year-old Cheryl whispered, "Bibsy, is that your boyfriend?"

Smiling, Bibsy introduced Jake to Kalvin and the three children, Cheryl, Buster and William. The men shook hands.

"Nice family you got here, Kalvin. And that's a nice lookin six-shooter, Buster. You fast with that thing?"

Buster showed off his best draw, then smoothly put his toy weapon back into its holster as Martha came into the living room wiping her hands on a kitchen towel.

"Jake, this is my sister Martha I been tellin you about."

"How do you do, ma'am?"

“Fine thanks. Martha’ll do just fine, Jake. Or you can call me Sister like the rest of the family.”

“What do you mean like the rest of the family? I sure don’t call you Sister, that’s for sure.” Jake and Bibsy laughed at Kalvin’s sly grin.

“We won’t get into all of that, Kalvin. You two care for anything to eat?”

“No thanks. But whatever you got cookin in that kitchen sure smells good. Collards ain’t it?” Jake was sniffing the air.

“Yes it is. And I stuffed two chickens to go along with that. You’re sure welcome to stay for dinner. There’s plenty. Really.”

“That sure is a temptin offer and Lawd knows I hate sayin no to a good home-cooked meal, but I really can’t stay.”

Martha shot a confused quick glance at Bibsy before saying, “Where you rushing off to on a Sunday, Jake? I thought this was supposed to be a day of rest.”

“Gotta get back and see what devilment my boys been into. And I got a good drive ahead of me.”

Bibsy caught the look Martha and Kalvin exchanged with the mention of his sons and knew they were already passing judgment on him. However, their actions only confirmed it was time to go. By now she was aching to live her own life without scrutiny.

"Well, I can understand that," Kalvin added. "How far away is home, Jake?"

"Bout thirty miles northwest of here. Langston County. Upstate New York a little ways."

"Isn't that where they're building that bridge I read about in the paper?"

"Yep. That's the place. Plenty of work up there now with the bridge and all that highway construction, but it's gonna mess up a lotta things too. Already they sayin you can't hunt cept certain times of the year. Don't know how they spect folks to eat the rest of the year."

Kalvin knit his brow in apparent confusion. "Not too many stores near where you live?"

"Oh, there's stores. But there ain't no need for too many of em. Most folks up there go out and fish, hunt or raise whatever food we need."

Kalvin said, "You're not leaving right this second are you? You at least have time for a drink don't you?"

"Oh yeah. I always have time for that."

"Well come on and sit down a second." He stuck his head out the doorway.

"Baby, will you bring in some glasses and ice for us?"

Jake took a seat on the couch and stretched his long legs under the coffee table clear to the other side of it.

“You know not too long ago during the Second War when there wasn’t no meat in the stores, everybody hunted. You could make money off it. ‘Specially from folks livin in The City.”

“Oh man, do I remember that! There wasn’t a specka meat in the markets then. Not a speck. And when there was, it was so expensive it might as well not even had been there cause nobody could afford it.”

“Folks is sayin pretty soon they’re gonna try to stop us from huntin in the county altogether. Sure will have a time on their hands stoppin me though.”

“You sound like a man who likes hunting for the sport of it.”

When Martha sat two ice-filled glasses and a pitcher of water on the coffee table, Kalvin jokingly grabbed her around the waist before she left the room.

“Nah.” Jake poured more water than scotch into his glass, “Ain’t no sport in it. Not for me anyway. I’m jus too stubborn ta go out and pay for food when there’s plenty right there around me that’s free. Folks will always change the rules whenever there’s big money ta be made.”

“You know what they say, money talks. But Jake, some people see shopping in these supermarkets as a sign of progress.”

"Oh yeah? Tellin me I gotta spend money for somethin I been gettin free all along is progress? That's a good one."

"Judging from Kalvin's mood, you two must've had some time at that dance last night," Bibsy said to Martha when she returned to the kitchen.

"Yeah, it was nice. It was supposed to end at one o'clock but it was just getting good by then. Even the band was having such a good time they agreed to play an hour longer. We had a ball. Bibsy, I was surprised you didn't want to go."

"You two don't need me always stuck up around you, Sis. You need to be alone sometimes. Besides," Bibsy widened her eyes to exaggerate her point, "I had a nice time myself last night."

"So I see." Martha casually rocked her thumb toward the living room.

"First I went to the Regal on Lenox, but things were kinda dull there. So I left and went to the Big Top down the street. They had a nice crowd and things looked like they were kinda jumpin in there, so…"

"The Big Top, Bibsy? Didn't we tell you that place is a dive?"

"Yeah, I know you and Kalvin told me not to go in there, but it looked okay when I peeked through the window. Anyway, I felt like tryin someplace new. I wasn't in the mood for any of those fancy clubs you and Kalvin go to."

Martha didn't mask an impatient tone, "So that's where you met Jake?"

"Yeah. We caught each other's eye soon as I walked in. He was sitting at the end of the bar. I went to the opposite end, you know where it curves around, so I could get a better look. I could feel him looking at me and I glanced over at him a coupla times. Then one of the men at the bar gave me his stool and asked what I was drinking. Before I could answer, Jake was standing there with us telling the man I was with him."

"What'd the man say?" Martha said while unable to control her laughter.

"He said, 'She didn't come in here with you man,' and Jake said, 'I was supposed ta meet her here. Ain't that right baby?' I just went along with it and said, 'Yeah, I was supposed to meet him here.' Then Jake called the bartender over and told him to give the man a drink and paid him. He told me to grab the empty booth in the corner then said to the man, 'Here's your stool back, no hard feelings, right?' "

"Well do tell! If that ain't the height of boldness. What happened after that?" Martha leaned in closer.

"The man just shook his head and grumbled something under his breath and got back on his stool."

"Sounds like you two are having a party all by yourselves." Kalvin and Jake joined them in the kitchen.

"What's the joke?" Kalvin reached in the freezer for an ice tray.

"Bibsy was just telling me how she went into the Big Top last night and a man at the bar gave her his stool and asked what she was drinking and Jake popped up and told the man she was with him."

"I was watchin her from the time she walked in the place. And I believe she was watchin me." Jake stole a glance at Bibsy.

"Well like I always say, if you're slow, you blow. And there ain't nothing slow about this man, I'll tell you that." Kalvin said. "Did your sister also tell you she was going off upstate to live with Jake on a farm?"

"What! Bibsy, you didn't tell me that."

"I was gonna get to it."

"Well, I'll be. When did you decide that?"

"This morning."

"I told you this guy is a fast mover. Didn't waste no time. Last night must've been something else."

"Shh, Kalvin, the kids'll hear you." Martha looked to see where the children were before adding, "It sure must've been some night."

"Now don't you start too, Sister. I'm goin in the bedroom and get my clothes together." Bibsy left the kitchen and headed down the hallway.

"It's not a farm. I'd be stretchin the truth mighty far sayin that."

"I'll tell you something, man," Kalvin objected, "My parents were born in the West Indies and you might convince them there's a difference. But me," he pointed to himself using both thumbs, "Hey, I was born and raised right here in New York City, and any place that has chickens and pigs and vegetables coming out of the ground is a farm to me."

"No, it's a long ways from a farm. We jus raise enough to feed ourselves. Sometimes I sell what I have left over to the market in town. Or just plain give it away. When the weather starts gettin nice like this, we eat mostly fish."

"Sounds more and more like a country farm to me." Kalvin went on. "But then again, I'm strictly a city man. Don't mind going to the country and getting a little fresh air once in awhile. But when you're a homegrown New Yorker, you just can't stay away too long."

"I'm the same way about where I live. Like to get away now and again. Come into The City. But I jus can't stay away." Jake turned to Martha. "Your sister's in good hands. I'm not gonna let nothin happen to her. If she's not happy livin my kinda life, I'll bring her back to you myself. That's a promise. And I always keep a promise."

Stepping away from the flour she just poured into a mixing bowl, Martha sat at the kitchen table, eyes blinking in bewilderment, "It's just that everything is so sudden, that's all. You just met for goodness sakes!"

"You ever get a certain hunch to do something? I got one of my hunches about this and something tells me not to let her get away," Jake said.

"She'll still be here if you come back next week. Or next month," she pressed.

"Martha, calm down." Kalvin said. "Now your sister's a grown woman."

"Yeah I know she's grown. Whew, this is so sudden!" Martha wiped perspiration from her forehead. "I guess she knows what she wants…and once Bibsy makes up her mind about something, that's it anyway. I hope things work out for the best for you two. I really do."

Martha's face was making a completely different statement from the words she'd just spoken, and Kalvin reacted with, "What if....," he paused in search of the right thing to say, "what if, you two give it a week just to think about this. I mean, it'll give you time to sort things through and set things up on your end. And it'll give Bibsy a chance to settle her business with her job and everything."

"Yeah." Jake rubbed the stubble on his face. "I know this sorta caught y'all off guard and it seems like we're bein hasty, but we ain't. We thought about it. Talked about it. And made up our minds. Simple as that."

"After just one night?" Martha said with her left eyebrow raised.

"Sometimes you gotta do what your gut says do." Then his hands shot up as though he was refereeing a ballgame. "Wait. I tell you what. If she thinks she needs more time ta think about it, I'll go along with that. And I'll be back. But I don't need no more time. My mind's made up."

"Understand it's nothing against you personally, man. It's just that we're the only family she's got up here and, well, we sort of feel responsible. You know?"

"You don't haveta explain nothin. Really. I understand. Anyway," Jake held out his glass for the ice Kalvin was offering, "I don't want you all tellin her momma I dragged her daughter away from here without givin her a chance ta think twice about it. Then again, even if I had that in mind, I don't see how I coulda pulled it off with that woman in there." Jake was motioning in the direction Bibsy had gone.

"Yeah, you know her alright." Martha said as she looked at Kalvin.

"Martha," Kalvin said, "Why don't you go talk to your sister and see what she wants to do. Now remember, the man's got time to make so don't make a whole afternoon of it."

With an overstated sigh Martha said, "I know. I know." She reached for a glass from the cupboard. "But I think I'll even have a drink on this one."

"Oh, oh. Watch yourself now." Kalvin's chiding was playful. "You want me to fix it for you?"

Martha's broad smile emphasized her prominent cheekbones and the generous gap between her two front teeth. "I can pour my own drink, thank you."

"You kids better stop running through this house," Martha shouted when she saw one of her hand-crocheted doilies perched cockeyed on the arm of the hallway chair.

"We're playin hide-n-seek, Ma," came a whisper from the shadows.

"I don't care what it is you're playin. You ain't gonna have this place lookin like no pigsty," Martha snapped back. A short search on hands and knees turned up the straight pins that had fallen to the floor, and she repinned her handiwork mumbling all the while, "All I do is clean. Other people's houses, then mine. One to the other." She got up rubbing her knees then headed for her daughter's bedroom where Bibsy kept her clothes.

She entered Cheryl's bedroom and closed the door behind her. "Bibsy do you have any idea what you're about to do?"

Bibsy stopped to look up from her task of carefully folding and positioning her clothes into the suitcase. "Yeah." Bibsy shrugged and continued packing. "What's the big deal?"

"The big deal, Elizabeth, is that you don't know this man. And you're about to go off with him to live somewhere you don't have any family and don't know a thing about."

Bibsy hadn't heard her big sister call her Elizabeth in years and it was enough to indicate the extent of her displeasure. "Calm down, Sis, it's not like I don't have any money and can't get back if I need to. I've been saving." Bibsy pushed the suitcase aside, sat down on Cheryl's bed and lightly patted the chenille bedspread, an invitation for Martha to join her. "I don't want you to worry about me."

Martha sat next to her sister. "Money can't fix everything. What if he tries to hurt you?"

"Jake wouldn't do that." Bibsy laughed. "Just because he's big don't mean he's evil and mean. And you know I can handle myself, in spite of my size."

"Yeah, I know you can." Martha's worried expression remained.

Bibsy perked up despite Martha's evident frustration. "Well Sister, looks like I'm gonna have a family after all."

"Oh, there's children too. I forgot about that." Another pronounced sigh. "It's not as easy as it looks, Bibsy. Raising kids is a challenge."

"He's been raising em on his own all this time, and they ain't babies."

"I know you always wanted kids, Bibsy." Martha took a sip of the drink she seemed to have forgotten she had in her hand, then simply said, "I guess this is a good thing for you then."

The vague reference to Bibsy's barren state was typical of how their family handled very important subjects. A sliver of silence and eye contact was the brief and sole acknowledgement of the botched abortion that left Bibsy sterile ten years prior, at seventeen. Letty's arrangement of the procedure was once the most scandalous, but hushed, hottest topic within the family, made even more so because they were practicing Catholics. However it wasn't long before the issue was relegated to the family vault along with other secrets that might taint the Randolph name.

Martha rubbed her forehead, then picked up the conversation unsteadily, "I want to be happy for you two…but I can't help being scared for you, Bibsy." Martha sat quietly before continuing at a very measured and deliberate pace, "I was just wondering if you might not want to go out with him for at least awhile before you…"

"No, Sis. I'm going now." Bibsy's voice was calm considering the enormity of the decision she was making. It was as though she'd reconciled the move in her mind much longer ago. "When my mind's made up about something…you know me…so please, let's not get into a big thing about it."

"But there's so much you don't know…or understand...."

"Like what?"

"Like what kind of person he is, for goodness sakes! You can't tell that in one night."

"I can't really explain it, but I feel different around him, Sis. And he keeps me laughing."

"That's nice Bibsy, but there's more to life than that. What kind of family is he from? What is all this stuff about living with animals and such? You don't know anything about that."

"Sis," Bibsy laughed again, "you worry too much. He's the one. I can feel it. He's different."

"He sure is that."

"You making fun?"

"No…well, I'm sorry." Martha blushed. "But he is different from the men I'm used to seeing you with."

"You mean the ones you and Kalvin been fixin me up with?"

"You can call it what you want. All I know is that you never seemed too interested. And some of those fellas were falling all over you….most of em had good steady jobs too. What's Jake do for a living?"

Bibsy hunched her shoulders and got up to continue packing.

"Bibsy, honey, you don't even know how he makes a living?"

"Look, Sister, whatever it is, he's doin alright enough to raise two boys by himself. That's a lot, and it's all I need to know."

Each of them stared the other in the eyes, giving nonverbal homage to the painful motherless life Bibsy and their sisters endured, and Martha escaped.

"But there's so much more to life than...."

"Sis, please don't ruin things by gettin into a big deal about this. My mind's made up and that's that. If it doesn't work out," she hunched her shoulders again, "then it doesn't. But we think it will. And there ain't no need for six months or a year of courtin to find out what we already know." She handed Martha the keys to the apartment. "I don't want to leave with us being ugly with each other. Especially after you and Kalvin been so good to me." Martha stood and they hugged, with Bibsy saying, "Don't think I don't appreciate it."

"Keep the keys, Bibsy, just in case."

"Nope." She forced the keys into her sister's hand, "I know this will work out. Don't ask me how. I just know. And even if it doesn't, I'm twenty-seven-years-old and it's time for me to be on my own now. I'll make it, Sister. So don't worry about me."

"What should I tell Mom when she calls and asks about you? Do you plan on getting married?" Martha quickly added, "The only reason I'm asking is because you know she's gonna ask. You know Mom."

"We ain't made no plans like that."

"Mom's gonna be furious, and you two are barely getting along as it is."

"Tell her whatever you want. She don't care nothin about me. If she did, she wouldn't have let Mary, Cora and me grow up in St. Cecelia's like she did.

"Wasn't just her doing, you know."

"No, but she coulda stopped Pop, but didn't. She jus went along with it. Didn't haveta be that way." Bitterness oozed from Bibsy's pores as natural as perspiration during a heat wave. "Now that we're out and grown, she wants to play the good mother. It's too late for that. I don't need her now."

"Bibsy, don't be disrespectful. She did the best she could. At least you all finished school and got a good education. Soon as I could read and count, they took me outta school so I could learn how to cook for the family. From where I stand, your life wasn't so bad."

"You always say that, Sis, and it's because you didn't live our life. Education ain't everything. Look at the jobs they had lined up for us when we graduated, nothing but housekeeping; a lot of good that education did us. Remember those friends of yours that went to Morgan State and wound up cleaning white folks' houses? And they did it because they woulda starved to death if they didn't. So don't tell me about no education, please."

"Yeah, I know. But I still say you're better off with it than without it, believe me. And as far as Mom is concerned, if she didn't care, she wouldn't have called and asked me to take you in until you got on your feet."

"No, I called you, you must have forgot."

"I remember well. She called the day before you did."

"You never told me she called first. So, that's why you did it, huh?"

"No. She didn't have to call. You know me and Kalvin would have done it anyway. Shoot, we wouldn't have met if it wasn't for you!"

The statement halted Bibsy's rising hostility. "Because you were too shy to go over and speak to Kalvin first. Ha! I remember like it was yesterday, him saying, 'Kalvin…spelled with a K because I'm special.'"

"I wasn't that shy. You're supposed to let the man make the first move."

"Says who? He was new in town. Standing back trying to see who was pairing off."

"I didn't know that at the time."

"Well, how were you goin to find out if you didn't ask?"

"He still says the only time he left New York was to go to Baltimore and find me, even though I know now that him and his brother were both down there looking for work in the Navy Yard after the Depression."

"Good thing you came to New York after you got married, or I wouldn't have had someplace to come when I left Baltimore. See how things work?" Bibsy pulled out each drawer, making sure she hadn't left anything behind. "Everybody except you could see you two were meant to be together." Bibsy paused a moment. "Sis, that's how I feel about Jake and me. Just a strong feelin I have. I think it's meant to be."

"I know you do." The women hugged. "That Jake better take good care of you, cause he'll have me to answer to. And I don't care one bit how big he is."

"I'll tell him you said so." Bibsy laughed, then turned from Martha and pulled her suitcase to the floor.

"You do that." Martha's hands were on her hips now. "See if I care."

"You don't have to get salty with me. It's him you're pickin a fight with, not me."

"But seriously, Bibsy. He promised me he'd bring you back if you're not happy up there. And he said his word is good, so don't think twice about telling him to bring you home if you're not happy. Or just call, or write, something. You need extra money?"

"No. I already told you I've been saving, I always did. That's one of the things they drilled in us at The Home. Don't worry, I'll keep in touch." Bibsy picked up a change of clothes she had spread on the bed. "Want to freshen up before we leave. Tell Jake I'll be out in a few more minutes. You know, Sis," Bibsy stopped and faced Martha once more. "After leaving St. Cecelia's, all I did was rent rooms the whole time I was in Baltimore. This is the first real home I've known. Always wished I could have lived with you growing up. Every time you visited us, I wanted to leave with you. Tried once or twice too, remember?"

"I remember. Guess it just wasn't meant to be. And maybe it's best we just accept that."

"Easy for you to say."

"Life is what it is, Bibsy. No point in stewing over things you can't change. You tend to get stuck in the past, always fretting about St. Cecelia's. Let it go. At least try."

"Sister, don't you think I've tried? It's not that simple."

Bibsy came into the kitchen, suitcase in hand, just as Martha was putting in a second pan of biscuits.

The children were gathered around the table, busy shaping their own biscuits from the leftover dough Martha always saved for them. William was putting the finishing touches on his airplane biscuit.

"Ma! Will just stole some of my dough. See, he's putting it on the tail of that ole stupid airplane," Cheryl screeched.

"I did not. It was mine to begin with. I let her borrow it and I need it back now."

"He did not. He said I could have it. See Ma? He always gets his way."

"Oh shut up." Buster joined the argument. "Girls are so stupid. 'See ma….'" He mocked his sister.

"Hush that fussing, will you! I won't have any name-calling in here. And if you all don't stop messing with that dough, it won't rise atall."

Bibsy stood off in a corner of the big kitchen watching the children as intently as a good movie.

"Better say goodbye to Bibsy. She'll be leaving us in a little while."

The children left their places at the table and charged toward their aunt.

"Bibsy, Mom says you're movin to where there's animals and huntin and stuff."

Buster jumped from his place at the table and charged toward his aunt. "When can I come to visit so I can help Mr. Jake hunt for animals?"

"Me too."

"I wanna come."

"Soon. Soon as I get settled in. I'll write Sister and invite you all up." Bibsy bent down and hugged all three at the same time, then looked in her purse and gave each a dollar. After thanking her, they made a game of running through the apartment waving the bills like flags.

"Bibsy, I keep telling you, you'll spoil these children giving them that much money."

Stationed at her usual post, Mrs. Tilson spotted Bibsy and Jake leaving the building. "Where you goin with that suitcase, Tiny, on vacation or somethin?"

"No m'am. I'm movin today."

"No foolin?" She leaned further over the ledge. "Whereabouts?"

"A place called Haverton, upstate aways, in Langston County." Bibsy answered without turning or stopping.

"Who you know up that way, Tiny?" Mrs. Tilson was shouting now, as Bibsy and Jake got further away.

“Me!” Jake yelled back pointing to himself.

They took a last look at Mrs. Tilson’s window once they crossed the street, but it was empty.

“She couldn’ t even wait until we pulled off.”

Jake stood on the sidewalk and took a long stretch. “Some folks wouldn’t have no business if they didn’t have other people’s business to tend to.” He looked up at the sky. “Sure is a nice day to go fishin.”

Chapter Three

Jake turned onto the ramp towards the George Washington Bridge. "Time ta get back ta fresh country air and folks that's familiar."

"Alright by me." Bibsy settled into her seat. "You ever live in New York City, Jake?"

"Naw, jus visit. And sometimes I visit the hell out of it too. But they didn't make this town for me ta live in. I like a little more distance between me and the next person. Don't believe it was meant for folks ta live stacked up like a decka cards."

"Oh, it ain't that bad once you get used to it."

"Not me. I could never get used ta livin like that."

After paying the toll, Jake worked his way over to Route 9W, a major road propped up on both sides by a series of small New Jersey towns before it wound its way into New York State and eventually the state capital, Albany. Being Sunday and the bridge behind them, traffic thinned. Jake clicked on the radio and turned the dial to a faded blues tune. Jake's slow moving vehicle kept pace with the easy tempo of the music ambling from the truck radio.

"You like the blues?" he asked.

"It's okay."

"You gotta listen to the words real close, they're tellin a story."

Due to the car's scratchy reception, Bibsy couldn't hear the words very well and found herself paying closer attention to the crying guitar than the lyrics. Sitting quietly taking in the tranquil landscape, she listened to Jake hum along.

She lit a cigarette. "What are your two boys like, Jake?"

"Wild and crazy like their daddy."

"Oh go on."

"No, they're good kids. Junior spends most of the summer fishing or swimming. He could fish all day long and never tire of it."

"What's Robert like?"

"That boy loves sports, specially track and football. That's all he thinks about. Keeps him busy and outta trouble I guess."

"I like them already. How old are they?"

"Let's see..." Jaked rubbed the stubble on his face. "…Junior is thirteen and Robert is...eleven, now."

"Who keeps them when you come to New York?"

"They keep themselves. If they need anything, they'll just go next door to Cousin Gus and Aunt Carrie's place, or somebody else on The Beach. We all keep an eye out for one another. How come you never got married and had a buncha kids yourself, Tiny?"

"Never wanted to get married, because I don't like the idea of bein tied down. I been tied down all my life." Staring at the dashboard she continued with, "And I can't have kids."

"Oh that's tough." It was evident Jake was caught off guard because he seemed surprised by Bibsy's answer. "Well, you got two now, two hard-headed boys. And if they're any trouble, you jus let me know."

"No, they'll be fine. Only trouble I'll have is if you want any more."

"Want more!" Jake's eyebrows snapped to attention. "No m'am. No thank you.

Mattera fact, that's the best news I had in years." He rolled down the window and let loose a 'yeeeooowww' that set dogs to barking from a distance and faces in a passing vehicle look back at them.

"You know," she said laughing, "You're a real nut."

"I always thought it was a damn cruel joke the way God tied baby-makin ta love-makin the way He did. With all His powers, He could've put it with somethin else. Somethin people didn't like to do so much. Don't you think so?"

"I think you're crazy." Bibsy continued laughing all the while thinking she could see herself with Jake a very long time. Easy.

After the abortion, Bibsy secretly hoped and prayed for a child, even imagining God would use her to perform a miracle like he did with Mary and Elizabeth in the Bible. After Sister Joseph told her Elizabeth was the patroness of pregnant women, she'd always considered having children a birthright, after all, her name predicted it. Eventually, she had come to believe Sister Mary Margaret was right in the end, that God had punished her for being so angry and defiant. Finding satisfaction knowing her least favorite nun was in the process of being proved wrong, Bibsy sat back comfortably enjoying the rest of the ride upstate.

Small towns gave way to the Palisades Park anchoring the road with swollen forests on either side. Occasionally they saw a patient farmer sitting roadside, allowing robust produce to self-advertise with prices hand-written on pieces of cardboard. The further they traveled, the more traffic thinned, and drivers offered the courtesy of waving or honking their horns at each other in passing. Jake picked up a young white boy hitchhiking; he climbed into the rear of the truck and got off several miles uproad.

"How'd your wife die, Jake?"

"TB." Jake's tone didn't invite more conversation, but Bibsy pursued anyway. "Oh, that musta been terrible. Did she suffer long?"

"What made you bring that up?"

"Oh, I don't know, probably all the talk about the boys earlier."

Jake took a moment before saying, "As I look back now...knowing her, she probably did suffer." He cleared his throat, a gesture seemingly more to collect his composure than aid his speech. "When Gertrude first took sick, we thought it was just a bad cold, and she started takin tonic three times a day. When that didn't work, she changed tonics. Every time somebody came down The Beach sellin a new tonic from their wagon, she'd buy it. We all useta tease her about all the tonics she was tryin, cause she never let on how sick she was."

"Why didn't she go to the doctor?"

"People up here don't go to doctors much. And colored folks hardly ever go bein that doctors won't come to The Beach or other colored sections of the county. We gotta come ta their office if we're sick. So nobody goes. Most people won't spend money to go to the doctor anyway cause most times a homemade potion will do the trick. Less they think they dyin, that's different, then we jus go on to the hospital, cause at least they got a colored section there. At least they did. To tell you the truth, I don't know what's in there now. Ain't heard of nobody goin there in a good while." Jake spat out the window, "Gonna make a stop at the store pretty soon. Better get whatever you need now. Won't be comin out this way again for a spell."

"We must be near the house, huh?"

"Jus a little ways more. There's markets in town, but I try ta keep my friend here in business. We go back a long ways together. His daddy and mine worked in the brickyards together."

"Sure is pretty up here." Bibsy rolled down her window completely, "And the air smells so clean. I can see why you like it here."

"Yep, whenever I get tired of it, I go someplace else for a while, and when I get back I preciate it even more. Nothin like it. Nothin."

Barking dogs were heard the moment Jake turned from Route 9W onto a long dirt path. Scuffling across an open field, two dogs aimed for the pickup. Jake pulled the truck into a lot next to an old splintery building with a faded General Store sign across its front.

"I ain't gettin outta this truck with them dogs carryin on out there like that."

"Them dogs ain't gonna bother you none. One of em ain't even got no teeth."

"Oh yeah? Says who? They act like they got more than enough teeth to me."

"Everybody round here's got at least one dog. Can't let them creatures know you're scared, sure enough will bite you then. Bibsy, never let nothin livin sense that you're scared."

"I ain't scared," Bibsy replied to the challenge. "I just don't want no dogs thinkin I'm supper."

"Well come on then." Jake got out of the truck. "Git! Go on away from here."

Following Jake's lead, Bibsy stepped from the truck shouting at the two sniffing hounds, then Jake grabbed her hand and they walked through a cluster of unconcerned chickens. When they got to the store, Jake swung open the creaky wooden screen door and a tiny brass bell jingled as they entered.

Taking time with the anxious hound that greeted them inside, Jake was still bent over stroking its side when he said to Bibsy, "Just let im sniff ya and he'll go on. Ain't that right, fella," Jake said with an assuring hand on the animal's back as it became acquainted with Bibsy's scent. "Just doin your job. Right fella?"

A voice came from a doorway at the rear of the store. "Be with ya in a minute, Jake. Who's your company that's got my dogs so riled up?"

"A lady-friend. Come on out here and meet her proper. What you got cookin back there that's smellin so good?"

"Rabbit." A white man wearing a worn and dirty Brooklyn Dodgers baseball cap and wide black suspenders stepped through a curtained doorway wiping his hands on a rag. His big frame and heavy boots made the wide weathered floor planks bounce as he moved across the room. "And don't tell me you can't stay for some. No excuses." Now across the counter from them, he extended his hand to Bibsy. "My name's Casey, Dan Casey, but everybody just calls me Casey. And I'm the only man in the county who can out-cook Jake. Betcha he didn't mention that, did he?"

Jake waved his hand at his friend. "Aw man, there you go puttin out lies again. I taught you how ta cook."

"Taught me....?"

"Listen." Jake waved away Casey's last remark. "This is here is Bibsy."

"Bibsy?" Casey looked at Bibsy, then at Jake.

"Yeah, that's her name. No questions."

"Ok, whatever you say. Glad ta meet you, Bibsy. Don't mind us. We're always kiddin each other. Plan ta stay long up here in these parts?"

"I'm gonna try. Looks like nice country up here. So quiet and peaceful."

"It sure is that." Jake said. "Most all the time."

"Sometimes it's too quiet and peaceful for my friend here." Casey brought a bottle of whiskey and three shot glasses from behind the counter. "So he's gotta hi-tail it down to The City for a change of pace every now and again. Care for a drink, Bibsy?"

"No thanks. Mind if I look around?"

"Help yourself. I'll warn you though, most everything on these shelves been here awhile."

"So Case, anything new happen while I was gone?"

"You only been gone a coupla days. Gotta stay away longer'n that if you wanna miss out on somethin." Casey gulped down his whiskey in one swallow and placed his glass firmly back on the countertop. "A fella did come by here yesterday though. Wearin a suit an showin too much teeth ta be trusted."

"What'd he want?" By the time Jake placed his glass on the counter and wiped his mouth with his shirtsleeve, his demeanor changed so dramatically, it shifted Bibsy's attention away from the rack of yellowed magazines and comic books.

"Aw, you know folks is always stoppin by wonderin if I'm sellin this place."

"Guess they figure you'll break down one day."

"Only trouble with movin, is you got nowhere ta go that feels like home. But I'll tell you, Jake, the prices they been throwin at me lately is awful temptin. Ever since that damn Dewey went blabbin to the papers about land in Langston bein a good investment, prices been goin through the roof."

"All becausa that bridge they gonna build. But your family's been round here damn near long as the dirt. That's gotta count for somethin too."

"Yeah." Casey refilled their glasses. "Jake, you know business ain't nothin what it useta be. I'm told these new supermarkets is takin in real good money. Nobody seems to care about where their food comes from no more, or being waited on one person at a time. Hell, that's how you get to know people. Everybody roaming through the store pickin up stuff without bein helped...I don't understand how that's better, but that's jus me. I know I'm the last general store for miles, cause the paper come by and did a story on this place a coupla times already. Folks don't wanna live like we're useta livin, Jake. They say life's too hard our way. It's old fashioned."

"Oh, you jus listenin ta the sales pitch of that fella come in here wantin ta buy the place. He'd tell you anything ta get holda these fifty acres you got here. No tellin what somebody'd do with all these woods. But I'll bet you good money, the first thing they do is chop it all down ta build."

"I know," Casey said, "and it'll be over my dead body."

Jake drove down The Beach road slowly, weaving in and out to miss the biggest dips in the road along the way. Even so, Bibsy kept bouncing up and down like a doll in the rear of somebody's car window. She didn't mind the bumps so much as that it called attention to how lightweight she was. She eased her hand down around the right side of the cushion where Jake couldn't see, and tried to hold herself to it. That helped some, but not much.

"Road kinda rough for ya, huh?" Jake mused. "It might not be the smoothest ride, but it serves its purpose."

"Oh yeah? What's that?" Bibsy's right arm had begun to cramp.

"Keeps them folks away that ain't got no business down around here. After every spring rain we useta bring truckloads of sand and dirt to fill in the holes. But no more," Jake snatched Bibsy closer and put his arm around her. "You gonna bounce yourself clear outta the damn window, woman. Come on over here."

"No I ain't neither, cause I was gonna hold onta that seat for dear life."

Their laughter created suspicion among the people they passed walking along the road. The pickup approached three women standing off to the side, knee-deep in conversation. As if on cue, they all swung around straining to see who was sitting next to Jake.

"Keep that up, the whole bunch is gonna wind up with a tough case of whiplash."

Jake honked his horn and waved to the ladies. Bibsy leaned over and put her face just outside the window and waved too. The women politely returned the greeting then resumed their huddle.

"Now you gotta tell me whose toes I'm steppin on?"

"Baby, ain't nothin to worry about. It's just you an me."

"Uh huh, I've heard that before, too."

Jake's house was situated at the very end of the mile long crater-filled Beach Road. Bibsy stood looking around while Jake unloaded the staples. He bought things in such massive quantities, there wasn't much Bibsy could help with except the few things she'd picked up for herself like sanitary napkins, a carton of Viceroys, Dixie Peach hair grease, toothpaste, comic books and romance magazines, some of which she'd read already. Jake heaved a fifty-pound sack of chicken feed onto his shoulder, and large sacks of sugar and corn meal under his arm, saying, "Get the door for me, will ya." Once inside, he called for his sons, "Junior! Robert!"

Junior came from the back of the house into the front room as Jake was swinging the corn meal and sugar onto the kitchen table. He turned to the boy. "Where's your brother?"

"Him, Cousin Gus and Aunt Carrie went huntin early this mornin. Cousin Gus said he had a taste for rabbit lately." Obviously not wanting to stare but glancing every now and then at Bibsy, he went on, "I been fishin all day."

"Yeah, I figured you'd be fishin on a day like today. What'd you catch?" Jake peered into a bucket on the floor in the corner of the kitchen. "Whoa! Look at the size of them catfish! You did alright son."

"They was practically jumpin right in the boat. I'da stayed and caught some more if I'd known we was havin company." Junior gave Bibsy another side glance.

"Oh, I almost forgot." Jake went over and brought Bibsy to where they were standing. "Son, this here is Miss Bibsy. She's gonna be stayin here with us from now on."

"How'd you do, Miss B…Bibsy. Did I say it right?"

"Yeah, Junior, you did fine," she said.

"Glad ta meet you." Junior looked at the floor, the walls, the furniture, everywhere, as if trying to focus on anything other than her.

Bibsy felt sorry for the boy; the way Jake put their introduction. But she figured he must be used to the way his father said things by now. She thought it peculiar that Jake Junior didn't look like Jake at all. The boy had a face that would move an artist to draw. Big rounded eyes sunk deep in their sockets with irises so large hardly any white showed. The rest of his face seemed full of sharp corners. His jawline was squared off almost at right angles, framing a prominent chin and cheekbones. Put all together it gave him a very distinct appearance. No, the boy didn't get his handsome features from his father. Jake was a good-looking man, but his son's face made you want to stop and study it. The realization that Junior must have a strong likeness to his mother made a tinge of jealousy creep up in Bibsy unexpectedly, making her feel awkward and foolish. She cleared a space on the couch to sit, lit a cigarette and reminded herself that the boy couldn't help which way he came into the world. And his mother, Jake's deceased wife, was just that.

Bibsy looked around the cluttered room and was surprised to find herself at ease amidst so much junk. Jake's place was so unkempt he couldn't have made a worse mess on purpose. Now that she thought about it, everywhere else she'd lived had been very orderly and spotless; and she'd been expected to help keep it that way. To this very day, Bibsy knew every square foot of St. Cecelia's. Through an organized rotating monthly schedule, she and the rest of the students moved from the school, to the dormitory, chapel, rectory and even the surrounding grounds. Cleaning, sweeping, polishing, scrubbing, raking, shoveling...until there was no visible dirt or disorder.

She looked over in the far corner at the unmade bed; the work clothes hanging from nails on the wall; the empty whiskey bottles and beer cans; dirty dishes and clothes strewn about; the wooden milk crates serving as living room tables; the tall stack of newspapers in another corner of the room; and was amused by it all. Jake was right, the house wasn't used to being kept up. But more important to her was that it didn't matter to him.

Bibsy turned to see Jake and his son busy in the kitchen and watched Junior take a big metal object that looked to her like gigantic bowlegged scissors off a nail on the kitchen wall and lumber outside with it. When he came back the metal tongs were clamped onto a block of ice which the boy put into the top half of the ice box.

"Hate to bother y'all," Bibsy began, "But that long ride and bumpy road sure got me in a bad way. Will somebody point me to the bathroom?"

"Ain't none." Obvious embarrassment twisted Junior's face.

"Gotta use the outhouse." Jake motioned to his son to show Bibsy the way, then forced a smile adding, "You'll be ready to go back to New York when you git back. You gonna haveta wait til tomorrow though. Ain't goin back there tonight."

Bewildered, Bibsy went out the door Junior held open. Not knowing why Jake was talking about her wanting to leave so soon, she figured it must have something to do with the toilet. She'd never been in an outhouse before, but as far as she was concerned it was simply a bathroom that happened to be out of the house. They rounded the back of the house then strode hastily across a dirt yard adorned with random patches of grass. Bibsy thought Junior had a clumsy walk about him, like his body hadn't yet gotten used to the height it was carrying.

After they had gone about a hundred feet, Junior started slowing down. "I'll wait for you right here, Miss Bibsy." He motioned to a decrepit wooden shack the size of a closet just up ahead.

Bibsy ran the rest of the way, but when she opened the door such a foul smell met her she leaned back and stood staring into the stench-filled blackness. Pressure on her bladder reminded her why she was there and she stepped inside holding her breath, leaving the door ajar for a sliver of light. Bibsy pulled down her panties, braced herself in a squat position reserved for public toilets, and watched her urine travel into a long dark tunnel. She couldn't even see where it ended, just heard its echo splash at the bottom. Bibsy thought she might have to throw up when she finished because the smell was making her stomach sick. Holding her breath as long as possible and taking short breaths in between, just enough to hold it again, created a lightheaded effect.

So caught up on the smell, it wasn't until she finished that Bibsy noticed the flies buzzing around which she tried to wave from her head and still keep her balance. Not bothering to look for paper, she fastened her clothes and rushed from the shed.

A safe few yards away, she took a long deep breath of fresh air that she'd now developed a new appreciation and even respect for. Turning to get one last look at the outhouse, she was surprised at its harmless outer shell. A "humph" was all she would say.

Bibsy took her sweet time catching up to Junior who was standing at a distance busy with a pocket knife peeling bark from a piece of wood. She picked up a rusted hubcap then tossed it aside to examine a large brick structure in the center of the yard. The bricks were old and weathered with chunks missing.

"Sometimes, Pop cooks on that thing in the summertime," Junior said. "He says my granddaddy made it." Then quietly added, "Ready ta go back ta the house, Miss Bibsy?"

She felt it strange that any shyness would come from such a giant of a kid, but didn't say so. She just looked up at him, smiled and said, "Yeah."

When they neared the house and heard voices, he said, "Sounds like Cousin Gus and them is back."

"Oh, yeah. Your father told me about them."

Chapter Four

The German shepherd sprung up and started growling even before the door opened, and everyone in the room fell quiet as Bibsy walked in.

"Quiet down, girl."

"Rain, hush up all that fuss."

After sniffing Bibsy's shoes and legs the dog lay back on the kitchen floor far from Jake whose swift movements in his corner kitchen captured Bibsy's attention as much as the strangers present. She couldn't help noticing with particular interest the way his brow knit in concentration as he poured cornbread batter into a frying pan atop the wood stove. His seriousness to the task of cooking reminded Bibsy of Martha.

He looked up as if trying to interpret the expression on Bibsy's face, then boomed in her direction, "How's my city gal? Feel any better now?"

"Glad to be in here smelling that fish, that's how." Bibsy had a pronounced clip in her voice. "Ain't you going to introduce me to your company, Jake?"

"Oh, she's a spitfire. I like that," Gus said.

"Me too," smiled Carrie. Four silver braids peeked from the sides and back of the kerchief she wore tied around her head framing her cocoa complexion. "Gotta say what you mean in this world. Those that don't git jus what they deserve. Nothin."

"Cousin Gus, Aunt Carrie and Robert, this here's... which one of your names you usin today, baby?"

"How many names she got? She some kinda convik or something?" Gus egged on.

"Don't listen to Jake. He's crazy." Bibsy laughed. "Just call me Bibsy. I kinda like that one. That's what my family calls me."

"Told you she had a buncha different names."

"Oh, go on, Jake," Bibsy said.

"Bibsy, huh? That's different. Well, welcome to Haverton, Bibsy." Gus said. "I'm Gus, and this here's my better half, Carrie."

"Glad to meet you all." Bibsy turned to Robert sitting in a wobbly wooden chair with an opened schoolbook spread across his lap. "Your father told me about his boys. Don't see how he could miss tellin me how big you two are. And I'd thought you'd be little, like my sister's kids."

Beaming, Robert straightened up and stuck out his chest as if that would make him appear even taller and more grownup. "Glad ta meet you Miss…Miss Bibsy." He stood and shook Bibsy's hand showing off a several inch height advantage. He wasn't as tall as Junior, but Junior was taller than everybody in the house except Jake.

"Grrr," Rain started up growling again at Bibsy.

"Quit it, Rain," Carrie snapped. "You even gettin on *my* nerves now."

Bibsy casually searched the room for Junior who'd come in behind her but now seemed to have disappeared. It took a moment or so to find him amongst so much disorder, but there he was, seated in a corner way on the other side of the front room. His long body folded into an odd double-jointed position, his back against the wall. He'd tuned out everybody in the room and was reading a paperback. Curious as to what it was, she thought better than to ask, especially since it looked like he was at a good part of whatever it was.

"What you all drinking?" She looked at Gus and Carrie's glasses of clear liquid. "Water, gin or vodka?"

"Lightnin. Corn liquor. You ever had it before?" Gus's face, especially his eyes, which curved upwards at the corners like two smiles, hinted a friendly easygoing nature.

"Can't say that I have. And no offense, but I don't care to try anything else new today. That outhouse was enough for one day. Any whiskey in the house?"

Carrie went to the kitchen cupboard and got a glass, the whiskey bottle, a jar of water, put them on a crate near Bibsy and said, "Here, honey, help yourself. I don't pour nobody else's troubles." As Bibsy fixed her drink, Carrie went on, "First time usin the outhouse, huh? You must not be from the South. You'da found plenty of em down there. I can tell you ain't from The City neither. Where's home, Bibsy?"

"Baltimore. I was born in Ellicott City, Maryland, but I was raised in Baltimore."

"Maryland." Carrie and Gus exchanged glances before Gus picked up the conversation. "Uh huh. A lotta folks think Maryland's in the north but it's right on the Dixie Line. And from what I remember from comin up north through there, now mind you that was some time ago, they had their Crow laws in that state jus like way down south."

Carrie slipped in, "Got em up here too, jus ain't in writin. Don't think cause there's no 'colored only' signs that it means we're welcome everywhere up here."

Jake cut in. "You all come on and eat your supper now cause it's ready," he said while putting two steaming plates on the table. "Robert! Junior! Junior, git your head outta that book and come on."

As the boys settled into their chairs Rain moseyed over to Jake's guests and growled again once she got near Bibsy.

"You need ta put this dog out." Carrie called to Jake. "She actin right foolish here tonight."

Jake pulled together food scraps and tossed them into an old pot without a handle and went outside with Rain at his heels. Once back inside, he finished serving the food to his guests. The adults ate where they'd been sitting, with their plates on their laps.

"These tomatas the ones R.J. brought over from his garden yestidy, Jake?" Carrie asked.

"Yep."

"I'ma fry mine like this for breakfast tomorra." Carrie went on. "They sure got a nice taste to em. Can't believe he got his first batch already."

Jake joined his company in the living room. "R.J. cares for that garden like it's family."

"Better than his family if you ask me," Carrie said.

After supper Jake brought out a shoebox clanging with dry cell batteries and put four of them into the radio. Turning the channel selector carefully, his ear was at the receiver. Finally a clear sound of a trumpet came through accompanied by a band in the background.

"Don't tell me we done lucked up on ole Louie this evenin. Hot dog!" But before he could sit down the station faded. He tried to retrieve it but each attempt brought only piercing sounds, static or silence across the airwaves. Jake moved the radio to different areas of the room. Nothing happened. Frustrated, he began spinning the knob to a spot he seemed more certain of. "Can't get much on this thing on account of so many mountains up here. Most radio signals just ain't strong enough."

"Don't matter." Bibsy waved her hand in the direction of the radio. "Was an old song anyway. Musta heard that thing a million times."

Two chords from a guitar and Aunt Carrie came to life. "Now here's my music. Low down country blues. You all can have that jazz stuff."

After a few songs, Jake spun the dial again, stopping when he heard the familiar nasal monotone delivery of the news, "*.....negotiations are currently underway that could potentially mark the end of the Korean War conflict. The United Nations is backing an agreement between...*"

"They finally gonna end this thing." Gus's squinting eyes peered at the radio as if doing so allowed him to see who was talking. "I believe Truman was just lookin for a good excuse ta put America's two cents in it. Now let's see if Eisenhower gonna end it like he said."

"The whole mess wit the Japs ain't even cold yet." Jake said. "And here we are again in somebody else's mess."

"Conflik." Carrie joined them. "White folks got more ways of talkin bout killin people than a little bit. Conflik. Humph."

"You right, Aunt Carrie. I ain't got no conflik wit no Koreans." Jake sipped from his glass. "I know how they can end it tomorra. Let them folks that's got the conflik with each other, let them fight it out. War would be over in a day. And I'm tellin you I'd put money on that one."

"They could get in the ring and make a big prize fight out of it." Bibsy joined in.

"Yeah. It'd be bigger than the Louis/Schmeling fight back in '38. And that was big." Gus said.

"Lawd, the bookies would go crazy." Jake laughed.

"We up here talkin all this war stuff, Jake we gonna miss The Shada."

"Oh yeah, Pop. Hope we ain't missed it already."

"Only The Shadow knows."

Junior shut his book. "That was corny, Robert."

"Hush up," Aunt Carrie scolded the boys while Jake resumed his position at the radio in search of another station. "Gonna miss the openin wit alla that talkin, and I like that first part."

They sat quietly as the program opened, "*Who knows what evil lurks in the minds of men? The Shadow knows.....*"

The show scared Bibsy. She didn't like the idea of evil lurking in invisible places and bad people running rampant in the world, because it reminded her of her youth at St. Cecelia's. The way the organ heightened the dramatic scenes gave her the creeps. However, watching the enthusiastic faces of the others present, she was sure no one else was frightened. Especially not the boys, whose laughter during the most tense moments irritated her. She could see everybody else attentively listening and enjoying themselves, but by the time the program ended, Bibsy found that she'd already finished the drink she had and was halfway through another.

After the program Jake clicked off the radio and lit two kerosene lamps handing one to Robert, and the boys said goodnight then headed toward their room.

"See if you can get your school lessons done steada all that comic book reading you all do," Jake said before they were out of earshot.

Carrie excused herself to use the outhouse. When she returned, she fished around the kitchen awhile then rejoined the group with an empty can she placed near her feet.

Bibsy watched her bring out a small round tin from her housedress pocket, open it, and pinch a measure of brown powder which she placed just inside her bottom lip before putting the tin away. Before long streams of saliva-snuff mix spewed from Carrie's mouth every so often into the can she placed by her feet. Bibsy had to fight the urge to stare, but to everyone else it was as uneventful as if she were chewing gum.

After refreshing their drinks they all stayed up talking for about an hour more. It turned out that Cousin Gus and Aunt Carrie weren't related to Jake at all. Their families originated from the same southern town, Richmond, Virginia, and had known each other three generations now. Carrie picked up the "Aunt" part of her name during her days as a midwife. She'd even delivered Jake in the very room where they were sitting. Gus's family was so large and he was so well liked that everybody called him "Cousin" Gus whether they were related or not.

"You know what brought us to this hole-in-the-wall town?" Gus asked Bibsy.

She'd wondered what the draw was, but couldn't bring herself to ask. "What."

"Bricks."

"Bricks?"

"Yep." The old man shook his head in agreement. "All up and down this part of the river, other side too, useta be nothin but brickyards. But it was season work, ya know. April til about Labor Day was the brickmakin season. Mack, rest his soul, that was Jake's daddy, he was sorta the leader. You know, back when things got started. Well, Jim O'Malley who owned one of the bigger yards would contact Mack when it was time ta round up the men for work."

"You mean you all came up here every year to work, all the way from Virginia?"

"Oh yeah." Gus assured her. "Even with meal money taken out, the pay was a lot better'n what we was gettin tenant farmin them fields down south."

Gus picked up his glass to take another sip, and seamlessly as if on cue Carrie brought the old tin can near her face, spat her snuff-laden excess saliva into it and continued the story. "He'd send Mack the money ta git the men far as D.C. You see, cause there was so many colored folks leavin them tabacca fields ta come north for work, they made up a brand new Crow Law sayin folks couldn' t travel cross the Virginia state line ta work."

"Had ta sneak out in small groups." Gus picked up the story without missing a beat when Carrie stopped again to spit into her can. "Cause there'd be bout fifteen to twenty of us altogether. Some would be hidin in the bottom of wagons. You'da thought it was the Underground Railroad all over again. Anyway, when we got ta Washington, we'd meet up wit Mr. O'Malley, cause him and Mack already worked out where ta meet and all that beforehand, and he'd bring us the rest of the way.

"That was always some trip. I believe O'Malley got as much a kick outta it as us. Folks would stop and stare at this white man leading fifteen or so colored men from the train and through the city streets. We'd get off the train at Penn Station, course we had ta sit in separate cars from O'Malley the whole ride, and walk across town to the pier together, then take the ferry over ta Jersey, then another train up here ta Haverton."

"These houses was the quarters he had set up for us when we got here," Carrie added. "They a little rundown now, but they useta be pretty nice. O'Malley'd be done cleaned up and aired out the place before we got here, cause they'd be closed up the whole winter.

"They musta really needed workers ta go through all that." Bibsy thought out loud. "They all did that...go south for workers?"

"Yeah, most of em. I'm tellin you brickmakin was big business back then. Humph, with all them buildins goin up in New York City? And Haverton had the best bricks, too." Gus continued. "From the way I heard it, once the white folks stopped comin here from Canada and Europe so much, they started lookin south for colored workers. And a lotta I-talians was comin up this way at the same time we did. They worked in the brickyard with us too. When was that, Carrie…1904 when I came, wasn't it?"

"Yep. And I came in 1905, the year before the landslide."

"Oh yeah, remember that? All them years of diggin up that clay finally took its toll. The brickyards kept diggin closer an closer to people's houses and stores till the clay pits was almost downtown with everybody else. That was pure greed. That's what that was." Gus explained. "Never seen nothin like it in all my years."

"A good twenty people died."

"I remember my pop sayin it happened in the middle of the night when most people was sleep." Jake said. "Took damn near half the town. Five whole streets, gone."

Seeing Carrie was in the middle of another thought, the group waited patiently while she spat into her can again. "That was a terrible thing," Carrie managed finally. "People was running round in their night clothes. Screams everywhere. Houses caught fire."

"Yeah, from the wood stoves turnin over." Gus continued. "That there was the beginning of the end. Right there. Folks really got spooked after that. Some thought it was the end of the world. A lotta white folks that could afford to, moved up to Stone Point and Grass Point after that. Guess they thought the rest of the village was bout ta go too."

"Isn't that how Holy Mount Baptist got their buildin, Gus?" Jake joined in.

"Yep. They useta go from house ta house prayin with folks. Specially after the slide. They useta come on The Beach too, cause back then a lotta colored folks lived down here. Then they started holdin they service in the basement of the white church."

"Presbyterans." Carrie added.

"I don't know what they were." Gus continued. "Then they finally bought the buildin. White church moved more in town away from the water. Scared I guess. I don't blame em."

"Ain't as many folks down here now like it useta be, but boy it was brimmin wit colored folks back then. People would take in family members, mostly from down south, and be sleepin all on top a one another til they got on they feet, cause the work was so plentiful. And this here house useta be the dining hall."

"Boy, could Mack handle a pot!"

"That's how I learned. From watchin my daddy."

"I saw how relaxed you are at that stove, Jake." Bibsy said. "I sure did catch that. How old were you when you learned to cook?"

"I don't know...just kept watchin him and one day I was helpin, then before you know it I was cookin on my own." You could tell Jake was pleased Bibsy was enjoying herself.

"Yeah, I remember Jake and Gertie used ta fight all the time over how ta cook certain things." Carrie said.

"Hush up, Carrie." Gus looked at Carrie then nodded toward Bibsy. His smiling eyes transformed into a stern gaze. "What you tryin ta do?"

"What'd I say? Well, I didn't mean nothin by it. She knows Jake was married before, right?"

"If not, she sure knows now, Carrie." Gus said.

Amused by the couple, Bibsy laughed and acknowledged that she knew.

"At least there won't be anymore fightin over who's right or wrong in the kitchen." Jake said looking at Bibsy.

"I don't cook." Bibsy stated flatly before turning to Carrie with, "What were you sayin, Aunt Carrie?" Bibsy could feel jealousy making another appearance and didn't know how to contend with competition from a deceased woman. This would be a first she thought, but now she was curious as to what kind of person Gertrude was.

"Oh yeah, where was I? Let me see. Oh, I remember...I didn't come up right away." Carrie went on. "Gus came first. But you know I started wondering...." They waited while Carrie spat again before resuming her story. "The men came back home with so much talk bout this brick-makin stuff and workin side by side wit these white men ta get bricks made. And the contests and games the men would make up among themselves ta see which yard could outdo the other. They even had their own baseball teams. Well, come the second year I decided ta join im. I wasn't makin no headway tenant farmin that tabacca field. Couldn't stand Gus bein gone so long without me no way. Factory work and housework up here paid jus as much, and the work wasn't as hard. So...."

"Oh, those was the days."

"Yeah. They sure was. Work was so plentiful, folks tried ta hold down two and three jobs at a time. Women and children could even hack a third at the end of the day ta pick up some extra change."

"Aunt Carrie, why don't you tell Bibsy about the time you made that bet with my daddy."

"Oh Lawd. Your daddy had me the talk of the town... shoot…the whole county, for years. They even had it rit up in the paper." The fond remembrance took her back a few paces, softening her roughened features. "Well see, in the evenins the men'd sit round the dinner table and brag about how much clay they hacked, or whatever job they was doin in the yard that day. So, I said they should allow womens ta work in them brickyards. I work jus as good as men do. Worked alongside men most of my life in the fields down south."

"How she could compare tabacca wit brickmakin, I don't know." Gus chuckled.

"So Mack bet me five dollars I couldn't last a day. Now it would take me almost a week ta earn that much money doin housework back then."

"I tried ta talk her outta it. Told her she could hurt herself. Brickmakin's men's work."

"Well, I was determined, so I sent word ta Mrs. Gavin, the woman I worked for, that I needed to switch my work schedule one particular day cause I had somethin ta tend to, and went and worked in the yards that day."

"What happened? Did you win the bet?"

"See, O'Malley and his men knew me too good around here, so I went down the road a coupla brickyards away to DeNelle's place, that was another big yard around here. All the yards started work early, so I showed up just before daybreak dressed in men's overalls with a cap pulled down over my head. I hid behind the burnin shed till the others got there, then just walked in behind em and did whatever they did."

Gus and Jake couldn't hold back their laughter.

"What happened then?" Bibsy was smiling, anticipating a comical outcome.

"I didn't know I got in with the crew doin the hardest job."

"You always tell it like that, Carrie. And I been tellin you for dern near fifty years, they was all hard jobs in them yards. You jus don't wanna cept that."

"Well, the other men told me later that that was the hardest job in the yard."

"They jus said that cause they didn't wanna hurt your feelins."

Carrie dismissed Gus's last comment with a wave of her hand, spat into her can and continued. "I was in this pit, cuttin the clay like I seen the men do. Break time came and I'd sit off to myself. When the sun came up good and strong, the men commence ta takin off they shirts ta keep cool. And there I was still wit long sleeves and a cap on my head. I wasn't bout ta cut off my hair for this bet. The sweat was pourin off me in buckets. Everything I wore was soaked enough ta wring out."

"That's what you get. Bein so dern stubborn. You lucky Mr. Gavin did spot you, fore you passed out in that heat an busted your head wide open."

"Of all the yards ta choose from, I had ta pick that one."

"Couldn't put nothin past Gavin. Lucky for you, he was a sharp foreman. As a favor he was doin double duty coverin two yards that particular day."

"And it hadta be that day. He stared at me for the longest time. I could see his boots from under the brim of my cap but I wouldn't look up at him. I'd already recognized his voice from hearin him talk to the other men. I jus held my head down so he couldn't see my face, till finally he sent word for me ta come up top. Said he wanted ta talk wit me."

Gus and Jake started up laughing again.

"I thought his eyes was gonna pop outta his head when he saw who I was."

Bibsy smiled with a puzzled expression. "Gavin?" she said, "Didn't you say that was the name of the lady you worked for?"

"Yep. And her husband had to be the one to fill in for DeNelle's foreman that very day. My luck didn't run too good. The only bright spot was Mack paid up anyway. But it was years before I lived that one down."

"What a shame. And they put the story in the newspaper?"

"Sure did. Folks around here laughed on that one a good while. A good while."

Stretching her legs, Carrie massaged her knees still smiling at the memory. "Gus, we better start headin home soon."

He and Jake were still chuckling from Carrie's story while Gus managed, "I'm ready whenever you are. Musta heard that story a thousand times and it still gets me."

Carrie got up yawning. "We better let these young folks get some rest."

"How you gonna see your way?" Bibsy pointed at the window. "Look how dark it is out there."

"We know our way home from here. Besides, there's enough moonlight tonight ta see."

Gus assured. "Done walked this route too many times ta count."

After they left, Bibsy said, "Jake," with a pained expression, and it was the first time Jake heard her voice with anything less than confidence.

"Yeah? What is it, baby? You alright?"

"No. I have to go to the bathroom again. Bad."

"Oh shoot. I thought somethin was wrong."

"It is. It's pitch black out there."

"Don't worry, I'll walk you. Ain't nothin out there no how. Maybe a few night critters, but they're more scared of you than you'd be of them."

"I don't think so. Let's take a lamp too."

"There's no need for a lamp, Bibsy. I know my way to the outhouse."

"But how am I gonna see inside that place? I gotta see, Jake."

Jake got one of the kerosene lamps and escorted Bibsy outside. She felt more confident outside than she thought she would, until she heard a noise behind them. She turned to see that it was Rain, and it was the first time since she'd been there that she was glad the dog was around. Once they got to the outhouse, Bibsy took the lamp and went inside. She exited feeling both relieved and triumphant. The experience still wasn't pleasant. Just better.

Jake was standing a respectable distance from the door when Bibsy emerged from the outhouse wearing a brand new look of accomplishment. He took the lamp, blew out the flame and put his arm around her shoulders as they headed back to the house. Bibsy couldn't believe how casually they walked through the dead of night. When they stopped to admire a crescent moon and a sparse sprinkling of stars in a blue velvet sky, she thought she could gaze forever at that sky and dream with wide open eyes, it mesmerized her so. Their small trance was interrupted by Rain's whining sounds. Jake patted the dog on its neck and they once again moved on toward the house.

Chapter Five

Jake woke first, gently roused by the distant chirping of nested birds; the sound that had awakened him most of his life. As he listened to birdsongs he collected his thoughts, one of which was his woman's body felt so perfect where it was, next to him. He considered staying home, but the recollection of the measly five dollars in his billfold was enough to coax his size thirteens from underneath the covers and onto the floorboards.

He quickly slipped into yesterday's clothes as his bare frame challenged the early morning chill already settled in the house. Afterwards he went into the kitchen to start a fire, then back to the front room sifting through a pile of clothes. Once he had his change of clothes draped over his arm, Jake strode back across the room to the window to gauge the time of day. He'd owned a watch once. Won it in a poker game. Lost it the same way. Kept forgetting to wind the thing, so it was useless to him anyhow.

While prying open eyelids enough to see, a raspy voice spoke, “Didn’t think there was anyone who was used to getting up before me. What you up so early for? It’s still dark outside.”

“Won’t be for long.” Jake studied the hilly landscape across the river. The slightest trace of light formed a halo above the treetops. “Be fully lit up out there before you know it.” He took his clean clothes to a room in the rear of the house and returned with a metal basin that he brought outside to fill. When he came back Bibsy was sitting on the edge of the bed wearing the covers around her shoulders. “The fire will warm things up in a few minutes.” Jake glanced at her while slow-walking and balancing the water-filled basin, talking as if speaking to it rather than her.

“I’m gonna go in the back room and wash up a bit before I start breakfast. You coulda stayed in bed cause you’ll just be in my way.”

“I’m used to getting up this early all my life. Can’t go back to sleep once I’m awake. Never could. Anything I can help with?”

“No, thanks. Nothing at all.”

Bibsy quickly changed into her clothes even before the room warmed up because she didn’t know when the boys would wake. She combed her hair, figuring to wash after everyone left the house. From her suitcase she took a fresh pack of cigarettes, stuffed them in her pocket and headed for the front door.

With just a smidgen of daylight present, Bibsy spotted a perfect place for quick relief a dozen or so steps near the dilapidated chicken coop behind the house where a thicket of tall weeds blocked any view. After washing her hands, splashing her face and rinsing her mouth at the water pump on the side of the house, she noticed a small pen with a couple of pigs snorting and rooting around the ground for food.

Lighting a cigarette, she headed toward the sound of the river. Making her way through snatches of grass she watched the wetness from the morning dew collect on the tips of her polished white sneakers. Acquainting herself with the earthy smells, she took in deep full breaths of air. The sound of moving water intensified as Bibsy continued down a path cut through shoulder-high thatch.

The trail emptied directly onto the waterfront. Its beach covered with rocks and pieces of red and grey brick, round and porous from time and high tides. Leaning against the remains of a breaking wall was the perfect spot to observe the willful water. Its presence so powerful. Gradually more light shone above a rolling treed horizon on the river's Westchester bank, as daylight steadily approached. Every once in a while a glint of sunlight would peep through an opening between branches, catch a dewy leaf just right and sparkle prettier than Christmas.

"You had me worried there after awhile. First, I thought you'd jus gone to the outhouse, till you didn't come right back." Jake draped his flannel shirt over her shoulders.

"Just admiring all this. Thanks for the shirt. Mornings are kinda chilly up here, huh?"

"Yeah. Till that sun takes a stand and warms things up."

Rain had stood several feet away and now sidled up closer with a pathetic whimper.

"Will ya look who's jealous?" Jake bent down on one knee, scratched the shepherd's back and began stroking her head with slow firm motions stretching Rain's eyes back each time. "Feel put out, huh?" He kept stroking. "I'm not puttin you out. Jus gotta move over some, ole gal. This here's ma lady."

The dog put one paw on Jake's knee and he stood abruptly, saying, "Nope. Nope. That's enough. Go on now. Be glad when y'all git useta one another." Rain lay back on the ground.

"Me too."

"It'll come. In time." Jake tapped his thigh twice and Rain came obediently to his side. "Rub er back like this. Git a feel for er. Nothin ta be scared of. She loves bein noticed."

Feeling the short bristly hair on the dog's back, Bibsy began rubbing it smooth. Eventually she began stroking her, noticing the tightness of the dog's muscles under Rain's coat. Soon, the dog's tongue dangled from her mouth and she danced with excitement.

"What's gettin into her now?"

"She loves this stuff. Gettin attention from both of us at the same time, she can barely control herself. Okay girl, go on now before you won't be worth a plug nickel."

Increasing brightness in the sky refocused their attention back across the river where the sun began cresting above treetops. It came up slow and steady, almost bashful, like it was being nudged onstage.

"Now ain't that a pretty sight."

"Sure is." Bibsy thought if only she had a view of God's handiwork like this every morning, instead of that dark scary chapel guarded by all those bigger-than-life marble statues, there would have been more sense to morning prayer while growing up, and she might not have rebelled against it.

With a friendly bark, Rain ran to meet Robert headed toward them on the path.

"Hey, Pop, Junior wants to know if you want us to fix eggs for you and Miss Bibsy or go on about our chores." He began searching the sky to see what they were looking at, and without looking at Bibsy directly said, "Mornin, Miss Bibsy."

"Mornin, Robert."

"Pop, what y'all lookin at?"

"The sun comin up."

"Oh," he said, before looking at the two of them and adding, "Ain't you seen that a slewa times already?"

Junior was at the pump washing a stack of dishes with a rag and a bar of Octagon soap, handing them off to Robert who dried and piled them onto a sawhorse. Hens devouring seed off the ground and doing their familiar strut and peck blocked the doorway when Jake and Bibsy returned.

Shooing the chickens from their path, Jake called to his sons, "Y'all git ta the pig slop yet?"

"We already tended to that, Pop," Junior yelled over his shoulder, then, "Mornin, M'am."

"Mornin, Junior." Bibsy turned to Jake with one foot in the doorway of the house. "You sure there ain't nothin I can help with? Sounds like there's a whole messa work to be done."

"No. You jus go on in there and sit at the table and wait for your breakfast. We got everything covered. I'll put another pot of coffee on cause I know the boys just about drained the first one. It'll just take a minute."

Bibsy had never heard of children drinking coffee and remembered feeling grown up when she had her first cup of tea, but was a fully grown woman before being introduced to coffee. However, not wanting to be critical she chose to keep that bit of information to herself.

"I'll have your eggs ready in a few minutes. How you like em?"

"However you make yours. Don't make a fuss cause I've learned a long time ago to eat whatever's in front of me."

They were still eating when the boys came in and put the dishes away on an open shelf in the kitchen. Once their chores were done Junior and Robert seemed a bit hesitant about going over to a cardboard box to dig for clean school clothes, but they did it anyhow wearing the bravest of faces.

Junior shoved his selection of clothes at Robert saying, "Here, take mine in the room for me."

"Which way you headed this mornin?" Bibsy asked Jake between mouthfuls.

"Over to one of the construction sites that's crawling all over the county like roaches. They buildin like crazy around here."

"Makin what?"

"Every damn thing. The new bridge, but highways mostly. Houses too...but the parkway and the thruway is where most of the work is right now.

"Well, I'm gonna nose around and see what work I can pick up for myself. Any suggestions?" Before Jake could answer, Bibsy included. "And I ain't lookin for no housework."

"There's a few factories in town that hires a lot of the women around here. I think one makes curtains and there's another one that makes sweaters. Over on Hudson Street. And there's a chicken processin plant in town too if you don't mind that kinda work, but it's dirty."

"I'll check them out. If I can't find them on my own maybe you can show me where it's at when you get back."

"Sure. In the meantime, why don't you take a walk and see the town? Best way I know how ta learn your way around. People are pretty friendly up here."

"I might just do that."

Bibsy considered straightening the house when everybody left, but washing up in a basin of icy cold water took the edge off that idea. Instead, she took Jake's advice and headed toward town.

Jake's was the last house on Beach Road, emptying right at his front porch. All the other dozen or so homes lined both sides of it. Some were single story like his, others two. Some were strung together four in a row, a long porch sectioning off each. Whether it was propped up on bricks, missing rungs or bowing to greet the ground, a porch was affixed to each house. Sitting on one was an elderly woman rocking in a chair and stringing beans. Small children lit up her yard. The woman nodded a greeting when Bibsy passed.

"Mornin." Bibsy waved.

"Nice day for a walk," the woman said without taking her eyes from the bowl in her lap.

"Yes, indeedy."

Further down and across the road, a heavyset white woman with an apron pocket swollen with clothespins narrowed her eyes at Bibsy but gave no welcoming gesture, nor did Bibsy initiate one. The woman lifted a metal tub piled with wet laundry onto a small table while two young children with dimpled knees and outstretched arms chased a reddish hen through her front yard.

She draped a sheet over the clothesline and yelled into it. "How many times I tella you, leave them chickens alone."

Continuing down the road she saw a woman on her knees pulling weeds from a vegetable garden. A dog shot from her yard and was halfway across the road aiming straight for Bibsy before the woman could get herself up from the ground. She shook a dirt-covered fistful of greenery in the air. "Trap, git your ass over here!"

The animal stopped but stayed in the road barking wildly. A few faces appeared at windows and a couple of the empty porches were suddenly occupied as the woman repeated, "I said git your ass over here," and went back to her garden once assured the dog heeded her command.

Bibsy heard a voice say, "Who is that? Never seen her around here before."

A wave and smile acknowledged the woman's help as Bibsy made a mental sign of the cross in gratitude and continued on.

On the porch of the last house on Beach Road, a man stood with his arms folded as he stared her down. "Hey! What's your name? Where you from?"

"Who are you, the sheriff?"

"Yeah." Smiling, he came down from the porch in his bare feet. "Yeah, I'm the sheriff." He walked half hopping alongside her, keeping an attentive eye on the road for sharp objects. "And the new law startin today is you can be arrested if you don't tell me your name."

"Bibsy. What's yours?"

"Bib…what?"

She knew her unusual name was going to create an adjustment for people, but she was determined to be identified on her own terms.

"Bib…sy, I said."

"Ok, ok, Bib…sy. That's different. My name is Mason T. Brown. Everybody just calls me Mason T. Where a pretty lil thing like you come from so early this mornin? Don't tell me you live on The Beach, cause I wouldna missed that. Just cause I work two jobs don't mean I ain't keepin up with what's goin on around here."

"Moved in yesterday with Jake Tucker. You know him?"

"Git outta. here." He stood back eyeing her up and down. "Jake done found him some brown sugar sho nuff." He caught up once more, this time exercising more caution now that they were on even rockier ground. "That's my buddy. We tight. You know, Jake is the one who's like the sheriff over here, not me. Or maybe our mayor. He knows everybody and everything. Showed me where ta hunt and everything. Well, I'll be doggone."

They'd gotten to the entrance of Beach Road, where a railing lined with at least a dozen mailboxes shaped like loaves of bread, each covered with different stages of rust.

"Well, it was nice meeting you, Mason T. You better get inside and put on some shoes before you stub your toe."

"Yeah, you're right. I don't like walkin round like this. Just came out on the porch cause I heard Trap goin crazy."

"What's wrong with that dog? He always act like that?"

"Nope. Only with people he never seen before. That's why everybody came out, cause Trap don't act up that bad unless it's a total stranger. He's even worse when somebody white comes down here."

"Maybe he should be on a leash."

"That's somethin you won't never see around here. Where you from?"

"The City. But I'm originally from Ellicott City, Maryland."

"The City and Maryland, huh?"

"Yeah. Why?"

"Just askin. I like The City. There's always something happenin there. Too much happenin for me though.

"Me too, sometimes."

"I went to the Savoy Ballroom a coupla years ago. Man, those colored folks was dressed to the nines...that's a show right there all by itself. And the dancin...wow!"

"Yeah, it can be quite a show."

"But I'm from the south originally. A small town in South Carolina. Jenkinsville. Everything's movin a little too fast for me in The City...the people, the traffic, the subways. Oh, the first time I went on the subway, I rode past my stop three times, so busy watching people on the train. I'ma fish outta water down there. Things is kinda quiet up here but the people is friendly, most of em. Since you from Maryland, you'll like it up here.

"I think so. It'll be a nice change." She began inching away. "Well you have a nice day Mason T. Nice meeting you."

"You too, Bibsy," he said with a smile, "And welcome to Haverton."

In some parts of downtown Haverton there were still brick sidewalks paying tribute to its heyday, and the shops often had names like Bricktown Hardware, Bricktown Towing Company or Bricktown Bakery. "In town" was a tight network of streets that snaked their course while nestling a dense array of houses and shops. There was a New Main Street and a Main Street. The widest streets were Broadway and Main, and where they intersected was considered the center of town and called "The Bank Corner" by locals, because during Haverton's glory days there was a bank on all four corners. Two were left, and one of those was about to fold.

Hi Tor Mountain was a section of the Ramapo mountain range considered part of the Adirondacks.

It bordered western Haverton, cradling the town between it and the Hudson River. The three mile distance between the river and the mountain felt a lot less, as if the mountain was close enough to touch. Curious, Bibsy thought. Gus would later say The Tor was haunted because it's where the Indians buried their people before, and even after, the white man came. Bibsy thought perhaps Gus might be right because she had felt an extra presence whenever the mountain was in her view.

The tallest building in town, actually the only tall building, was the once grand Landmark Hotel with its three levels of verandas. There were no other competing structures so Hi Tor loomed mightily as Haverton's backdrop.

Bibsy instinctively ventured toward a part of town where she saw mostly colored people, and their rundown houses tended to be even closer together on litter-strewn streets. Small dirt surfaces replaced what would have been front lawns in other parts of town. Despite its appearance Bibsy felt more at ease seeing her own people. Familiarizing herself with Haverton was so much easier than the New York City maze she had to memorize, and even write down directions to ensure she'd find her way to and from her sister's Harlem apartment. Appreciating the scarcity of people on the street, it was easy to let her guard down, and those people she did pass tended to speak or nod an acknowledgement. Each stop brought increased confidence in her ability to find her way around the village. Bibsy now allowed her curiosity to guide her down one street and back up another, making frequent turns without losing her bearings. Determining from the kindly expressions on people's faces, she knew she'd be obliged if she got turned around and needed directions back to The Beach.

She came across Emma's Beauty Shop on Clinton Avenue and stood next to a black cameo on the storefront window without realizing the symbol indicated a colored hairdressing establishment. Peering through the plate glass window into the empty shop, it wasn't until she spotted a curling iron and a jar of pink curling wax on the counter that she was certain the shop catered to colored women. Bibsy checked the hours of operation on the door and made a mental note to return the next day, Tuesday. Even though she hadn't set out looking for a beauty shop, she thought it was a good idea especially since Martha wasn't around to do her hair anymore.

At St. Cecelia's they were taught it was vain to primp and focus too much on their outward appearance. And vanity was a sin. Venial, but definitely a sin. The nuns didn't dare venture into black hair care and assigned the older girls the task of grooming the hair of the younger students. All the girls wore the same cornrow style, even neat lines as straight as pews from front to back, nothing fancy. Ever. The girls with naturally straight hair got to wear two pigtails. None of the students were allowed to wear their hair loose at any time.

When Bibsy left school she couldn't wait to get to a beauty parlor and explore the particular hair-care ritual that would include the hiss of a straightening comb and the clank of curling irons that transformed her head of thick healthy hair into a tamed mane of bouncy curls that shined like new patent leather. She loved suddenly being able to freely run her fingers through her hair, a gesture magically elevating her into adulthood. However, the practice required that she ignore the occasional burn, the gradual weakening and eventual breakage of her hair due to consistent pressing and curling.

Bibsy set out the next day headed for Emma's and this time Trap's owner came over to Bibsy with the dog on a leash and introduced herself.

"Hi, I'm Ida," she said to Bibsy after the wildly barking dog attempted to pull the woman across the street upon seeing Bibsy, but Ida yanked him back. "I hear you're Jake's new woman. Jus let him sniff you. Once he gets your scent a coupla times he'll leave you alone."

"You sure?"

"I'm very sure. This here is the smartest dog in Langston County. I'll put money on Trap over any of em."

Standing very still, reluctantly Bibsy patted Trap like Jake showed her to with Rain, allowing the dog to get acquainted, all the while replaying in her mind Ida's words, "new woman," and considered the possibility of revisiting the conversation she and Jake lightly touched on while driving down Beach Road.

Once Ida was satisfied Trap had sufficiently captured Bibsy's scent, she abruptly pulled him away. "Okay. That should do him for now," she said then headed back toward her garden. "Just a couple more times and you'll be fine."

Bibsy hoped so. "Thanks," she said to Ida's back. She'd never lived among any dogs. Even though there were no pets at St. Cecelia's, now she thought it would have been a nice experience, even an escape, to have grown up with one or two of them around. Just none like Trap.

When Bibsy walked into Emma's Beauty Parlor there was one woman in the chair getting her hair done and no one waiting.

"Hi." Bibsy said as she entered. "Do I need an appointment?" She added, though hoping she wouldn't have to return home and come back another day.

"No, come on in. I gotta coupla hours before my next customer. I'm Emma. You must be new in town," she smiled but quickly returned her attention to the section of hair that she slid the curling iron from.

"Yeah, moved over to The Beach a few days ago. My name's Bibsy."

"What'd you say?"

"Bibsy." She was beginning to wonder if this was worth it, but held her ground because it was too late to turn back now and rename herself."

"Well, have a seat, B...Bibsy. There's some magazines over on the table by the wall you can look through. I'll be finished with Pearl here in no time."

"You got people on The Beach, Bibsy?" Pearl said with her chin resting on her chest and stretching her eyes to get a glimpse of Bibsy.

Opening an Ebony Magazine, Bibsy said, "Moved in with Jake Tucker a few days ago." She stared at the magazine but allowed her peripheral vision to monitor the two women. It was a technique she and other girls mastered at St. Cecelia's because their survival required being aware of everything at all times; even as they were expected to keep their eyes cast downward displaying deference at all times.

"Oh really?" Emma finished another curl and stood back holding the curling iron upright eyeing Bibsy for a long enough moment that Pearl could also look up to get a good glimpse. Then she gently nudged Pearl's head back down and continued curling.

At the mention of Jake's name Bibsy felt the air in the shop become weightier, invisibly competing with the odor of heated hair. With her eyes glued to the open magazine, but her attention squarely on the two women, she decided to close it and look up at them because she needed to carefully scrutinize their reaction to her next question.

"You know Jake?"

"Girl, everybody knows Jake." Pearl said. "Where're you from, Bibsy?"

Preparing for the upcoming interrogation, Bibsy felt her guard rise. "The City."

"Oh." Even though Emma was speaking, Bibsy could tell Pearl wasn't missing a beat. "You know each other long, Bibsy, you and Jake?"

"Long enough." Bibsy said before realizing how that may have sounded, then decided to change the subject. "You know of any places hiring around here?"

"What kinda work you lookin for…day work… housekeeping?"

"No. Not if I can help it."

"You too good to do housework?" Pearl said, just as Emma was removing the cloth draped around her neck. "It's a decent livin. I have five women that I work for. It's not that bad. And it feeds my family jus fine."

Emma said, "Pearl, everybody don't wanna do housework."

"I cleaned enough in my lifetime. That's all." Bibsy said. "I don't have nothing against it. My sister does that kinda work and my mother always cooked for people. Nothin wrong with it. It's just not for me." Bibsy didn't understand why she always had to explain why she didn't want housekeeping work. She understood it was the most plentiful employment out there for colored women, but vowed never to get on her hands and knees to scrub another floor for anybody once she left St. Cecelia's. "Jake said there were some factories around here."

"Yeah, there's a chicken processing factory." Pearl said as she was paying Emma. "But if you don't like housework, you sure won't like that. Killin and guttin and packin up chicken parts all day...and the place smells to high heavens. But they're always lookin for help."

"There's other factories around too, Pearl." Emma motioned for Bibsy to sit in her chair as Pearl made her way to the door. "There's the curtain factory on Route 9W and Better Sweaters over on Hudson."

"You all can help yourselves. I'll keep my housework, cause my ladies treat me real good. You all have a nice day now. Nice meetin you, Bibsy."

"You too, Pearl."

"I'll see you in two weeks, Emma."

"Right."

"You have to get up a minute," Emma said to Bibsy after the door closed. "Have ta give you a boost in the chair like I do the kids." Bibsy slid out of the chair and waited for Emma to go into a back room and return with a makeshift booster seat fashioned out of wood which she draped with a couple of folded towels. “Here, that should do.”

Bibsy let the comment slide even though she would never get used to people comparing her to children due to her height. As a child, one of her secret wishes was that God would make all the short people in the world tall and all the tall people short, so each could know how it feels. Just for one day she wished she knew what life would be like as a tall person or even average height. However, she was grateful that anyone who knew her for any length of time didn’t continue to make such comparisons.

“How you like livin on The Beach, Bibsy?”

“It’s okay. Takes some getting used to but it’s fine with me.”

Escorting Bibsy over to the sink and beginning to shampoo her hair she said, “It would take a lot for me to get used to livin without plumbing and electric. I don’t know how they do it over there.”

Emma towel-dried Bibsy’s hair, sectioned it off in loose plaits and put her under the dryer with the Ebony she had earlier. Bibsy sat there getting increasingly bothered by the whole process. She hated primping and the whole extravaganza of it. She knew some women spent hours at it, and she even enjoyed watching her sister delight in the whole ordeal of looking good to go out. But for her it was one of those things in her life she’d gladly eliminate if she could. So she sat there steeling herself for the rest of the haircare experience.

"You know Jake was married before, don't you?" Emma said when she began straightening Bibsy's hair.

"Yeah. He said his wife died from TB." Bibsy couldn't help but wonder what Emma would have said if Bibsy hadn't known.

"Yeah. It was so sad. Gertie. That's what everybody called her, but her name was Gertrude. Anyway, she was like a lotta people who live on The Beach. Don't trust no outsiders. Not even doctors. She useta be a regular customer of mine. A good woman. I useta get after her about that cough though."

"Yeah, I heard she was a good woman." Bibsy said, unaware how else to respond in that awkward moment.

"But I'll tell you...Jake Tucker sure do love him some dark-skinned colored women. That's for sure. You know what they say, the darker the berry, the sweeter the juice. Must be true, huh?"

"I don't know about that." Bibsy wished Emma would be as attentive to the straightening comb coming too close to her scalp as she was to gossip. "Ouch," she said as she felt pain travel quickly from the back of her head down her spine like an electric shock, and knew she'd have to nurse that sore spot for at least a day.

"Oh, did I touch you? I'm sorry," Emma said and curbed the conversation for awhile.

However, the silence didn't last long. As soon as she put the curling irons in the flame she said, "Jake useta date a coupla women in town after Gertie passed but none of em lasted long. They couldn't handle livin on The Beach."

Smiling with that bit of news and realizing she'd forgotten to mention anything to Jake about his past women after Ida's comment the day before, she said, "Oh yeah?" Bibsy never made it a habit to plan too far ahead anyway. Right now she and Jake were enjoying each other's company, and that was that. Emma's prying nature was already getting on her nerves though.

"And Jake loves his likka. You know that already I guess."

"Where's those factories you mentioned before?" Bibsy said. "Can I walk to em from here?"

"Oh sure. Maybe you should go there when you leave since it's not far from here. And besides, you'll be lookin all pretty. Better Sweaters is the name of the factory and it's jus a few streets over."

Bibsy looked into the mirror when Emma twirled her around. "Thanks. It looks nice," she said while lightly patting the rows of stiff curls on her head.

"You want me to comb it out for you? You should if you're goin ta check out that job today."

"Yeah, maybe so."

Emma pulled Bibsy's hair into a pageboy style with a fat loose roll of bangs across her forehead. "This is how I seen them women wear their hair in The City."

Bibsy thanked Emma and paid her three dollars. After double-checking her directions to the sweater factory, she headed toward the door.

"You wanna make another appointment? Same time in two weeks?"

With some hesitation she finally said, "Yeah."

"If you can't make it causa work, come in an change it, hear? And don't forget to roll up your hair at night, Bibsy."

"Okay. I will," Bibsy said, knowing she wouldn't, but was unwilling to spend more time there explaining. Besides, she needed to walk because her feet felt tingly from her legs dangling from the booster seat for so long.

Standing outside the long one-story brick building examining a sign across the front that read "Better Sweaters" she ventured inside where she was met at the door by a beefy looking white man wearing shirtsleeves and a ready smile.

"Hi." Bibsy said to him when she walked through the door and adjusted her eyes to the florescent lighting and the dust holding vigil in the air. "I was wondering if you need anymore workers?" She yelled above the din of the machines while smiling in an attempt to turn on as much charm as she could muster after the beauty parlor experience.

"It depends." He shouted back. "What kinda experience you have? You ever worked in a factory?"

"Yes."

"Come into my office a minute. Can't hear a thing out here."

Bibsy followed the man through rows of industrial looms and sewing machines into a dingy office off the far side of the floor. She noticed all of the women wore head scarves and most smiled or nodded as she passed through the narrow aisles.

He offered her a seat in the only available chair as he sat behind a desk in the cramped office. "What factory experience do you have?"

"Worked in the garment district in The City where they made men's dress shirts."

"What was your job there?"

"Collars and cuffs mostly."

"Oh. That's not so easy."

"Not too many people wanted that job. And I was pretty good. Fast too."

"Where you live?"

"The Beach."

"Well, why don't you fill out this application for me. I'll be back in a few minutes. By the way, my name is Dave." He shook her hand then handed Bibsy the application. She filled out the brief application using her best St. Cecelia's penmanship knowing most people were impressed by it, especially after realizing most colored people's cursive writing was usually poor. She wasn't sure about the address but hoped Beach Road would be sufficient.

When Dave came back and looked at the application he said, "Nice handwriting. Where'd you learn to write like that?"

"Catholic school in Baltimore," she said as she watched Dave press his lips together and nod approvingly. Landing a job had always been easy for Bibsy because she knew how to play up the things that impressed most employers in interviews. It was the one benefit of St. Cecelia's Bibsy felt she'd earned the right to use.

"Well, I need another buttonholer. You think you can do that?"

"Yep. I'm a quick learner."

"Let's see." Dave pondered. "You live on The Beach so I can't call you...aw hell, why don't you start next Monday? Can you do that? I'll have Evelyn train you. She's the best I have over there. I'll give you a tour of the place and introduce you to her."

"Thanks. What time you want me here on Monday?"

"Eight o'clock sharp and you've gotta punch in on time every morning."

"I'm useta that too. Thanks again."

Heading back home that afternoon, Bibsy was pleased with herself for having landed a job so quickly. Ever since she'd been out of school she had her own money and knew it was her best insurance in case things didn't work out between her and Jake.

Chapter Six

It was only noon and already hot. Wide open windows stood at the ready to greet a mid-summer breeze that never came to call. Surely in no time the sun would start throwing flames from the sky.

Lying next to Jake and propped up on one elbow, Bibsy said, "What you wanna do today?" Her index finger lightly tracing the hairline framing his face.

"More of what we jus did."

"Ain't you the greedy one."

"Yep. That's me." Kissing her breast. "Greedy."

"What if the boys come back?"

"They won't be back no time soon. Screen door's locked anyway."

Each stroke and every kiss increased her desire for the next, and their bodies created a natural rhythm with no awkward missteps, just fluid movement. His kissing became mouthing and tongue tickling as her elbow gave way and she slid down beside him. She kissed his face, then neck and the tightly curled hairs covering his broad handsome chest, wrapping her legs around him as she went. Her body was throbbing to be quenched when he entered, so very gently and lovingly. Soon, the bed sang a springy squeaky rhythm keeping time with their music. And its song went on and on and on. Long after, their bodies still molded as one, they enjoyed the deep dreamless perfect sleep that only good lovemaking brings.

The sun had fought its best fight and was in slow retreat when Jake and Bibsy woke. Untangling sticky sweaty bodies used up all their energy and they could only get as far as rolling onto their backs, before resting again, allowing counterfeit breezes to dry them. Revive them.

Jake made the first move out of bed. Before actually getting up, he sat on the edge of the mattress stretching, making loud roaring noises that made her laugh.

"What are you thinkin?" she said.

"Oh, jus how lucky I am. That's all."

Once bathed and dressed, they went for a drive. No particular place in mind, just hoping for a breeze along the way.

As the truck made its slow lumpy trek down Beach Road, Bibsy fanned herself with a piece of cardboard. "Can we stop at Louie's for something cold to drink?"

It was the store closest to The Beach and owned by an Italian family. Attached to the rear of the grocery store was their kitchen, upstairs the parlor and bedrooms with two rental apartments above that. Still chewing, Louie entered the store from the kitchen. His wife Julia soon followed, as one of their five children peeked at Jake and Bibsy through the curtain partition.

"Hot enough for ya, Louie?" Jake asked as they trod a sawdust-covered floor to the freezer chest.

Louie made a grumbling sound and fingered the white handkerchief tied around his neck.

"It's days like this I wish we still lived on The Beach." Julia said. "No air gets between these buildings, they're too close."

Louie made another grumbling sound no one understood except probably his wife.

"It's hot down there too, today." Jake swished his arm through bottles floating in cold water that had been ice that morning. "No more beer, Louie?" Jake's disappointment erased when he spotted an ale.

"They cleaned me out today." Louie managed. "Beer. Sodas. Not much left."

Bibsy reached into the chest and came out with a cream soda.

"Where's the boys?" Julia asked. "They've gotten so tall, so fast. Gonna be like their poppa."

"Probably over at the swimmin hole." He opened their bottles on the side of the freezer chest. "Least that's where they were headed this mornin. By now they're probably over to the junkyard lookin for somethin or other."

"What I wouldn't give to be a kid again. Just take off and swim all day." Louie untied his handkerchief and wiped his brow.

Julia waved her hand at her husband. "He'd never close the store long enough to go swimmin for a few hours. He's glued to this place."

Julia's remark sparked life into Louie. "If I did, you'd give away the whole place to your sister and that no good bum she's married to. Look," Louie pointed at Jake. "This man has lived on The Beach all his life. And he always pays his bill with me. Jake knows his credit is good here anytime. Anytime." Louie ran the handkerchief through glistening thin hair. "But my own brother-in-law won't pay me. The only thing he knows how to do is lay on his goddamned fat white ass and make babies."

"Louie!" Julia shrieked, crossed herself looking heavenward. "God forgive him." She smacked him on the arm. "Watcha your mouth."

"Just because he's livin on The Beach don't mean he's gotta rely on handouts and shame the family. He could be savin a fortune livin there, but he's a dope."

Jake downed the ale and searched for another. "How's your brother, Frank?" He didn't want to hear Louie carry on anymore about his brother-in-law, Jimmy. Whenever he was in a bad mood, he'd start in on the poor guy. On occasion, a white family would move to The Beach on their way to owning their first home or business. Jake knew Louie would never admit it, but what he hated most was Jimmy didn't mind living amongst so many colored. "Saw your brother Frank at the job site the other day, talking with the foreman."

"Oh Frankie's doin good. Real good." Julia's enthusiasm clearly welcoming the subject change.

"The way the builders are crawlin all over this county like hungry rats, he'll probably be a millionaire in another ten years," Louie said. "Things are changin too fast for me."

"Me too," Jake said.

"I miss the old days though," Julia said.

"You wanna live on The Beach again, Julia?" Jake said with a smile.

"Well, no. That's not what I mean. Those were rough times. I mean...remember how many people useta come from all over the east coast to Haverton to our festa, Jake?"

"What you mean useta? They still do. I'm glad they moved it over to the school.

"Yeah. But even the festa's changin. It's not like the old days." Julia shook her head.

"What's wrong?" Louie said. "You still get to dance the tarantella, don't you?"

"You know what I mean, Lou." Melancholy tinged Julia's voice. It's becoming more like a carnival. It started out as something sacred. I notice more and more people are showing up after Mass is over. It's not right."

Julia turned to Bibsy. "We useta have open air Mass right on the steps of St. Peter's Church. Seeing thousands kneel right on the hard ground," Julia clutched her breast, "was a beautiful sight. Then it got so big we had to move to the field by the school."

Having associated Mass with dimly lit churches and chapels throughout her lifetime, the idea of having Mass outdoors seemed right for this place. With thoughts drifting to life at St. Cecelia's, Bibsy got fidgety and impatient and wanted to leave. She moved toward the door and when Jake didn't get the hint she said, "I'll wait for you in the truck, Jake."

"Okay. I'll be there in a minute."

"Don't leave me out there in the heat all day, Jake." Bibsy said before the screen door closed behind her.

"She's kinda feisty, huh Jake?" Julia said chuckling.

"Nothin I can't handle." Jake drained the second bottle of ale and put a dollar on the counter.

Louie's tone became confidential. "Jake," he said, "it doesn't look good. Frank says once the new highways are in place and the bridge is finished, The Beach is gonna haveta go. They're planning on putting a power plant big enough to get electric to the whole county. They expect thousands more to move here once the bridge is finished." He hunched his shoulders. "It's what he said the big shots are saying now. All the open land and farms are bein bought up and their makin a killin. You better put somethin aside because he said in a year, two at the most, it'll all be gone."

Julia nodded in agreement with Louie. "It's true, Jake. Remember he told us a whole year before it was in the paper that the bridge was gonna be built. Better take heed," she added before leaving to attend to a crying baby.

"You know he's always been in good with all the right people in county government and knows this stuff way ahead of everybody else. He tried to tell that bum relative I was just mentioning, but he won't listen."

"Louie, they been sayin things like that for as long as I can remember," Jake said. "You know that talk's been goin around for years. How many times have you heard that The Beach is gonna be sold?"

"But it's not like before, Jake. Look at the way they're buildin now. You know the woods where I useta hunt, the place your father showed me years ago? The place that guy owns...you know him...whatshisname..."

"Who, VanDenmeter?"

"Yeah, that's the one. The guy musta had what… over seventy acres?"

"Easy."

"Well, there's houses goin up there now."

"No shit."

"A whole development. They practically built a fucking little town on all that property."

"He was always a greedy sonofabitch. But that's jus one person, Louie. Besides, that was vacant land. They ain't gonna put out all the people on The Beach with nowhere ta go. There's too many of us. Most of em is there cause ain't that many apartments nowhere else in the county – not if your skin is a certain color." Jake started heading toward the door. "I ain't gonna worry bout it, but thanks anyway."

"What's wrong?" Bibsy asked when Jake got behind the wheel of the truck and sighed instead of starting up the truck right away.

"Aw, jus talk." He turned the key and slowly pulled away from the curb. "There's always been talk about the town pushin us off The Beach, and it's startin up all over again. That's all."

"Yeah, I heard women at the hairdresser say that too. Why would they push everybody off?" Bibsy said. "Where do they want the people there to move to?"

"That's jus the point. Don't nobody have a answer to that question."

When Jake pulled into the Esso station, the attendant got up from a desk where he'd been eating a piece of chicken and came out to wait on them. Jake had opened the truck's hood and was busy checking his oil and radiator when the attendant walked up rubbing his hands on the sides of his trousers. "Filler up, Ken." Jake said with his head still under the hood. "Looks like you been over ta the Baptist church again. You better watch out, you liable to start turnin colored from eatin all that down-home food."

"Well then, I'll jus haveta start changin. Regular, right?" Ken asked although he'd already started pumping the gas.

"Yeah, you know I don't put no premium in this ole thing. Just whatever it takes ta keep er movin." Jake clamped down the car's hood. "What they got over there at Holymount, the usual?"

"Yep." Ken dug into his teeth with his pinky fingernail before cleaning Jake's windshield. "If you goin, you better get over there soon, cause they'll be closin the kitchen in another," he checked his wristwatch, "forty minutes."

Three women wearing white bibbed aprons sat at a long serving table waving fans with a prayerful white Christ on one side and Holymount Baptist Church printed on the other, when Jake and Bibsy came to the church's side entrance.

"Well, look what the wind done blew in," said a fourth woman standing near the door when they entered. "Come on in. Ain't seen you in ages. Who's this?" She smiled. "I heard you had a lady friend stayin at the house."

"Yep." Jake introduced Bibsy to the foursome then said to Bibsy, "Notice how fast news travels around here."

"Oh, that's old news," one of them laughed.

"Sure is. Come here and let me get a good look atcha, honey," said the elder among them.

Bibsy took a shy step forward and smiled good naturedly at their inspection. "Can I trouble you for one of them fans? If you got an extra one to spare." Bibsy said. "Sure smells good in here."

One of the women reached into a shopping bag and handed Bibsy a fan. "You ain't feedin this poor chile,

Jake? I'm surprised at you." She got up and headed for the stove.

"Yeah, it's your turn, Sister Williams," said a voice at the table.

"I know, I know. Why you think I got up, Sister Thomas? What would you like, Bibsy?"

Jake answered. "What's good today?"

They spun around as a team. "What you mean what's good, *today*? Everything's good. Jus like always."

"Don't come in here startin no mess, Jake Tucker. It's too hot for that."

"Humph, you think you the only one can cook? I been cookin fore you was old enough ta smell yourself."

"Take it easy, ladies, you know I'm jus teasin. Ain't too hot for a little fun is it?"

"Yeah. Matter a fact, it is."

"Any ribs left?"

"Some, but they almost gone."

"Fish is all gone and so is the collards."

"Can I have chicken, string beans and corn bread?" Bibsy said.

"Sure can. And, you, Jake?"

"Same thing, with some ribs on the side. And gimme a coupla chicken dinners for the boys."

One of the women still seated had been staring at Bibsy the whole time. "Scuse me, but you sure look familiar," she finally said. "You related to the Millers over in Kancy?"

"Unh, unh. Ain't related to nobody around here."

"Where you from, honey?"

"The City."

"Oh, but you sure do favor them. Don't she, Sister Williams?"

"A little."

"Not a bit." Jake stated. "They ugly. The whole bunch of em."

"Watch your mouth, Jake." The woman by the door took Jake's money and carefully handed Jake two paper bags. "You know the Millers is related to Sister Larkin over there," she motioned to the heavyset woman at the table, "by marriage."

"That's right." Sister Larkin said without expression. "Don't you go bad-mouthin my family."

"Oh yeah?" Jake said with no hint of embarrassment, then, "Shows you they at least tryin ta pretty-up the family."

"Git on outta here boy, you a mess."

Upon leaving Holymount Baptist Bibsy reflected on the easy conversation inside, something she'd never witnessed inside a church growing up. And it wouldn't have mattered that they weren't in the sanctuary. Bibsy was conditioned to conduct herself in silent reverence anywhere in God's house. Or anywhere for that matter, because they all stayed under the close scrutiny of nuns everywhere they went. Only nuns and priests spoke freely, but even they maintained a quiet and solemn conversational tone. Loud talk didn't exist, and laughter was muffled as though it was unnatural and something to be ashamed of. Unless asked a direct question, children didn't speak. Even then their responses were expected to be respectable, yet barely audible with clear enunciation. It was a rule that stuck, especially after meeting the acquaintance of their black leather strap on enough occasions.

Bibsy woke the next morning tired and with a sense that something wasn't right. Fairly soon she realized why, that dream again.

"You had a fitful sleep last night," Jake said when they were having breakfast. "I had to grab hold of you to quiet you down. Musta had a bad dream, huh?"

"Oh yeah?" Bibsy laughed attempting to make light of the issue, and her concern, because she didn't know if she'd talked in her sleep, and if so, what she said. "It ain't nothin, jus have bad dreams sometimes. That's all."

"Don't tell me I'm causin you bad dreams, now." Jake said. "It got so that you yelled out. That's when I grabbed you."

"Really?"

"You don't remember?"

"Not one bit." She laughed again, disguising the terror inside upon the realization that the nightmare must have been the result of being inside that church yesterday, bringing up memories of St. Cecelia's.

"Something you wanna talk about?"

"No. It ain't nothing serious…just some childhood mess."

Chapter Seven

Mid-July brought a string of hot days and one night the house was so hot the boys slept on the front porch on pallets, leaving the heat to keep its unmerciful vigil inside. Jake suggested they go for a swim since neither of them could sleep. Bibsy agreed but let Jake know she wasn't going in. Jake put on a pair of swimming trunks under his trousers and they tiptoed across the porch as the boys' snores competed with the cadence of crickets echoing throughout The Beach.

"I'll watch you." Bibsy said. "Cause I just got my hair done the other day."

"Well, suit yourself. It'll cool you off though."

The swimming hole was one of several defunct clay pits left from the brickyard days when dozens of them dotted the Haverton and Stone Point shoreline.

The Hudson filled in a few of them over the years, making perfect swimming ponds. The prized yellow and blue clay lining created a smooth surface and kept the water cooler than a concrete pool. Children and adults preferred these ponds to swimming in the river because the Hudson had a reputation for a deceptively deadly undertow which had taken enough lives over the years to earn the respect of locals.

The pond nearest The Beach was wide enough to take several strokes across and deep enough for diving. Beach residents maintained it by regularly skimming debris and any little creatures using their finer-grade fishing nets. There were two other swimming holes in Haverton, but no one used the one by The Beach except its residents.

Spending good money on regular hair appointments, Bibsy wasn't about to throw it away so quickly just to cool off. But she had to admit, she was beginning to dread those trips to Emma's more with each visit. She'd already begun to get a simple wash and press just to cut down on her time there. The curls didn't last long anyway because she covered her head with a scarf at work and wore it pinned up other times.

With every hair appointment Emma wanted to know how she was managing living on The Beach as if she anxiously waited for the time when Bibsy would come in and tell her she'd had enough. If she were to leave she surely wouldn't tell Emma, but simply get up and leave one day without broadcasting it.

"I don't know how you can manage livin with no indoor plumbin," she'd say. "Gertie useta complain about it all the time."

Bibsy usually replied, "We're managing alright." Then she'd quickly change the subject. Hearing about what Gertie used to do and say was beginning to wear thin as well, and Bibsy knew Emma was cruising toward a time when Bibsy would have to tell her about herself. But first she'd have to find someone else to do her hair because she didn't want to cut off her nose to spite her face.

If anything, knowing that Gertie complained about The Beach was motivation to stick it out. The one thing she absolutely couldn't adjust to was washing clothes by hand, and after only a couple of weeks there Bibsy insisted Jake take her and the boys to the laundromat in town on Saturdays. Supplying the necessary components to get the job done, she taught Junior and Robert how to do their own clothes because she said they were old enough to. Excited to have any modern convenience enter their lives, the boys didn't complain. They began warming up to Bibsy after that.

Sitting on the damp clay edge of the swimming hole with her feet in the water, Bibsy watched Jake take a running dive into the water and come up with a big grin on his face.

"Oh I wish you'd come in and enjoy this with me, baby. The water feels good on a hot night like this," he said while treading water.

"No, that's alright. I like watching you."

The full moon cast a warm mellow glow over the area and created a soft natural spotlight over them. Jake's wet muscular torso glistened in the moonlight as he took several laps. She was fascinated by Jake's command of the water. He was an excellent swimmer and looked as if he was having the time of his life. Bibsy had never been swimming and realized she'd never even been to a beach before, but was now so impressed with how easily Jake navigated the water, a wide smile was affixed across her face.

"What you thinkin about?" Jake said breathlessly when his head popped up in front of her.

"Where'd you learn to swim like that, Jake?" Bibsy said reaching out to him. "I can sit here watchin you all night."

He hoisted himself up and sat beside her and said, "Lotsa people swim down here." He was still catching his breath. "This swimmin hole been here long as I can remember."

"Boy, I guess I missed out on a lotta things growin up."

"Never too late ta learn. I can teach you if you want." Jake's large rough hand enveloped hers. "And you know I'm not gonna let nothin happen to you."

"I know." She was sure of that. "But I don't even have a bathing suit."

"Bibsy, ain't nobody down here but you, me, Rain and the crickets right now. Wear your birthday suit."

"Oh, no. I can't do that. Unh, unh." She said. "I see you got on swimming trunks."

"You want me to take em off? I will if it'll get you in the water."

"No. No need for all that." Bibsy said. "But I could take off my dress and just leave my bra and panties on."

"There you go. Now we're gettin somewhere."

While Bibsy removed her cotton shift, Jake found a truck-sized inner tube nearby that the kids often used and threw it in the water then he got in and draped Bibsy across the rubber tube and gently pushed her around the pond.

"Let your legs and arms hold you. Rest your head against the inner tube and relax. Don't worry, it'll hold you up. And I'm right here."

Confidence in Jake allowed Bibsy to loosen up. With her feet dangling in the cool water, Bibsy wondered what her life would have been like if she had access to something like this every summer while growing up. But the particular pattern of moon and stars in a purplish sky with a cricket chorus backdrop quickly brought her attention back to the present moment with Jake. His presence exuded comfort and safety. A sense of serenity overcame Bibsy so new it was foreign.

"How's that feel?" Jake said, and without even looking she knew his question was accompanied by his customary broad smile.

"Nice. Real nice. Peaceful."

"Yeah. It's funny how the water has a way of doin that, ain't it?"

"What was that?" Bibsy searched the water alarmed. "Something just brushed by me."

"Nothing to worry about, probably just an eel. It won't hurt you. I ain't never gonna let nothin hurt you, baby. You don't haveta worry bout that."

Within days Bibsy had her first swimming lesson that began with the two of them floating side by side under the moonlight staring at the stars. Even though Bibsy barely held onto Jake's calloused fingertips, simply knowing he was nearby she felt secure in the water.

"If you're ever in water and think you can't swim, jus lay back and relax on your back like this, and you'll float. Pretend like you're layin in bed. Let the water carry you til somebody comes. You fight it and start splashin around, then you're sure ta drown in no time."

Jake and Bibsy made regular nightly trips to the swimming hole after that, and he held her firmly even when they were being frisky and playful. Because Jake didn't showboat as Bibsy knew he surely could have, her confidence grew steadily and so did her ability to swim. He was so patient and encouraging until the depth of water, an occasional eel or dark of night was inconsequential. Bibsy also noticed her night vision improved and she could distinguish things in the dark that she couldn't before.

As swimming became more of their regular routine, she and Carrie got into the habit of doing each other's hair in the cornrow style of Bibsy's youth. Each plaiting the other's hair. Bibsy enjoyed spending time with Carrie and getting to know her. She especially enjoyed never needing to go to Emma's shop again.

Carrie and Bibsy were fishing from Carrie's favorite spot, one of the rotting platforms along the Hudson that had once been an active loading dock during brick-making times. The place offered shade in the afternoon from a crooked tree, its base stood underwater during high tide. Their dresses were pulled above their knees, with legs swaying with the river's current. The fish weren't biting but the women were too satisfied to search for a better spot. It was enough to just be outdoors lazing away a Saturday morning. Bibsy pleasurably sending clouds of cigarette smoke into a cloudless sky. And Carrie, with her snuff-dipping, happily spewing rounds of dark saliva to the ground.

"What'd Jake say bout them men from the power company that was seen leavin from down here yestidy?" Carrie asked.

“Not too much. Said he didn’t know why somebody didn’t try to scare em off with their shotgun like usual.”

“He’s right too.” Carrie nodded in agreement. “I got a bad feelin about the whole mess, to tell ya the truth. Got a right foul smell to it.” Carrie set a fixed gaze ahead as though trying to bring the far shore into better focus. The old woman’s expression was making Bibsy uneasy. The whole idea of using shotguns to scare off people didn’t sit well with her either, but she never said so.

“What’s eatin you, Aunt Carrie? A few guys from the power company came and took pictures and did some measurin. That’s all.”

“No, it’s more’n that, Bibsy. A lot more. You don’t understand yet.”

“Understand what? Explain it to me then.”

“You see,” Carrie took time to allow her bottom jaw to work the snuff around in her mouth, “That was real bold what they did. Strangers don’t come down here. At least they never did before.”

“The power company’s from around here, ain’t they?” Bibsy quipped. “How you figure them strangers?” She was hoping to lighten the mood but her remark seemed to make Carrie sink further into it, redirecting her far-away gaze squarely at Bibsy.

“They’re strangers if they don’t live down here. And strangers don’t come along The Beach without somebody who we recognize as a friend. This place is known for stray shots. Specially when outsiders come snoopin around. That's the way it's always been."

"Oh." Bibsy was annoyed that Carrie was suddenly so serious. "I thought you meant people from out of town when you said strangers."

"Don't haveta be. Bein colored don't automatically make em one of us neither."

Carrie kept aiming for the same spot when she spat and the mess was beginning to puddle.

"Everybody around here knows that. Now, white folks will go anytime they want upriver a ways.

To Stone Point, for instance. But down here, they stop right there at that dirt road and send word, by one of the children usually, to get whoever it is they wanna see." Her eyes softened a touch when she said, "And shoot, durin the Prohibition days folks would line up at the beginnin of that dirt road to git the strongest shine in the whole county. Yes they would. Whoops! I got a bite!" Carrie held a tighter grip on her pole and began reeling it in. "Must be a good size. Or jus feisty. I'm gonna haveta stand up for this one. Here, hold this pole a minute til I get up. And hold tight ta that reel. Don't let it spin out."

Bibsy held her own pole between her knees and took Carrie's, but only had it a hot minute before Carrie was on her feet snatching it back. She reeled it in slowly, patiently.

Once it was out of the water, Carrie grabbed first the line, then the fish under the gills squeezing the mouth open to retrieve her hook. "This one's still got a lotta fight left in im." She threw the thrashing fish into the bucket of water and waited for its jerking movements to slow, then worked the hook from its mouth.

"Whoa, that's a big one! What kind is it?"

"Carp," Carrie answered as she worked the last prong of the hook loose. "And Mr. Carp, you gonna taste mighty good." She tossed the fish into the bucket, rebaited her hook and cast the line into the water once more.

"You sure are fast. Takes me forever to get the fish in the doggone bucket. I'm careful. Take my time. But still, that hook gets stuck in my finger damn near every time. I don't even bother if it's a catfish. I either cut the line or leave those ugly slimy things right on the hook for somebody else to take off."

"Hooks won't bother you after awhile. How long you been up here now Bibsy, a month?"

"A month? I been here two months goin on three. Seems longer than that to me. I guess cause nobody acted too friendly in the beginning, colored or white."

"Some will speak no matter what. Others won't. A lotta people from The City come up here talkin bout how nice everything is, and wind up goin back in no time cause country life don't suit em. Maybe they jus wanna wait and see if you gonna stay before they take the time to get ta know you."

There wasn't a part of Bibsy that didn't believe she and Jake would see old age together, and she felt bragging on it was certain to foul things up. So her response to Carrie was, "Whether I stay or not ain't nobody's business but mine. Since when is the whole town in on it?"

"They ain't." Carrie wasn't put off by Bibsy's testiness. "I think you did pretty good. I seen where new folks been here six months to a year before anybody'd take to em. But that quick tongue of yours makes people decide right fast if they wanna be bothered or not. Don't haveta figure on it too long."

"I don't care. Ain't lookin for no friends. I'm just sayin everybody don't speak when you pass em on the street. But truth be told, most of em do."

"Takes time. Course, bein Jake's woman won't hurt you none around here. Everybody on The Beach and most of the town knows Jake. Plenty of em still remember his daddy too. Boy, those sure was the days." Carrie went into herself with that memory without apologizing, until she was ready to continue. "Folks left down here now ain't got the heart oldtimers had. Notice you ain't seen no police cars come round here."

"Hmmm, now that you mention it...."

"Too many men have come down here lookin for trouble and found it. Wound up missin. Or shot by accident, cept it wasn't no accident and they knew it and we did too. But it keeps outsiders away. Only a fool would come searchin for trouble in a backwoods place like this with all the tall grass and twisted trees along here. And a liquor-lovin trigger-happy bunch as is down here…pure foolishness! It's awful strange that they start takin the liberty now though. Ain't like the power company to take such a big chance wit they men. They got somethin up their sleeve," Carrie said. "Jake's gonna haveta find somethin else ta fix besides fish for his poker game tonight, cause they ain't bitin worth a damn."

"You think you'll feel up ta doin hair on Sunday?" Bibsy said.

"Yeah. After I get supper started." Carrie said. "I'm glad you and Jake took up swimming.

"How'd you know about that?"

"Girl, ain't no secrets on this beach." Carrie took another snuff pause before adding, "Now that's somethin Gertie woulda never done. She wouldna done nothing to mess with her regular hair appointment in town. And I know how much Jake loves the water. And now I got somebody to scratch my scalp regular. See how things work out?"

Finally, Bibsy thought, there was something she didn't have to compete with Jake's ex-wife about.

"Aunt Carrie," Bibsy began with hesitancy, "you ever miss not having kids of your own?"

"Umm." Carrie was thoughtful and measured her response accordingly, "I useta, a good while back. But to tell you the truth, I helped raise so many that it really don't feel like I didn't have none. But I guess it woulda been nice to give Gus a child. I think he woulda liked that. But over the years we raised a whole heap of kids together."

"Oh." Living with Martha, even for only several months, and now Jake and his boys, Bibsy witnessed the vibrant dimension children added to households, and it was such a stark contrast to her own childhood where any natural childlike curiosities were choked off and never saw the light of day.

"Why'd you ask?" Carrie glanced at Bibsy briefly before turning her attention back to the river. "You pregnant?"

"No." Bibsy said. "I wish I could be." Usually cautious with personal information, their regular hair braiding sessions allowed them the opportunity to bond more deeply. Because Carrie wasn't prone to gossip, Bibsy gradually began to trust her enough to divulge some aspects of her past, like growing up at St. Cecelia's. "Soon after I got out of school I got pregnant and my mother made me have an abortion." She paused a moment before continuing, "Something wrong happened…and now I can't have kids."

"And now you want kids." Carrie kept her gaze straight ahead at the gently rolling Hudson.

"Well..I wish I could have Jake's kids. But I can't."

"You know, Bibsy." After spitting out all her snuff and wiping her mouth with a rag she kept in her housedress pocket, Carrie continued. "I useta waist a lotta time tryin ta figure out why God would not want me to have chilren. But then I realized how much a blessin I could be to so many of em that's already here, and I stopped feelin sorry for myself. If you love kids, there's a lot of em already here. What does it matter that you didn't bring em inta this world? There's a heap of em already here, and all of em needin ta be loved. Even those that got mommas and daddies, they still need it too."

Carrie's explanation made sense. And it was true that she'd been feeling sorry for herself for quite awhile. She shook her head in agreement, although it was still painful, "Yeah, that's true."

"And to tell you the truth, Jake don't need no more babies. He got two good boys there. I know, cause I helped ta raise em." She faced Bibsy now. "But they need a momma. And you can't ask for better kids than Junior and Robert."

"They are. And I like em both."

"Junior's sweet as can be. Now that Robert can be a handful at times, but he knows ta step back in line when you tell im."

"You're right. I was just wishing my life was different, and I could just have one."

"But don't miss the blessins you got right up under your nose. It done fell right in your lap and you can't even see it for feelin so much pity for yourself. Let go of what you don't have a chance of changin...an move on."

Bibsy thought Carrie was sounding a lot like Martha now. Except that even in her straightforward manner, her words were soaked in a tenderness and compassion that Martha's lacked. Letting go and moving on was advice she'd gotten all her life and it was always difficult, if not impossible. Because Carrie was also childless Bibsy knew she spoke from experience, and because she wasn't kin it was easier to hear. Gratitude. She had to give that one more thought. There were so many years of dwelling on what was missing; how she thought her life was so different from everyone else's. The women sat for a long stretch without speaking, enjoying the flight of the birds in the sky, the occasional passing boat and even the fish that weren't biting.

Plunkett was already sitting at the table eating when Mason T came to the house. Jake was at the stove frying chicken.

"Damn, Plunk, can't I ever beat you to a poker game? What'd you do, sleep over here last night?"

"Might have, if Jake let me." Plunkett laid another chicken bone on his plate. "What you know good, Tee?"

"Nothin new. Jus the same ole, same ole. Damned if it don't smell good in here." Mason T pulled out a chair and sat at the table with Plunkett. "And look at the pile of bones you got stacked on that plate. What you tryin ta do, grow that other leg back?"

"I lost a leg in Korea. Doctors ain't said nothin bout my appetite gettin stranded over there."

At first, people used to shy away from Plunkett when he was forced home from the service after his accident. Not out of meanness, but from so much pity it seemed to clog their minds and warp their tongues. People who'd known him all his life shrank from the obvious when they saw him and talked about the weather and other such things; ignoring the left pant leg blowing in the breeze or folded and pinned thigh high. It was Mason T's unchanging, easy up-front ways that rescued his childhood buddy from sympathy's slow sure death.

"I always said you guys ought ta be on stage somewhere. Maybe they'll let you reopen the Haverton Opera House on Broadway. "Y'all could pack em in the way they did in the old vaudeville days." Jake stopped to sip some whiskey. "Since you was almost the first one here, you can have a sample, Mason T. Jus one. Gotta pay up after that."

"Yeah, let me get a taste of that chicken before this man starts lickin the pots." Mason T used the table to tap out a tune while he glanced around the room. "Where's Bibsy and everybody?"

"They all went with Gus and Carrie to the store." Jake put a piece of chicken in front of his latest guest and handed him a bottle of hot sauce. "They'll be back soon."

Sweet Lou and Big Mabel came in together. They both lived on The Beach not far from each other. Sweet Lou worked for the New Jersey Railroad that came through town. He and his woman had eight children and there was rumor that he had three more elsewhere in the county. That's how he'd gotten the "sweet" part of his name. Big Mabel had earned her name honestly. She was also the only regular female poker player in town. No matter how much she was winning or losing, her expression stayed the same. Nobody's ever seen her smile. The two Weaver brothers came soon after. Charlie, the youngest, hit the number three days earlier and you could tell Lady Luck had paid him a recent visit. His eyes told. Besides that, he was more eager to play than usual.

"You playin tonight?" Charlie asked Jake.

"No. Gonna deal."

"Good."

"Yeah."

Some of the players fixed drinks as Jake pulled the cellophane from a new deck. He worked the cards until the stiffness yielded to him and shot between each other in a precision blur. "There'll be some ice soon's Bibsy and them git back from the store. Should be soon."

"Better be, or you'll have a buncha drunks on your hands." Mabel put fifty cents in a jar near the liquor, after fixing an Old Grand Dad and water.

"Okay," Jake said giving the final riffle to the cards before handing them to Plunkett for a cut. "Same as always. Stud's the game, in case you forgot. Nothin wild. Two-dollar minimum. And no bullshit." He dealt the first round of cards faced down. The next face up. Mason T had the high card, an ace of clubs, and made the first bet. Everybody placed their bets before Jake dealt another round.

Lou had two tens showing. "I'll raise it to four."

Rain's barking announced a car pulling up. "Here comes the ice," Jake said.

"Could be somebody else," Mabel said as she threw her hand in. Mason T junked his as well.

"No, that's her welcome-home bark." The bets were placed and Jake dealt the next round.

Charlie's brother, Wes, raised the bid to six with a pair of deuces and a queen showing. Plunkett had the third deuce and looked to be working on a heart flush. He matched the bid and said, "Gimmie the next one in the hole."

Bibsy, Gus, Carrie and the boys came in and greeted the players who returned their hi's without taking their eyes off the table. The boys made a loud racket pouring ice cubes into a metal tub filled with bottles of beer and soda.

"Got the change you wanted, Jake." Gus held up four rolls of quarters. "Couldn't get em all in the same place though. That's what took so long. How's the game goin?"

When no one answered, Gus came over to the table just as Lou exposed the winning hand, three tens. Jake counted the pile of bills and took out the ten percent house cut, then pushed the stack toward Lou.

Lou slid a two-dollar tip back to the dealer and said, "Keep it comin."

Before the next hand, Sweet Lou yelled to Bibsy, "Can I get some ice Miz Bibsy?"

Not lifting her eyes from the romance magazine she was reading, she said, "We went to the store and brought the ice in the house. The least you can do is get up and get it."

Sweet Lou looked at Jake as if expecting an explanation and Jake simply shook his head. "Don't look at me, she's got a point man. Get your lazy ass up and get your own ice."

Three hours into the game, Mason T pushed his chair back from the table. "I know when ta quit. That's enough for me," he said stretching. "Aunt Carrie, can you fix me a plate ta take home? That'll be my breakfast in the mornin."

"I might crash at your place tonight," Plunkett said to him. "Don't go reachin for your shotgun if you hear me stumblin around. If you got somebody stayin the night, let er know it's jus me."

"Or you're liable ta get konked upside the head with a fryin pan." Charlie laughed out loud at his own joke.

"What's your rush, Tee?" Jake said. "Things is jus gettin interestin." He dealt the next hand.

"A little too interestin for my money."

"You got more money than anybody here," Mabel said keeping a keen eye on the table as she talked. "Livin on The Beach and workin two jobs. You could probably buy the whole beach by now."

"Somebody's gotta have some money around here," Plunkett defended his friend. "He's got more sense than all of us put together."

Charlie raised the bet with two queens and a king showing. "Tee ain't foolin nobody. He's gonna go back south and live like a king one day. Cause they sure ain't gonna let im do that up here."

"This won't last forever." Mason T said as he handed Carrie two dollars and reached for a plate of food wrapped in waxed paper. "Anybody hear anything bout two lectric company guys on The Beach the other day?"

Sweet Lou's, "I'll see Charlie's two and raise it twenty," quieted the whole table. He was showing a pair of aces, with a jack kicker.

Mason T hung around to watch the outcome of the hand.

Wes threw his in. “Too rich for me.”

Big Mabel was working on a possible straight and said, “Sheeeet,” in a low voice, “I’m goin with my hunch.” She reached in her bra, pulled out a roll of bills, peeled off a twenty and threw it in the center of the table. “You’re bluffin, you ole dog,” she said. “Call it.”

Jake looked at Plunkett. “What you gonna do, man?”

Plunkett shifted in his seat staring at his pair of nines and a queen. He peeked again at his two hold cards, then dug in his shirt pocket and threw a twenty in the pot.

Jake said, “Charlie?”

Charlie double-checked his hold card and matched the bet on the strength of it and the three spades showing. “Call it,” he said. “I feel lucky.”

Jake dealt the final round of cards. “I’m gonna eat after this.

Plunkett beat out everybody with a full house. Gus was ready to step in and deal but the players wanted to break and eat or relax with a drink.

Bibsy handed Jake a plate of food. “Anybody else?”

“Nope, that’s fine.”

"I'll take a dinner. Same thing Jake's got."

"Me too."

"Give me a chicken sandwich and a soda."

"I'd like two pieces of chicken on one slice of bread."

When everybody was busy eating Carrie began pulling the children from the couch where they had fallen asleep with comic books in their laps. "Get up," she kept saying. "Go on in your room cause this gonna be my spot after while."

Mason T said, "Ain't nobody answer me when I asked about those guys from the power company. Y'all heard anything?"

"I heard they'd come over here but I didn't believe it," Wes answered.

Bibsy said, "I don't think it's such a bad idea if we have electric lights and running water. It'd sure make life around here a whole lot easier."

The quiet was thunderous until Jake said, "Maybe you oughta shut your mouth to things you don't know nothin about, Bibsy."

"You ain't my daddy Jake. Don't go tellin me what to do."

The room was still only a moment before Jake raised his voice with, "I ain't claimin to be your daddy. Just the same, you don't know what you're talkin about so you need to leave that subject alone, woman."

Bibsy eyeballed Jake over the romance magazine in front of her, "Jake Tucker, I ain't scared of you. You can raise your voice all you want. Humph," she said and began to flip through the pages. Then she got up and fixed herself a drink. "I don't know who you think you are." She mumbled under her breath.

"Can y'all hold off fightin til I can make me some money here tonight?" Mabel said.

"Better take care of that," Sweet Lou said to Jake nodding in Bibsy's direction.

"Man, you mind your house and your women, and let me mind this one, hear?" Jake said to him.

"Okay." Sweet Lou shook his head. "Only tryin ta help."

After several elongated minutes of everyone focused on the game, Mabel broke the starchy air after the next hand was dealt. "When I first heard about the power company nosing down here, I didn't believe it either."

"I still don't." Jake said. "But I'ma check in the mornin ta see if there's any markers on the road that those surveyors like to leave behind. Make em disappear if I see any."

"I'll help. What time you gonna get started?"

"Soon's I git a few winks. I'll make the boys help out too."

"I'll come by with my boys too. The more hands, the quicker we'll finish."

"Ain't nobody asked for no lectricity down here."

"If I seen em, I'da had target practice sure nuf."

"Wonder why they botherin us now, after all these years? Last time they tried ta put lectricity over here they almost lost one of their men."

"They jus tryin ta catch us off guard."

"They know we ain't gonna let them put no street lights up."

"The first thing'll happen is you'll have the police nosin around here regular."

"Then they'll sweet-talk everybody inta gettin wired for lectric in the house...causa them TVs.

"Yeah, that'll do it."

"Some of them shows is pretty nice though."

"I like them cowboys."

"Seen one of them cowboy shows over ta my sister's place the other week," Big Mabel said. "It was pretty good."

"Oh, oh, sounds like you ready ta pack it in. Plan on movin, Mack? Gettin too rough for ya?" Gus asked.

"You know better'n that."

"They best leave well enough alone if they know like I know," Carrie said from a curled up position on the couch.

"You seen how they did us over at the Mud Hole. Got everything over there now, and they said they was jus gonna run lectric wires. Got phone lines. Dug up the damn street ta put in water pipes. Send you a goddamn bill every month for every one of them things, too. We didn't ask for that shit."

"Shouldna let em in there in the first damn place." Jake started shuffling again.

"Shit, Jake, the Mud Hole ain't hemmed in like The Beach. We right there in the open." Wes wiped his mouth on his shirt sleeve before rubbing his hands on a nearby towel.

"Anyway, we playin cards right now, ain't we?" Jake started dealing another round. "Tired of hearin about white folks. They ain't gonna do nothin less we let em."

Chapter Eight

Bibsy kept a third eye on Rain ever since the dog walked up to her during that time of the month and sniffed between her legs. Only after Bibsy consistently threw something at her each time did Rain finally stop. She felt it was trouble enough going through the ordeal with an outhouse, no running water and only men in the house. Having a dog broadcast it to the world was too much.

Jake laughed, saying it was only natural because Rain's sharp sense of smell is what made her such a good hunting dog. He said there were so many dogs on The Beach that raccoons, skunks, possums and other such night critters kept their distance. Even squirrels, considered food by many Beach residents, were hardly ever seen on the ground.

Growing up she'd always wanted a dog because they seemed so naturally cuddly, especially the puppies. But of course animals weren't allowed at St. Cecelia's. When she first got out of school she got a dog from a woman she worked with who was moving and couldn't take it with her, but it ran away because Bibsy didn't have the heart to tie it up. Expecting to run into the same problem again, she never replaced the animal. The notion of letting dogs run free was brand new.

As Bibsy became more and more a part of the flow of the household, oftentimes being the one to feed Rain, slowly they softened to each other. Like the others in the family, Bibsy came to rely on Rain to announce visitors and ward off other animals, something especially useful at night when she and Jake had their routine swim.

Jake noticed Rain had slowed down since the beginning of the summer and finally one morning rolled her over and inspected her belly. Observing Rain's bigger and tighter midsection along with reddened teats, he pronounced, "This dog's havin pups." By the time August came, Rain had a litter of eight puppies. Six survived. Jake had just given away two to people on The Beach, and the other four were constantly underfoot, forever playful. The runt being Bibsy's favorite, she named Tiger. The boys thought it was a weird name for a dog, but Bibsy stuck to her choice.

Enjoying the sight of puppies scamper through the house tussling with each other, she looked through the mail she'd just brought in the house. Still no letter from Martha. Since Bibsy had recently sent her a third letter, she rummaged through her old suitcase where she kept her personal papers and pulled out a postcard where Martha had written the address, making sure she'd written it correctly. Looking again at the street address, apartment and zone number, she was hoping she'd copied it correctly. Bibsy held the postcard and sat a moment to contemplate her older sister's handwriting. Actually, studying it for the first time.

Martha tended to show Bibsy more compassion, maybe because she was ten years older and consequently wiser. Or, it was more likely since they hadn't grown up together were able to start off on a clean slate. Bibsy felt the orphanage ruined her relationship with Mary and Cora. Some of the nuns, Sister Mary Margaret in particular, masterfully played them against each other. Sixty young colored girls desperate for at least attention, if not affection, constantly jockeyed for any form of acceptance, and it played a significant role in fueling a fierce rivalry and jealousy between them that would last a lifetime.

While living with her sister those few months, what she cherished most was simply being among them in their everyday lives. Bibsy did think Martha worked too hard in their home and Kalvin could have pitched in more to help, after all, she worked every day just like he did. Looking again at the postcard, feeling something about it was off, Bibsy eventually realized it was the handwriting. She opened the screen door and shooed the pups out of the house, then made room on the couch and sat down to inspect the writing more thoroughly.

Every time she discovered another first she hadn't known, seen or done with her own flesh and blood, it wounded her in deep unidentifiable places. Then once again, the anger would creep up and flow through her body forming an emotional stampede aimed directly at Letty.

Why did she have to put them there of all places? Mom and Pop both had family. They took the oldest, why not them? They weren't bad kids. Why? She'd been asking herself those same questions since she was a child and still had no satisfactory answer. Her mother's explanation that she had to work and live-in help made more money than day work wasn't sufficient. What did money matter, she thought. We were her children. Bibsy knew too many colored women who'd raised their children alone. It was something colored women always managed to do. So, why? She was convinced that the family was hiding a significant piece from this puzzle.

Bibsy noted the stark difference in her sister's cursive writing. How unlike hers, their sisters or anyone at St. Cecelia's where everyone's penmanship was exactly the same. Sixty girls formulated each letter of the alphabet with the exact same style, height, slope and size. No flourishes. No deviations. No unauthorized curlicues. No singular identity.

The nuns at St. Cecelia's demanded the students execute the exact same penmanship with heartbreaking success. Expressions of individuality were rewarded with the force of a wooden ruler across bare knuckles, ensuring everyone would conform to their insistence of uniformity. Instinctively rubbing the back of her left hand, Bibsy recalled the pain with perfect recall. The recollection of the knuckles on her left hand swollen beyond their intended size was evidence of Sister Mary Margaret's particular teaching style.

"Put your hand on the desk, Elizabeth. You know the rules," Sister Mary Margaret demanded with pursed lips in her too familiar Irish brogue. "Quickly! Or you'll receive three strikes, instead of two." Other nuns would whack the backs of hands and be quickly done with it. But Sister Mary Margaret demanded her students make a fist, making the knuckles more pronounced, increasing the pain. Afterwards she'd linger there, hovering over her charges with a devious smile as if savoring their suffering.

Whenever she cried to her mother, as she always did when she was young, Letty chastised her further and told Bibsy she tended to be a troublemaker and needed to "stop all that foolishness" because it was just making it harder on herself. "Why can't you be like your sister, Mary?" was her familiar reply. Bibsy hated that her mother wouldn't stand up to the nuns. Feeling abandoned, she'd come away from her fruitless pleadings on those infrequent third-Sunday visits, feeling more hurt than from the punishments the nuns dished out.

Letty held a strong belief in the power of education. "With an education, you won't have to cook or clean for nobody. You can get you a good job and there's no better education than a Catholic school."

Bibsy looked down at the postcard, loving every off-centered, flat, misshapen loop and curlicue for merely being. Surviving. In the opposite slant of the letters characteristic of lefties, she saw what her writing might have been if it simply had the freedom to be. In the final moments she stared at Martha's script before putting the postcard back in the suitcase, she wondered if the reason her sister didn't write was because Martha was ashamed of her handwriting. Bibsy was heartbroken that her letters might have offended Martha and immediately decided to call her from Louie's on her way home from work the next day, but as if reading her mind, Robert burst into the house that evening saying Louie had a message from her sister to call.

"Hello?"

"Hi, Sis." Bibsy was excited just hearing Martha's voice.

"I got your letters. Sorry I didn't get to write back. Busy, busy, busy."

"I know. That's okay, Sister."

"I sure do admire your handwriting though. Wish I could write like that."

"Thanks, but I like yours better. They beat us to death to get us to write that way. They shoulda let us write however God intended us to."

"It sure is a whole lot better than my chicken scratch. Well, I know you're at a payphone so I'll get to the point. We're coming to visit in two weeks. And I probably won't be able to convince Kalvin to spend the night, so we'll probably be there early and head home before nightfall so the kids can enjoy themselves all day."

"Oh, they'll love the country. And I can't wait to see you."

"Yeah, me too. Kalvin found the bus and train schedule and he'll figure out the best way to get there."

"You want Jake to call you with directions?"

"No, I don't think so."

"There's a train station right in town. And I hear there's a bus that stops here from The City."

"We'll work that all out. You know Kalvin, he'll get us there. Anyway, two weeks from this Saturday. See you then."

"Okay. Bye, Sis."

Chapter Nine

The faintest breeze carried the sweet scent from hundreds of honeysuckles tangled in the brush along the riverbank. Placing her coffee-filled Mason jar on the ground and plucking one of the wildflowers, Bibsy carefully rolled its miniature trumpet shape back and forth between her thumb and index finger. Once her curiosity was satisfied, she tossed the bud into the water and watched its short-lived journey downriver.

Patiently waiting for Jake and the boys to finish working on the truck's engine so they could begin their planned visit to one of Jake's friends in Hillboro, she thought about how her family would react to her new home. Bibsy thought Martha, and especially the kids, would enjoy Haverton but wasn't so sure about Kalvin. She couldn't even imagine her brother-in-law outside of The City.

Inspecting another honeysuckle, sniffing it this time, Bibsy thought about her job at Better Sweaters and was proud that she'd caught on quickly how to negotiate the industrial button-holer. Because it wasn't an easy machine to learn, she and Evelyn were the only ones who weren't expected to rotate positions like the other workers who operated looms in teams of three or four; each group at a different stage of the sweater-making process. Every few weeks they'd rotate tasks, so if needed, there'd always be someone available and trained to fill in at any of the positions in case somebody quit or called in sick. Aside from the constant banter among the women, a new sweater style or color was the only relief from the constant monotony.

The job rotation reminded Bibsy of the way chores were organized at St. Cecilia's; switching off every month from cooking, to yard work, to washing clothes on a washboard, yet always cleaning. They cleaned the chapel twice a week. The older girls, creating scaffolds using ladders and wood planks, were the only ones entrusted to clean the floor-to-ceiling stained glass windows. And it was required that their work be done in silence, especially in the chapel where they were required to attend six o'clock Mass each morning.

Bibsy heard someone on the path and turned cautiously. Sometimes she'd hear something or someone, only to find no one was there, but was relieved when she saw Junior and said, "Hey," as he headed toward her. "You're not helpin with the truck?"

"Nah, I was just watchin. I don't like workin on no cars."

The river current was rough and they watched the smaller boats struggle to navigate the water's wrath that day.

"You like coming out here, don't you?" Junior said.

"Yeah. I don't know, but sittin here lookin out at so much water puts a different take on life. Makes everything look different to me. Problems get shrunk down to size. It's peaceful too."

"You know," Junior said looking at the bud in Bibsy's hand, "my mom useta love them flowers. Every time I smell em I think of her. She would bring bunches of em in the house and have the whole place smellin nice. Sometimes they'd be covered in ants though." A sweet smile brightened his face. "She sure liked them flowers."

It was the first time Junior mentioned his mother to her and one of the few times she welcomed hearing about Gertie. They shared the same connection of growing up without their mother. However, they preserved some memories of their mom, which is more than she had.

"Junior, how old were you when your mom died?" Bibsy said.

"Six. Almost seven. All the time I think of things I wished I had asked her, but I didn't think of em then."

"Oh yeah? Like what, Junior?" She found his statement intriguing and wondered what questions she might have for her own mother, if any.

"I wonder about silly things. Like what was her favorite color and what kinda things made her laugh."

"That's not silly, Junior. Why don't you ask your father? I'm sure he'd tell you."

"Naw, it upsets Pop to talk about her, and he jus waves his hand at me if I ask him stuff like that. He said when people leave this earth you jus gotta accept it and move on."

Junior broke off a honeysuckle branch and tapped it gently against his knee and watched a battalion of ants fall to the ground and scatter. They both turned when they heard footsteps on the path.

"Glad that's done." Jake was still lathering his hands and forearms as he came down the pathway. "We're ready to go now. Lost a little time cause I had ta plug that damn radiator, but we got it done."

Hillboro was a smidgen of a hamlet cradled against New York's southwestern sector along the Ramapo Mountain range. Although Jake used the back roads through the mountain pass that was familiar to locals, it took his fragile truck a good part of an hour to get there.

Preoccupied with the conversation she'd had with Junior, Bibsy now also wondered what kind of woman Letty was. She thought Junior seemed wounded by his mother's absence in ways she hadn't expected or even contemplated about her own mother. It was hurtful to acknowledge she didn't know what made her own mother laugh, or what her favorite color was, and yet Letty was alive and well. She didn't know anything about her father, nor did she desire to know since he'd done the unthinkable by bringing them to St. Cecelia's. If her father hadn't done such a horrific deed, Bibsy thought Junior's query might have sparked curiosity about him as well. But as far as she was concerned he'd been dead her entire life.

"Anybody come up that road must either be friend or family." Manny greeted them as the truck pulled up the last incline, emptying into a yard displaying an array of spent cars and trucks accumulated over the years.

His eyes were cloudy and moist, as if tears were on the verge of spilling down his weathered cheeks onto his prickly white stubble. Deep creases etched into a brow partially hidden beneath a sweat-stained brimmed cap.

After greeting Uncle Manny and a few of the others, the boys and Rain tumbled out of the truck and disappeared with a group of boys playing baseball in a nearby open field. A stream of people approached the truck welcoming them.

"Howdyado?" Manny said to Bibsy when they were introduced.

"Fine thanks."

"Brought you some catfish," Jake pulled a bucket from the back of the truck, looked inside and saw there was still some movement even though half the water had spilled during the ride. "I know how you like catfish."

"Sure do." Manny gave Jake a good natured slap on the back. "You just made my day, son."

After using their bathroom, which Bibsy gladly noted was located inside the house, Jake and Bibsy met Manny on the front porch where he'd set out old newspapers and was sharpening his hunting knife on a nearby stone. Jake went to the truck and got his hunting knife and pulled out his pocket knife as well, and it wasn't long before he was busy skinning catfish. Manny soon joined him.

"My name's Katherine, but everybody calls me Kate." Manny's wife looked like a white woman and in response to Bibsy's surprised reaction quickly added, "Don't worry, I'm colored. Everybody up here is."

"Yeah, all the ones tryin to be white, done already left. Livin white somewhere or other."

Jake shook his head laughing as Kate returned to the house, "Aw, come on Uncle Manny, don't start that up again."

Looking around, Bibsy realized quite a few could have passed for white, or maybe Spanish. Every now and again she'd see someone dark-skinned like herself.

"It's true. Ain't no need in lyin about it."

Kate stuck her head out the screen door. “Anybody want some iced tea?”

“Tell em, honey. Soma your folks passed over, didn’t they?”

“Oh, there he goes again. Manny, why you always bring that up around company?”

“Jake ain’t no company. He’s damn near family. Any time you know somebody long as we know Jake and his people, they family. And,” he looked at Bibsy, “Anybody Jake trusts to bring up here is family too.” Manny cupped his mouth pretending he and Bibsy were having a private conversation, “She don’t want to admit it, but some of her folks crossed over.”

“I’m not ashamed. They the ones should be ashamed.” Katherine looked at Jake and Bibsy. “Iced tea?” They shook their heads yes.

“Wish I’d run into em. I’d call em out so loud they’d haveta put me in jail for disturbin the peace. I’d let the world know.”

Jake held down the body of a large catfish with his left hand, and with the other leaned into his blade severing the fish’s head. “That’s probably why they moved away, cause they know you’d probably do just that.”

“Want me to get the fire goin Pop? Y’all cookin the fish outside?” Manny and Kate’s grown son, Josh, asked.

"Yeah son. That's a good idea. It'll keep the heat outta the house."

Some of the people dove in and helped Jake and Manny prepare the fish. Some went inside and helped with the food or brought some of their food to cook along with the fish. Others went home and brought back liquor or beer.

Kate held three glasses of iced tea in her hands as she pushed the screen door open. "Honey, you don't haveta stay out here listenin to Manny's mess if you don't want to. You're welcome inside if you want."

Bibsy laughed, "I'll come in and see if there's anything I can help with."

Bibsy went inside and came back moments later with a bowl of potatoes and began peeling. "We still in New York, Jake?"

Manny answered for him. "Yeah, you're in New York. But to tell the truth, we right close to Jersey, right over there." He nodded in the direction of the southwestern range of the Ramapo Mountains. "Got people over there too."

Kate joined them and began cutting up the potatoes as Bibsy peeled them. "Manny, you got family everywhere." She turned to Bibsy, "His folks helped to settle this place a long long time ago."

"Sixteen eighty-seven." Gently tugging at the skin with his knife, Manny exposed the pink flesh of a catfish.

"That's the year on the records at the Dutch Reformed Church. That's when my great-great-grandaddy along with a dozen or so other men bought land up here. He wasn't the only colored one neither, there was two others. Freed slaves who had money like him."

"Come on Manny," Jake laughed. "Bring on the history lesson."

"He does this every time." Josh smiled at his dad.

"The story goes, that my great-great-granddaddy was the son of a slave ship captain and his slave. He was Dutch and had lots of money, and left his baby son a good piece of change in his will when he died. When the boy got older…now, they lived in the part of The City called The Bowery, where lots of colored lived then. Anyway, when the boy got to be a man, he used his money to speculate on some farmland up here. Him and two other slaves that was free like him."

Josh jumped in to speed up the story. "They were part of the original settlers of Langston and Bergen County in New Jersey. Named it the Tappan Patent in history books. But white folks don't play up the fact that colored folks was part of it."

A woman in the crowd added, "I heard they drew the state boundary right through the middle of our people, putting half of us in New Jersey, and half in New York, cause we was gettin too much pull in Albany."

"Did you know they had a law back then that the freed slaves couldn't congregate with the ones that wasn't free?" Manny didn't wait for an answer. "That's why those three colored families that started out together, stayed close over the years, and their families married each other. Mixed in some Indians too, cause colored folks always got along wit the Indians."

Josh broke in, "Pop loves entertainin them college students that come around interviewing him for their thesis papers."

"I got em in there." Manny nodded toward the house. "They give me copies. Need ta let the world know we been in this county long as white folks have."

"I hear that young lawyer y'all had here awhile ago is helpin with all the schools down south now. Done made his way to the Supreme Court they say."

"Yeah, I seen it in the paper and the Jet Magazine too."

Manny mumbled, "Shoulda left the schools the way they was."

"Pop, how can you say that? Our kids had an elementary school that got cast-off books the white kids didn't use anymore. The children were taught in a rundown one-room shack, with an outhouse in the yard, while the white kids had a nice looking brick building with classrooms and indoor plumbing."

"We always took care of our own." Manny said. "We never had ta ask outsiders for nothin before."

"But Pop, Hillboro Elementary was the last school to integrate. We had ta do something drastic. The NAACP did it for us."

"You know your father won't ever change. Stubborn as the day is long."

"Pop, things are different now. Kids need education to get ahead. Our kids comin out of that school never did as good as the white kids cause they didn't have as good of a foundation to begin with. It wasn't separate and equal, it was separate and unequal. And the lawyer proved it."

"Thurgood. A strange name ain't it? But he's a smart man." Kate turned to Bibsy, "You ever hear of such a thing? Here in New York, a separate school for colored children?"

"No, I didn't know that happened up north. When was that?"

"Bout ten, twelve years ago."

"Nineteen forty two. Eleven years ago. And now, just like you said, Uncle Jake," Josh continued, "He's takin on the whole country. Usin a segregated school in Kansas to fight the whole system. I think he'll do it too."

"He's a sharp lawyer. I hope he wins."

"I hear over in Kancy, they're finally lettin colored folks inta the YMCA."

“Oh yeah? It’s about damn time. Things sure are changin pretty fast all of a sudden around here, ain’t it?”

“Not fast enough for me. Why is Langston always the last to get anything done?”

“Too fast for me. They threatenin to take The Beach again. Got some power company snoopin round.”

“Oh yeah? I don’t think they’ll bother y’all.” Manny said. “Some places they’ll think twice about bothering, The Beach in Haverton and The Hill over in Springville. You all can pretty much do what you want cause the cops ain’t comin round there. They ain’t stupid.”

“I don’t see them runnin too quick to your rescue either.” Jake said.

“Yeah, that’s true. But everybody up here’s related one way or another, and we’re a long way from the main road.”

“I see they got up here to put in them septic tanks. I was checkin out your hook up in the bathroom.”

“Wasn’t my idea, Jake,” he nodded toward Josh, “it’s this younger generation. They got different ideas about things.”

“It’s time, Dad.” Josh said. “It’s 1953. You can see the county’s changin.”

“Son, that’s always happened. Nothin new.”

"Uncle Jake, you better get you a piece of property. You and a lotta other folks been rentin too long."

"So they can do me like they did that colored doctor that tried ta have a house built over in New City?" Jake looked at Bibsy now. "They wouldn't let him build there cause he was colored, and they didn't care if he was a doctor or not. So he took the builder to court, and the man changed the name of the company. The colored fella took him to court again and the white guy did the same thing all over again. Changed the name of his company three times, til finally, the colored fella gave up. Feedin all his money to the courts and gettin nothin in return."

"It's a damn shame." Kate said.

"Sure is." Bibsy added.

"But there's places you can buy in the county. In colored sections." Josh said.

"What about Kancy? It's nice over there. And it's on the water. Lotta black folks over there, not on the water…but you know what I mean."

"See all that property them Jews bought in Ramapo?" Came another voice among them. "Betta put your name on somethin soon Jake, fore it gets outta reach."

"Speakin of Kancy, you heard what happened to Ray over there?"

"No. What?"

"They took his house to make way for this new thruway."

"You kiddin. That big place?"

"I'm not kiddin at all. That twelve-room house. Forced him ta take whatever they offered him cause the state said it was in the way and had ta go."

"Humph, they moved some of them other houses. The ones white folks lived in. Seen em on platforms, movin the whole house down the street."

"You know they didn't wanna see no colored person livin in a big house like he had. Think he might get too big for his britches."

"That was a big beautiful house, even had maids' quarters in it." Kate added. "I know they didn't give him what that place was worth, cause you can't even buy somethin like that today. They don't make houses like that no more."

"Not for colored folks to live in."

"Where's he movin to?"

"Central Kancy. You know his father-in-law Spence owns a buncha property over there too. He'll be alright."

"Yeah, I guess til they want that too."

"They better not try ta push Spence around. Cause he'll open his mouth and tell them politicians about themselves. Bring in the NAACP too."

"Uncle Jake, I'm telling you…you better get you a piece of land now before it gets outta reach. Once that bridge goes up, everything's gonna change around here. The Ford plant's moving here and it's gonna bring jobs and higher prices for these houses. You'll see."

"Humph, I got a home already and I ain't never leavin it neither."

Chapter Ten

Rain and her puppies kicked up a fuss as Robert ran into the house yelling, "They're here, Miz Bibsy! Your family's here! Mason T's got em in his car."

Jake and Bibsy wrapped up the chickens they were preparing for that night's supper and shoved them into the ice box, then went outside and met Mason T just as he was pulling his Chevy into their yard. Bibsy could see the children through the car window bouncing up and down excitedly pointing at the puppies.

"Look who I seen comin down the road," Mason T shouted from his side window. "Good thing Trap happened to be in the house. That dog woulda scared em half ta death."

As soon as he came to a stop the children swung open the doors and hopped out before he could even cut the engine. From the front passenger's seat, an older woman eased from the car, her movements graceful and sure. It was Letty.

"Thought I'd surprise you," she said as Jake approached and offered assistance.

Rain and her puppies were now barking wildly. "Don't mind them. This here's our welcomin committee." He gently took hold of Letty's arm and tucked it securely under his own. "Hi, I'm Jake Tucker."

"Hi," Letty held Jake's arm firmly and looked up at him. "I'm Elizabeth's mother. Mrs. Randolph." Once she steadied herself on the uneven dirt yard, she said, "What's the matter, I can't get any sugar from my own child anymore?"

Playing off her surprise at seeing her mother for the first time in over a year, Bibsy greeted her family and introduced everybody. The sight of her reminded Bibsy of the last time they were together just days before she'd left Baltimore for New York on a Trailways bus. Like most of their interactions it was an unpleasant parting.

"What happened to your hair?" Letty asked in a small polite voice that complemented her tasteful Saks Fifth Avenue adorned petite frame. Letty had a lifelong habit of shopping in the neighborhoods where she worked, but Bibsy always found her cruel yet predictable comments at odds with her syrupy voice and fashionable attire. Just as the nuns' evil deeds were contrary to who they were. The younger children were too caught up in the puppies to hear Letty's remark, but everyone else did, even Robert, who looked back at Letty after stopping in mid-action when picking up Tiger.

Not answering, but instinctively touching the hair by her left ear, for the first time in awhile Bibsy wondered what she looked like. They had no mirrors in the house and the only regular place she saw her likeness was when she went to the ladies room at work. The air at the job was so lint-filled the women regularly wore kerchiefs to protect their hair. No one ever commented on her hair. Jake never said anything was wrong with it, nor did the boys. She wasn't being talked about on The Beach, as far as she knew. Now she began to think maybe she was, and nobody told her.

Since she and Carrie began the habit of doing each other's hair regularly, Bibsy acknowledged it was a more pleasant experience than sitting among Emma's gossiping clientele, and besides, she and Carrie enjoyed spending that time together as each one plaited the other's hair. But more importantly for her, the hairstyle of Bibsy's youth was a perfect solution to her and Jake's nighttime swims. They spent so many evenings swimming in the clay pond during that very hot summer the natural braided hairstyle served her best, and that's how she was wearing it when her family came to visit.

"I just did my hair this morning. What's wrong with it?" It always amazed Bibsy how quick to the draw her mother was at igniting fireworks between them. This visit would surely be no different. The only difference was now Letty was humiliating her in front of her new family, and Martha bringing her was an additional dose of betrayal.

Jake had one foot on the bottom step of the porch helping Letty, when he stopped and turned in Bibsy's direction. "Ain't nothin wrong wit your hair baby. It's jus the way I like it."

"You want me to do your hair Bibsy?" Martha attempted to ease the tension. "Got a pressing comb and curling iron? I can do it while I'm here. I don't mind. You know I like to stay busy."

After assuring Letty's comfort on a porch chair, Jake positioned himself at Bibsy's side and said, "I love your hair and everything up under it," then put his arm around her shoulders, "specially when we go swimmin."

"Ooh, can we go swimming too Ma, Dad, please?" the children were saying.

"The kids can go swimmin if they want. Me and Bibsy usually take a dip at night when we got the swimmin hole all to ourselves. Right baby?"

"Why'd you haveta tell everybody that?" Bibsy waved playfully at Jake. An expression of immense gratitude spoke through her eyes though. "You're too much."

"Whew!" Kalvin fanned himself with his straw Stetson. "See, Martha, what'd I tell you about this man from the very beginning?"

Martha shook her head smiling as she reached down in a small travel bag she'd brought. "I knew about the swimming hole from the letters Bibsy sent, so I brought your swimming trunks and bathing suit. Cheryl, don't forget your bathing cap. Time to put on my walking shoes, too." She slipped off her heels and replaced them with flats while they were still standing in the yard.

"So we're all set then. Junior, you and Robert show the kids where they can change, then take em to the swimmin hole."

Letty pulled a pair of comfortable shoes from the Saks shopping bag she carried and put them on as well. "Can somebody show me where the bathroom is? It was a mighty long ride getting here. Especially that last little bit coming up this road."

Bibsy offered, "I'll take you, Mom. And it ain't a bathroom, it's an outhouse." She was glad to demonstrate to Jake and the boys that she was willing to become a part of those uncomfortable moments when a newcomer asked to use the restroom. Bibsy walked towards the porch, but before reaching the steps she heard Letty say, "Oh Lord, an outhouse," under her breath.

"I'll finish the chickens." Jake said, although it was obvious he never took his attention from Bibsy and her mother.

"Jake, I'll help out soon's I get these children situated." Martha said, avoiding Bibsy's gaze.

Not understanding why her sister didn't warn her about their mother coming, Bibsy decided to deal with that later. Right now Mom presented the bigger problem since she'd already embarrassed her about her hair; instincts and experience told her more was coming.

All week long, Bibsy straightened up the house in anticipation of her family's visit. She couldn't help doing some extras, like putting curtains up to the windows, on rods, instead of the dirty fabric nailed to the window frames that had been adequate all along. She spent a good chunk of her paycheck at Woolworths buying most of the things she hadn't previously needed, like table cloths and new towels and such. She also bought Jake and the boys some new T-shirts and swimming trunks. Seeing what it meant to Bibsy, Jake, Robert and Junior also pitched in, sweeping and picking up all the glasses, jars, cans and full ashtrays scattered all over and tidying up the yard, stacking most of the junk neatly behind the house near the chicken coop. Bibsy placed a piece of decorative cloth over the milk crates. Then she topped everything off with a light dusting. It wasn't the knees-to-floor spit shine required at St. Cecelia's, but Bibsy was feeling a little proud of the job she'd done in her new home.

She remembered the day she bought three dressers home from a secondhand shop in town. They were a set she'd been eyeing for a few weeks on her way to and from work every day. Knowing he hadn't moved them in awhile, Bibsy offered the shopkeeper thirty dollars for the set. When he refused, she headed for the door, a trick she learned from Martha who deftly negotiated with street vendors in New York City, and the shopkeeper suddenly had a change of heart and reluctantly took her offer. Jake grumbled some when she asked him to pick them up from the store for her, saying it was a waste of money, but he finally did. However, once the furniture was in the house, he wanted to pay her for what she'd spent, but Bibsy wouldn't take his money and that started a fight.

"You don't haveta spend your money on stuff like that, Bibsy. That's my job." He had said.

"I thought you said this was my home too. What... you didn't mean that?"

"Yeah, I meant it, but that's not what I'm talkin about. Buying furniture an big stuff like that...you don't do that. That's for me ta do."

"Why? Since when do you tell me how I can spend my money, Jake? If I live here, then I'm buying something for the house. Something we can all use. That's all. Don't seem right keeping a scorecard on this stuff."

"Woman, some things is for a man ta do."

"Why, because it's furniture? And secondhand furniture at that. Jake, come on now. Where's the rule book that says so? We all pitchin in ain't we? Can't you just say thank you and call it a day?"

"No. Cause it ain't right."

"Why? That's what I said when you bought me those house dresses and my first bathing suit over at Robert Hall's awhile ago. I didn't offer you money for those things."

"That's different. It wasn't furniture, Bibsy."

"It makes no difference."

"Yes it does."

"I'll tell you what, if you wanna give me the money, fine. I ain't gonna argue with you no more about it, Jake."

He gave her the money and that was that. Later, she would think it was really a silly fight and came to appreciate the stance he took, but she never told him. Junior and Robert tended to walk through the house now a little taller since the dressers arrived and even thanked Bibsy on more than one occasion.

With Letty's arrival, Bibsy was suddenly seeing her newly spruced up home through her mother's eyes and knew its improved state was a long way from anything her mother found adequate.

"This sure is a surprise. You visiting from Baltimore?" Bibsy said as they took their time walking across the yard.

"I'm working in New York now."

"Oh yeah? Sis didn't tell me that."

"On Eighty-second Street and Park Avenue. I thought it was time to leave Baltimore."

An excellent cook, Letty never wanted for work. She and Martha had a natural sixth sense with food that most people don't possess. So many years at the task of food preparation allowed them the critical judgment to determine exactly where, when and how to be creative with any recipe. Each was capable of whipping up anything from pies and yeast bread to seven course meals without breaking much of a sweat. Letty's skills were valued enough that wealthy people tried to keep her happy, usually offering a well appointed room in addition to a decent salary, with the standard Thursdays and every other Sunday off. Her ease in the kitchen both puzzled and angered Bibsy because she didn't share any of it. None. Bibsy was certain if she'd grown up around her that would have been different because it seemed how other women learned to cook.

"Thought it was a good time to move closer to my children."

"Oh." Always justifying the distance between her and her children, Bibsy was immediately suspicious of her mother's sudden desire to be near.

"You know I am getting up there in age now. Martha and Kalvin are talking about buying a house in Queens, and I thought I'd help them out. Said they'd make sure to have an extra room for me."

"Seems Sis forgot to tell me a whole lot of things. Sounds like you all got a nice arrangement planned out." So that was it, Bibsy thought, she was looking for a place to settle down in her old age. "How's Mary and Cora? When's the last time you heard from them?"

"They're both fine. Mary will be taking her final vows next year. Cora met a nice young man in Baltimore and it looks like they'll be getting married soon. By the way, are you and...and..."

"Jake."

"Jake. Did you get married or are you living in sin?"

"I guess you'd call what we're doing is living in sin, Mom. And we like it that way." Bibsy took an extended drag from her cigarette and exhaled slowly.

"You should be ashamed of yourself, Elizabeth. I saw a big Catholic church on the way here. Are you going to Mass on Sundays?"

"St. James is across town. No, can't say that I am. Mom, I had enough church growing up. We went to Mass every single day, except Saturday, and that was confession day, so we made it there on Saturdays too, church every day of the week. I figure I'm paid up for the rest of my life and probably somebody else's too."

They were at the outhouse now and Bibsy stood back, stamped out her cigarette, immediately lit another, and waited nearby for her mother. Looking at her Timex and seeing less than an hour had elapsed since Letty arrived assured her this day that she'd so looked forward to was destined to be long and painful.

"Lordhavemercyjesus," Letty exclaimed when exiting the outhouse still smoothing out her skirt. "Been a long time since I been in one of them." She looked at Bibsy and said, "Can't say that I miss it either."

"You get used to it." Still steaming from her mother's comment about her hair, Bibsy figured there was no point in feigning good manners now. Letty had blown that possibility.

The children raced past them in their bathing suits, headed toward the outhouse with a trail of puppies in tow and before long they heard Martha's children say, "Peeeuuu," with giggling in the background.

"Let me get to the point, before we get back to the house. The reason I came was to talk some sense into you, and bring you back home with us. Actually, it's good you're not married to him."

Stunned, Bibsy stopped and looked quizzically at her mother. "Back home? This is my home."

"Martha and Kalvin said you can stay with them again until you get on your feet. Hope you can get it right this time. Martha said she can easily get you a job doing housework…"

"I'm not goin anywhere. I'm doin better than I was, right here, Mom." Bibsy said laughing. "You can't see that?"

Now Letty began to laugh. "No, I can't." Her mother made a sweeping movement with her arms taking in the entire yard, ending with a gesture toward the outhouse. "Even you can do better than this, Elizabeth."

"I finally have a family, and I love it here. You think I'm gonna leave here to go back with you and Martha and Kalvin?"

"Don't tell me you actually like this life?" Letty said with more disbelief than question.

"Yeah, actually I do. I love it. And I love Jake too."

"Humph."

"What's that mean?"

"Nothing."

"Yes it does. It means something, or you wouldn't have done it."

"Well, I guess I've heard that from you on more than one occasion, that's all."

"You'll never forgive me for getting pregnant right out of school. Even after all this time. Will you? How long you plan on rubbin my face in that?"

"You have to admit, Elizabeth, with all your education and religious training...to jump in bed with the first man you meet was pretty stupid. And the way you left Baltimore, was shameful too. Going with a married man. Just shameful."

"Maybe if I'd grown up in a regular home and got my mother's advice about men along the way, none of that woulda happened."

"Oh, so it's my fault you got pregnant?"

"I'm not sayin it was your fault. I wanted to keep the baby. I was willing to own up to my responsibilities."

"What did you know about responsibility, Elizabeth, at seventeen?"

"What I do know, come hell or high water I would have raised that child. And I'd be able to have children today."

The silence that hovered around them at that moment was potent enough to touch.

Letty waved dismissively at her daughter. "I saved you from yourself, chile. You just don't realize it."

"You mean saved yourself. Thought you'd wind up havin to raise my baby didn't you? And that was more important to you than committing any mortal sin. And whose sin would that be Mom, yours or mine? Did you take that to confession?" As soon as Bibsy said it she braced herself for a blow and Letty didn't disappoint.

Her mother turned and faced Bibsy fully, then slapped her so hard she lost her balance and almost fell, but quickly righted her position. The two women eyeballed each other so intensely they could feel each other's body heat.

"You always did have trouble respecting your elders. Always did."

"I give it when it's given to me." Both relieved and ashamed at finally expressing the words that have fermented in a pool of anger for so many years, Bibsy could feel the moisture build under her eyelids, but willed the tears from falling. "When am I supposed to get respect? When you say it's time?"

"That's not how it works," Letty began moving toward the house again, "you have to earn respect."

"Humph."

"You know, Elizabeth, you've always blamed me for putting you all in St. Cecelia's. We thought we were doing right by putting all you younger ones there together. I made it my business to stay in touch, and so did Martha. Things could have been a whole lot worse. Did you ever think of that?"

"What's worse than livin with people who despise you, and watching them put on a face to the world that says they care? We knew what they were really like. Some of em would call us black nigger to our faces when nobody was around. We told you that and you still kept us there." Since high school Bibsy considered crying a sign of weakness and refused to allow herself that release.

The women stopped again. "It still could have been worse. You don't know what I've seen in my lifetime, Elizabeth."

"All I know is what I've seen in mine." She stamped out another cigarette and immediately lit another. "I hear people talk about their families up here all the time. I don't have no such stories because I don't know anybody. Not really. I know names, but I don't really know those people."

"You want a story? You finally got on my very last nerve with this mess. I'ma give you a story." With her teeth clenched Letty communicated through a mere slit in her mouth. "How's this, my grandmother was what you called in slavery times, a breeder." Letty looked Bibsy square in the eyes as she continued. "That means she was forced to sleep with and have babies with whatever man she was told to."

Bibsy looked away from Letty's intense stare and took a moment to comprehend what her mother had said. She struggled to understand the words Letty strung together…breeder…grandmother…slavery…but there was a void. When the concept eventually registered with her heart and mind, Bibsy gasped, but soon replaced with skepticism, because she didn't trust her mother to tell the truth. Not after years of hearing her promise to visit on a particular day, month, whenever, without showing up, she'd had more trust in Jake than her.

"I was told she had a total of thirteen children and only got to see two of them grow up. One was my mother."

"I don't believe you." Bibsy said. She knew Letty wasn't above lying to make herself look good. But for the first time in her memory, there was a raw openness about her mother. Having exposed an open wound handed down through time like a baton, no amount of high class polish could conceal it, and despite her skepticism, in her gut she knew Letty was speaking the truth this time.

"It's true. Very true. And I've never told it to anybody." Letty spat on the ground as though the gesture released any residue of the distasteful words she'd spoken. Bibsy had never seen Letty spit, publicly or otherwise.

"Why? Why not tell?"

"Some stories are too painful to pass on, Elizabeth. But you…you are one person who really deserves to hear it, because you think you know every damn thing and there's a lot you don't know."

"No, the problem is I don't know anything or anybody. Nothing at all about my own family."

"We did the best we could. That's all. One day you'll accept that."

But now she was curious. "What was she like? Your mother."

"She was a hard-working woman who told us kids over and over to do whatever we could to keep the family together. Never get separated. Of course, that didn't happen unfortunately."

"Why not?"

"Well, me and my two sisters left North Carolina together when we were young and stayed in contact, but we lost track of our three brothers. The way they were lynchin colored men, they just scattered. Never seen em again."

Although Bibsy didn't hear much about lynching when she was coming up, she knew what it was. That was one of the first things Letty told her children when they came out of St. Cecelia's. Bibsy pretty much summed up her warning as, don't do anything illegal or get white folks angry or they'll string you from a tree. However, she never told them about losing track of her brothers because of the fear of it. She never knew her mother even had brothers.

"They got away the best they could and we never heard from them again. The three of us made our way to Ellicott City together. I met your father there and stayed. My sisters went on and settled in Philadelphia and New York City. We stay in touch though." The telling of the family fissure planted a twisted and pained expression on Letty's face that was generations old. "So, when your father and me started having troubles...."

"What troubles?"

"Just troubles."

"Like what?"

"I don't want to get into alla that right now."

"Why not? I want to know why you and my father didn't stay together. I'm a grown woman now, Mom."

"You know you are the only one. The only one who keeps pressing this. You've always had a real stubborn streak about you that sure puts me in mind of your father. He was just like that. Lord knows he was."

"I don't know nothin about that. All I want to know is what troubles could you possibly have that made you put us there? Don't you think we should know? Finally."

"You know, raisin up this stuff is not goin to do nobody no good. Grown folks sometimes have troubles and the best thing for them to do is separate. Sometimes, that's the only good thing to do that's best for everybody."

"Mom, everybody wouldn't do what you did. Give their kids away."

"I didn't give you all away!"

"That's what it felt like. We kept telling you what it was like in there but you wouldn't pay us no mind."

"Damn it Elizabeth, he was a sick man. Died in a mental hospital. Kept talking out of his head. Wandering off and couldn't find his way back home. Things like that."

"Why couldn't you tell us that?"

"Because children don't need to know everything, Elizabeth."

"Well we're not kids anymore, Mom. Do the others know?"

"Martha does. She's the one that useta go out lookin for him all the time."

"What about Mary and Cora," Bibsy felt her temper rising.

"No Elizabeth, they don't know. Never wanted any of you to know. It's too much. Too much to handle. Especially for children. Being colored is burden enough to carry around in this world. Don't need nothing more."

Bibsy remembered his funeral. She was in high school and recalled peering into a casket at someone she knew was responsible for giving her life, yet she had no memory of him. She remembered feeling out of place because she had no sense of loss. Mary, who was the eldest and four at the time they arrived at St. Cecelia's, had told her that their father carried Bibsy in his arms when they were first brought there. As she got older it made her angrier knowing she was that young, and hated him all the more.

Bibsy's puzzled expression said it all. "If he was sick, why couldn't you raise us then?" Noticing her mother's discomfort by the direct question didn't deter her from pursuing it further. "I seen other women raise their kids by themselves."

"Jesus Christ, Elizabeth! Father, forgive me." Letty made the sign of the cross.

"Girl, you're gonna make me lose my religion out here. Can't you let it go? I had four children in the space of six years. You don't know how hard that is." She was shouting now. "Nobody ever talks about never having time in your day to even go to the bathroom when you need to." The memory of the distance that grew between her and her children with each new birth seared pain across Letty's face. "Plus I had a husband I couldn't even trust to stay with you all. I had to make money. As much as I could. Everything was left on my shoulders, so I did what I had to do." She quickened her pace back to the house. "At least you were put someplace where you'd be safe and taken care of. And you all got a decent education. Be thankful for what you did get and stop dwelling on what you missed out on. That's your problem."

"You coulda told me this stuff years ago. I been grown a long time now."

"Elizabeth, I was raised to believe you shouldn't talk about such things. Your father suffered, and so did I. It broke my heart to put you all there. I couldn't even bring myself to go with him to take you all there on the bus. I made him go without me."

"We blamed him all those years, because it was him that brought us. And you knew we blamed him, and you let us."

Letty just looked at Bibsy with her lips pressed tightly together.

Bibsy thought a moment before continuing. "Seems to me, by locking us all up you found a way to get your freedom altogether."

Letty swung around with a lethal expression framing her fine ebony features. She gazed long and hard at Bibsy before marching off toward the house muttering, "I'm through with you. That's it."

The women brought so much tension into the room, it was like a third person entered with them and it cut right through the Amos 'n' Andy slapstick blaring from the radio. After pouring a drink, Bibsy sat at the kitchen table with Jake as she opened a fresh pack of cigarettes. She resolved in that moment this would be the last time she'd see her mother. Taking in their discussion in the yard as best she could, she knew she still could never forgive her for what she'd done to them as children. It was too great a price.

Martha, meanwhile, was looking back and forth from Letty to Bibsy. She mouthed to Bibsy, "What's going on?" But Bibsy didn't answer.

Letty had retrieved her shopping bag off the porch when she came inside and sat on the couch and reached inside her bag and took out a pint bottle of Johnny Walker Red Label. "Can I get a glass? And some ice if you have it." She said to no one in particular. "Anybody care for some scotch?"

By the time the children came in the house they were excited, dripping wet and hungry. Martha and Kalvin looked relieved to busy themselves with the children while Jake set food on the table. But the atmosphere was so thick the children picked up on it right away. Even Rain began to bark, something she only did in the house when she sensed danger.

"What's goin on, Pop?" Robert said looking at everyone's expression.

"Nothin. Y'all get ready ta eat. Let that dog out too."

Martha and Kalvin's children were so enthralled by their swimming experience their jubilation took center stage, to the apparent relief of the adults.

"Ma, we swam in a lake."

Junior said, "That wasn't a lake, Buster."

"I floated inside a big rubber circle that we used like a raft." Cheryl jumped in the air as she described her experience.

The children continued their spirited conversation all evening, in spite of Letty and Bibsy nursing the hostility in the room and staying in their separate spaces for the remainder of the visit. Once everybody finished eating Kalvin said they should begin to make their way back home since they weren't sure how long it would take. Jake arranged for Mason T to drive them back to the train station, while he followed behind with all the kids who were thrilled to ride in the back of his truck.

Listening to the children laughing behind him as he drove, he looked at Bibsy who hadn't spoken since she and Letty returned from the outhouse and said, "Cheer up, it's almost over."

"You're right about that. I'm finished with her."

When they arrived at the Haverton train station Bibsy got out of the truck and gave her sister's children hearty hugs and goodbye kisses. She saw her sister and Kalvin headed toward her.

"How come you didn't tell me Mom was comin?" Bibsy said to Martha.

"I didn't know until last night. She happened to be there when I was gettin the kids' clothes laid out for the trip today and she just included herself. You know how Mom is."

"Yeah, too well." Bibsy said before saying goodbye to Martha and Kalvin.

She returned to the truck without acknowledging her mother who'd walked down the platform and stayed apart from the group. When they pulled off Letty had her back to them looking down the tracks for the train to come.

Chapter Eleven

"Let's put this day behind us," Jake said the night Bibsy's family left. He was already in the bed waiting for Bibsy to join him, patting the mattress hoping to entice her there. "Let me help you take your mind off things," he said flashing his distinctive grin.

"Not tonight, Jake. I need to sort through some things before I come to bed."

Bibsy was sitting at the kitchen table smoking her umpteenth cigarette of the day while staring off, attempting to cull something useful from the day's events. There was plenty, if only she could bypass Martha's betrayal and the heavy disappointment Bibsy captured in Letty's eyes, once again, which she could not.

"Your momma's gone now. And from the way things looked, she probably won't ever come back again."

"Thank God for that." Bibsy's gaze was fixed on the cast iron door of the wood burning stove. "You know she tried to get me to go back with them. She actually thought I'd go back to The City with them." Bibsy shook her head in disbelief. Sitting with both elbows on the table and her hands holding her head, she appeared exhausted and beaten.

"No foolin?" Jake sat up in the bed. "She thought she'd jus walk in here an take you away from me jus like that, huh?"

"Yep."

"So, that's what you two got so riled up about out there."

"It was that and a whole lot more." Bibsy exhaled a stream of smoke and automatically lit another cigarette. "I don't want to talk about it right now, Jake. Please. I'll be to bed in a minute."

"Bibsy you can't let people get the better of you. When folks start actin a fool, ya jus gotta let em go. Even if they family."

Bibsy was so deep in thought she didn't even hear what Jake was saying, but nodded as if she had. Fragments of the day kept replaying in her mind as Bibsy tried to grapple with her life: Jake, St. Cecelia's,

Letty, Martha, The Beach. She felt herself slipping into a sadness deeper than ever.

In the past, Jake easily charmed his way around whatever issues came between them, and they were a cozy twosome by morning. But this time it appeared Letty Randolph left something more than the scent of pricey perfume behind. And whatever it was would never be masked by cologne, no matter its cost.

"Bibsy," Jake said, "come on to bed." He studied her for a long while after she didn't answer, and eventually turned over and was soon asleep.

Bibsy remained in deep thought trying to unravel the day, but so many thoughts of her mother and memories of St. Cecelia's clashed inside her head it gave her a headache. She took her cigarettes and the kerosene lamp outside and sat on the porch.

In no time she began talking to herself.

"Why'd she haveta come?" Bibsy said as she settled into a chair and put her feet up on a wooden crate. "She knew damn well I wasn't going nowhere with her. Got the nerve to put her nose up at the way I'm livin. I'm doing better than anything she ever had for me. Humph! Martha shoulda never brought her here. Things woulda been just fine."

Rain crawled from under the porch and looked at her talking to herself then barked once as if needing assurance that she was alright. Shooing her away, the dog went back under the porch where she'd been, and Bibsy resumed her one-sided conversation.

"Where was she when I needed her? We was just kids livin at the mercy of them nuns."

Bibsy stayed out on the porch talking for quite some time, until the screen door opened slowly without her noticing.

"A breeder. Why'd she haveta tell me that stuff for? I don't even know what a…"

"Bibsy." Jake said standing in the doorway with just his briefs on. "Who you talkin to sittin out here in jus your nightgown?"

The sound of his voice startled her. "What?" She jumped up brushing ashes from her lap. "Ain't talkin to nobody. Just sittin here thinkin, that's all."

He came out on the porch, took what was left of the cigarette from her hand and threw it on the ground, picked up the lamp, then grabbed her by the hand and led her back inside to the bed. "You can think all you want in the bed then. Come on."

In the morning when Jake asked her why she was sitting on the porch talking to herself, Bibsy said she didn't remember it.

"Well I can understand how she mighta got the best of you. Whew! That woman jus come through here and upset the whole day, didn't she? And she ain't no bigger'n a minute, jus like you."

Jake went to check on the boys and found a note on Robert's bed saying they'd gone hunting with Gus and Carrie and would likely bring home supper but they didn't know what.

"Why don't we take a boat ride today? Let's get outta the house. Looks like the boys'll be gone all day. Gus and Carrie took em huntin."

"Sounds fine to me," Bibsy said, knowing she would have agreed to whatever he said at that point.

"I'ma put that smile back on your face or die tryin, so you might as well smile now and get it over with."

A barely visible hint of a smile brought out his famous wide grin. As soon as they finished bathing, they packed some food into the cooler, a couple of fishing rods, and Bibsy brought along a few romance magazines and a fresh pack of cigarettes. They drove to the store for soda and beer and then to the ice house to fill the cooler. By mid-morning they were on the water. His motor boat was a marine version of the truck he owned. Jake kept a pair of oars on his dilapidated boat just in case the motor gave him any problem. He even put brackets on it to hold the oars if he ever needed them.

Maneuvering the rudder, Jake headed to the middle of the Hudson, then downriver past Sing Sing prison and the lighthouse. He cut the motor when they were near Upper Kancy, nearing the river's widest three-mile span where they saw a group of kids crabbing on the shoreline. In the distance, metal beams of the bridge's ongoing construction spiked from the water jarring the lengthy tranquil scenery of the river in its full splendor. The drastic change in surroundings catapulted Bibsy from the pensive mood she'd been in since the night before, and it happened so quick and unexpectedly it was disorienting at first.

The expanse of the Hudson River from that vantage point was both breathtaking and intimidating. The river was massive, yet Bibsy wasn't afraid. Actually, she'd never experienced fear while in Jake's presence.

On the Langston side of the river mountainous brownstone rock formations jutted skyward commanding attention, its angular surface standing tall and majestic. Protective. On the opposite shore, Westchester County, the spectacular rolling treed horizon that greeted her daily came into closer view. Downriver Bibsy could see the concrete structure of the new General Motors plant spilling onto the river's edge. Sitting there in the middle of the river, flanked by two spectacular landscapes on each shore, was both overwhelming and humbling.

The water lapped against the sides of the boat, while birds played a faint random harmony in the background. Against the very palest of blue skies, rays of sunlight caught the ripple of the river's current. The day was crisp and clear, the sun swathing her skin with just the right amount of warmth. The vista drew Bibsy's eyes upward, and as she fully absorbed being in the midst of such lush natural beauty, warm delicate breezes danced across her face and radically dwarfed yesterday's issues.

Jake said nothing. Just sat watching Bibsy return to the person he knew her to be as they drifted ever so slowly downriver. Pairs of geese, ducks and swans took pleasure in the river as well.

Finally, his smile acknowledged her better spirits. "This puts things in better order, huh?"

"Yes it does. Yes it does." She reached out to take his hand and he guided her to sit beside him. "You know," she said when the boat steadied, "Seems like we been together longer than we have."

"I know. It does. Even the boys said so."

"Hmm. What else did they say? Anything bad?"

"Nah." Jake put his arm around her shoulders. "Ain't nothin bad been said. And it won't ever be."

It did make her wonder what they thought of her, but she decided not to pursue it. She didn't want to disturb their mood, this moment, in this place. It wasn't that important right now anyway. Nothing was. "It's so peaceful out here. God sure put this place together, didn't He?"

"Yeah," Jake laughed. "Pushes all that other stuff aside, don't it?"

Although not intending to, Jake's comment reminded her of her mother's visit and how upset it made her.

"And my mother wanted to take me away from all this."

"What about me?" Jake put on like he was hurt. "I don't count?"

"Of course you count. You count most of all." Bibsy slipped her arm around Jake's waist and leaned her head against his shoulder. "Thanks for doing this. It's just what I needed."

"I could tell." He said. "I don't know what happened out there with you and your momma, but whatever it was, ya need ta think twice about dealin with her again. I don't like anything upsettin my baby like that. Maybe the two of you oughta stay apart. Jus cause you're family don't mean ya gotta force yourselves ta be around one another."

"Yeah, you're right. I don't expect to see her for a very long time." Bibsy imagined seeing her mother at her funeral and wondered what that would be like. There was a similar distance she felt from each of her parents, yet she'd never even known her father.

"I got a question for ya," Jake said. "I know you don't remember none of it, but when you was sittin out on the porch last night you said somethin bout breedin. You plannin on startin up farmin or somethin?"

"Ha!" The idea of her being a farmer struck a funny chord, as she was having a hard enough time keeping up with Carrie and her vegetable patch. "That was just something my mother said out in the yard yesterday."

"Oh. I was wonderin. Not that I'm pryin or nothin. I jus thought it wasn't somethin I'd ever expect ta come outta your mouth, is all."

"Now I got a question for you."

"Okay."

"Mom says her grandmother used to be a breeder in slavery times. You ever heard of something like that?"

"I see." Jake said, instinctively clutching her shoulder tighter and drawing Bibsy closer. "I heard about it," he thought for awhile, then continued gingerly, apparently still giving it more thought, "mostly from oldtimers who come from down south. That's something you won't hear any white folks talk about," Jake said as he waved to a passing sail boat. "How you think I got the color I am, Bibsy? My father's grandmother was forced one night by the master who owned our family in Virginia. That's what my father told me."

Bibsy didn't consider Jake's complexion very often. However, she had a suspicion the reason he got along well with so many people was that he hadn't suffered the scars that dark-skinned children do. For her, Jake's color was never an important part of who he was and she'd not known him to try to gain favor because of it. She had noticed once when he came home from working outside during the summer his nose and cheeks were red from being in the sun all day. When she asked him if his face hurt he just ignored her and continued pouring slop into the pig pen. But Bibsy clearly remembered skin color being an important part of her life at St. Cecelia's, even from an early age.

When she was a very young girl, she didn't know what to make of being slighted because of her dark skin. She remembers that's just how things were. That it was never discussed was confusing at first. It was obvious to all the students that it was unfair, but when you're young and treated unfairly, it just makes you wish you were like the people who are favored. You don't question why, or try to make sense of it. That takes awhile. But when your designated place in the church to worship Our Savior is assigned to the back of the sanctuary, no matter what shade of colored you happened to be, where St. Cecelia students were the last to approach the altar for the Sacrament of Christian unity, the Eucharist, childhood's naiveté is fleeting.

Daydreams were a particular part of Bibsy's survival during her younger years there. She'd imagine living outside of the orphanage in a home with two loving parents like the intact white families worshipping together that she saw at church and in all the pictures she saw in stories they read in school, stories depicting the mother as a woman who stayed home while the father worked. She imagined having a mother who didn't have to work and a father who made lots of money and took care of the family so she didn't have to. She and her sisters would have all they needed, and they wore pretty new dresses each day, not the coarse cotton grey uniforms that made her skin ashy. The family would take drives to the country after Sunday Mass in their new car and there would be big feasts everyday. They'd never have to eat not-so-hot cereal or cold toast for breakfast. The children would never be punished, or ever hit. The single constant in her mind's eye was that she was always the most favored child, and her family was always white, because she'd never heard of white people being treated mean by anybody.

She remembered clearly the first time she began to daydream.

"Elizabeth," Sister Mary Margaret said, "take a seat on the stool." Bibsy would slink over and climb up on the wooden stool in the corner of the room, where Sister Mary Margaret would crown her with a foot-long black cone-shaped cap with the word dunce spelled out in large white capital letters all around. "Now, maybe the next time I ask you to recite The Apostles' Creed, you'll learn how to pronounce Pontius Pilate correctly." Then she'd spin around on the thick heels of her clunky black lace-up nun shoes and face a class full of snickering faces. "Now let's go on...."

As a young child Bibsy used to cry a lot. Whenever punished, hit or called names, she'd seek out her older sister Mary and sob until she was just too tired to continue. Mary would wrap her in her arms stroking her, trying unsuccessfully to get Bibsy to calm down; even as they both knew the only remedy was allowing her cry herself out. Mary's promotion into the upper school separated them, and she eventually had to learn how to stop crying on her own. However, the tears didn't really go away, they just hid out in that newly formed thicker skin she acquired.

Whenever there was an opportunity for one of the students to represent the school publicly, most often the girl who was the lightest and had the straightest hair was chosen, like being selected to crown the statue of Our Lady in the May procession. That never went to anyone as dark as the Randolph girls. Even the smartest dark-skinned students like Mary weren't chosen. With the wide spectrum of shades that colored folks came in, the competition for favor wrapped around the slightest variation in skin color and hair texture among girls who clamored intently for the tiniest morsel of acceptance.

There was a light-skinned girl with whom Bibsy did develop a friendship. Her name was Angela. She was sent to St. Cecelia's at thirteen from the Good Hope Hospital Annex, a place where young colored pregnant girls stayed until they delivered their babies before they were forced to give them up for adoption. The whole school knew as soon as the nuns announced to everybody where a new student had arrived from, that if it was Good Hope, she'd just delivered a child.

After Angela and Bibsy became friends she told her that it was her father's brother who got her pregnant, but because her father was a doctor and she was from a well-to-do colored Catholic family in Washington D.C., she wasn't allowed to come back home. She said her mother told her it would hurt her father's practice and be a constant reminder of the shame she'd caused the family. They placed her child in a colored orphanage in Philadelphia, and Angela never got to see or hold the baby she delivered.

Angela cried a lot in her private time when she first came, the way Bibsy used to. Except she'd muffle her sounds in her bed pillow so the nuns wouldn't hear, sometimes crying all night until she dropped off to sleep. It was funny how the children knew not to complain or call the nuns on her or any of the girls that recently came and needed to adjust. They were just kids but knew instinctively that the new arrivals needed to get it out of their system, knowing the nuns would punish the rule-breaking girls unmercifully if they told. The last time one of the students told on another, the accused received a wet strapping. That meant the child was immersed into a tubful of water, then had to get out and while dripping wet was subjected to a beating with a leather strap while her were pores open.

At first, Angela kept saying to the nuns that it wasn't her fault, that her uncle forced her, but they encouraged her to keep quiet or she would find herself in more trouble than she'd already caused. The nuns' cruelty was legendary enough to silence any human being.

Bibsy found out the hard way that the road to survival was silence. Not a month passed from her First Communion when the confession became a regular part of her life. Bibsy came up with the bright idea of using it to everyone's advantage by telling the priest what the nuns were really doing to them, especially Sister Mary Margaret.

"Bless me Father for I have sinned. It has been a week since my last confession. Father, Sister Mary Margaret is mean. Some of the others are too, but she's the meanest. She calls us black niggers sometimes, she beats us…."

"Ahem, ahem." That was his sign for her to stop talking. "My dear child, you are here to confess your own misdeeds, not those of others. Those who displease God will have to answer Our Savior for themselves. You must have sins of your own you'd like to confess."

"I don't like Sister Margaret, Father."

"You know hating is a sin. God doesn't want you to hate His children."

"Father Timothy." Bibsy recognized his voice. Actually all the children knew the only priest from the order of Josephite Fathers assigned to St. Cecelia's. "Am I a child of God too?" She said.

"Of course you are. What other sins would you like to confess? Remember, there are others waiting in line behind you."

"I still don't like being here and I hate my mother too for putting us here. I'm finished, Father." Bibsy was so disappointed. Her hands were sweating so hard the white mother-of-pearl rosary beads she clenched shined from her perspiration.

"For your penance, I want you to say ten Hail Marys, ten Our Fathers, and ten Acts of Contrition."

"Thank you, Father. "Bibsy exited the confessional booth with her head hung.

The next day after Mass, Sister Mary Margaret asked Bibsy to follow her to the principal's office. Bibsy was scared because she noticed Sister Mary Margaret's customary smirk was more pronounced than usual, and the only person known to be meaner than her in all of St. Cecelia's was Mother Agatha. When they arrived, Mother Superior sat behind a large wooden desk. The additional lighting of the desk lamp highlighted the puffy lined face protruding from her bonnet, making her advanced years more evident. Wire rimmed glasses sat on the very tip of her nose and she looked over them whenever she spoke. Bibsy was directed to one of the chairs across from her, and Sister Mary Margaret sat solemnly in the other. It was Bibsy's first time in the principal's office except when it was her turn to clean it.

The Mother Superior began with, "Elizabeth, are you aware that you're named after a very important person in the Bible?"

Bibsy nodded yes. She'd been told this many times before.

"You're not a horse, or a mute. You have the gift of language, child. Use it."

"Yes, Mother Superior," She managed, barely audible.

"Speak up child. And sit up straight."

"Yes, Mother Superior." Bibsy straightened her posture.

"Tell us who was Elizabeth in the Bible, child."

"She was related to the Blessed Virgin Mary," she said nervously. She wasn't told to be prepared for a quiz, but this was one story she remembered because it was that of her namesake. "She didn't think she could have children because she was so old. But God blessed her with a child, John the Baptist. He jumped in Elizabeth's stomach when she met Mary who was pregnant with baby Jesus. She's the patron saint of pregnant women."

"See, she's not stupid." Mother Superior looked at Sister Mary Margaret whose trademark sneer was absent at this meeting. "Do you realize how fortunate you are to be a student here, Elizabeth?"

"Yes, Mother Superior." Bibsy's mind raced through the events of the last few days trying to determine what may have warranted her sitting there, but nothing surfaced.

"There are so many girls who would love to be in your place right now. Like those poor souls living in the alley behind this school." Mother Agatha was referring to the vagrant colored families living behind St. Cecelia's who relied on church handouts for survival. "Is that how you want to end up, Elizabeth?"

"No, Mother Superior."

The alley families could be heard cussing day and night. St. Cecelia students were given constant reminders that they were not only better than the alley families, but better than most colored people. And the goodness and mercy of the Franciscan Sisters of Mill Hill, England who committed their lives to work among the coloreds and Indians in the United States made it so.

"God has blessed this school to teach you colored girls Christian decency and civility so when you leave here you can become a welcome help to a fine Baltimore household. Don't you want that, Elizabeth?"

"Yes, Mother Superior." She lied.

"And you probably know all the rules of this school as well. Don't you?"

Bibsy shook her head, then caught herself and said. "Yes, Mother Superior."

"To make sure you remember all the rules of our good school, you'll be going without supper for a week." Mother Agatha said.

"For what? What did I do?"

"While you are here, you need to learn never to question authority. Do you understand? Is that clear?"

"Yes, Mother Superior."

"As I was saying before you interrupted me, during the supper hour I want you to stay in the dormitory and write one hundred times, the paragraph in your catechism stating the purpose of confession as it is appears there. Secondly, because you so rudely interrupted me, you are to write the Act of Contrition one hundred times as well. And I expect perfect penmanship, or you'll have to do it all over again."

"Yes, Mother Superior." Bibsy knew better than to ask anymore questions or even show displeasure at her punishment.

"You may leave now. You're to begin your assignment tonight."

Sister Mary Margaret walked her back to the dormitory saying, "Elizabeth, the number of black marks you're collecting on your soul is mounting, and you need to spend more time in a state of atonement, asking God to forgive your sinful nature if you ever expect to make it into heaven. If you keep this up, you are certainly destined to burn in hell."

Without them mentioning Father Timothy and the confessional, she knew what got her called into the principal's office, even though she'd never be able to prove it.

In spite of the betrayal, Bibsy used all the avenues at a good Catholic's disposal through the years, from the rosary beads that were blessed at her confirmation, to novenas selected for intercession and God's grace... hoping for relief from the nuns' cruelty. But by the time she got into her teenage years, she learned to simply do what she was told, memorize the church doctrine as outlined in her Baltimore Catechism and recite passages as needed, and never attempt to make sense of it.

She went to her room and picked up a fresh tablet, opened her catechism to ensure accuracy and began to write: 'Oh my God, I am heartily sorry for having offended thee, and I detest all my sins because I dread the loss of Heaven and the pains of hell. But most of all for having offended thee my Lord, who art all good and deserving of all my love. I firmly resolve with the help of thy grace to confess my sins, to do penance and to amend my life. Amen.'

In the dormitory after their evening prayers, the girls took out clean tablets every night and helped Bibsy fulfill her punishment. They were careful not to complete it too quickly as to draw suspicion; and since they all had the same exact handwriting, the nuns never knew the difference.

"They used to beat us at St. Cecelia's even if we had the wrong expression on our face. We'd have to lay across the bed and lift up the skirt of our uniforms to the waist so we could get the full affect of the leather strap. They were so mean, Jake," she said, "I hate my mother for putting us in there."

"Maybe she didn't have no choice. Did you ask her why?"

"That's some of what we was talkin about yesterday, too. She said our father took sick and had to go in the hospital. He died in a mental hospital and she had to work because there was no one else left to make money."

"That's some tough luck. At least you all were together."

"That's the same thing she said. What does that matter? That we were all tortured together? Humph!"

Bibsy shared with Jake some of the punishments and humiliations she suffered at St. Cecelia's including details that surprised even her, and momentarily the purging had a cleansing effect. Maybe it was the boat and being on the river. Or the warmth of the sun. Or Jake's attention to her every word. More likely all of those things simultaneously.

"On the outside it looked like they were all so religious, but they were the meanest people I ever seen. I can't tell you all that went on there, Jake, there was so much. But it was hell. Pure hell."

"Well then I'll never bring it up again. Together we gonna make us some new memories. Things worth rememberin."

That night they lay in bed holding onto each other not saying a word, but each could feel the other's embrace more so than anytime before. Jake's touch was calming, soothing, creating a peace so very foreign to her.

She snuggled into his chest, “Please, don’t ever leave me, Jake Tucker.”

“I’ll always be right here, baby. Don’t worry.”

They drifted off to sleep cuddled in each other’s arms. Through the night, when either of them moved or changed positions, their bodies sought out the other as if by magnetic pull and they automatically rearranged their embrace without waking.

Chapter Twelve

Bibsy sat at Carrie's kitchen table helping can fruit and vegetables. Having been at it for a few hours, there were still a few bushel baskets filled with apples, peas and squash that Gus brought home from a local farm that still needed to be done. Quart and pint-size Mason jars lined every inch of her kitchen in neat rows as they divided up the canned food between their two houses. They'd already canned most of the produce from Carrie's garden in mid-summer and she'd had a bountiful harvest this year. Especially string beans.

When the Red Skelton program ended and Carrie turned off the radio, both women were still smiling from the comedy. "That man is something else," Carrie said. "But I gotta save my batteries. I hear he's on the television now. Wonder what he looks like."

"Seems like a lotta shows are switchin over to TV." Bibsy said. "Aunt Carrie, how much longer you think we'll be able to live down here. Some people on my job say they gonna tear all this down."

"Ta tell you the truth, Bibsy, I don't know. Rumors like that have always cropped up from time ta time. But this time it feels a lot different. Jake don't think so, but me an Gus do. In the ole days every time a house became empty there'd be another family movin in by the next day, a week at the most. You notice them two families that moved out this summer?"

"Yeah."

"Well, them houses is still empty. Every year there's less and less folks down here. It's sure got me worried alright."

Bibsy was grateful for Carrie's honesty, but her response also created more worry about Jake. As much as she wanted to believe him, she'd not heard anyone else match his certainty about their lives remaining the same. Making matters worse, she'd seen him more preoccupied as the weather cooled and began to miss him.

"Jake and the boys are out there chopping wood every evening after supper. Even weekends. Don't seem like he's got time for nothing else lately."

"Gus too. And come this winter you'll be glad they did. There's some mean winters up here, girl." In the middle of counting filled Mason jars she stopped without looking at Bibsy and added, "He'll git back to you once he gets the house ready so it can stand up to the cold weather that's comin."

"Every time you turn around, he's fixin something else. Got so much wood, til it's practically stacked up to the roof."

"You'll be thankful before too long. Mark my words."

It was the first time since she'd been there that Bibsy felt the better part of Jake's attention was elsewhere, and it frustrated her. She'd grown accustomed to having him all to herself. Fishing together on the boat. Sitting on the riverbank after their evening meals. Their late-night swims. She enjoyed being in his presence even when there was silence between them. But lately, with all the extra chores he attended to after working all day, whenever they were together he was dozing off and at night he was usually asleep before she got into bed.

Getting dinner started by the time he came home from work helped. Sometimes they'd eat at Gus and Carrie's place and she'd help Carrie with supper. With Jake and Carrie's guidance Bibsy managed to cook a few meals on her own. Chicken and fish was what they ate all summer, and she eventually got the hang of that. There were a few mishaps, like cooking the fish too long, the chicken not enough, and not knowing when the vegetables were tender enough, but gradually, Bibsy developed a better sense of the timing and confidence in the kitchen began to emerge.

Carrie looked around at the dozens of jars of beans, squash, tomatoes and corn, and wondered aloud if it was enough to make it through the winter months. "Gus got a good price on those apples over at the Phillips Orchard yesterday. Probably had a good harvest this year. Along wit the peaches we put up last month, we should have plenty sweets this winter."

"Should be. We got the whole back room at the house practically filled with jars of food." Bibsy was concerned they were taking up too much of the little space they had, but she knew Jake was against buying anything but the most necessary staples from the store.

"These jars might keep you from starvin in a few months. We gotta dig ourselves out whenever it snows. Sometimes that can take days."

Bibsy and Carrie moved the jars of string beans to the floor in the living room and dragged the bushel of apples nearer to the table and began the process of coring, peeling and slicing. "By the way, you need ta get yourself ready for the winter, Bibsy. Get yourself some long johns and flannels, so you'll be ready for the cold weather."

"I can buy sweaters real cheap on the job. I'll pick some up for you and Uncle Gus. I got the boys some for school, and I was planning on getting Jake a...."

"That's nice. Real nice. I preciate that, but I ain't talkin bout sweaters and such. I mean it gets reeeal cold in these houses when it gets inta the thick a winter. You gotta remember, these houses wasn't meant for winter use. You gonna need more'n a sweater."

Bibsy hated that Carrie tended to make things sound so urgent whenever she made a point. Like the world was going to break out in flames or something if people didn't take heed to whatever she was saying. But she also noticed the mood on The Beach shifted since the summer. Those same people she'd witnessed being relaxed and laid back when the weather was hot, now attended to their neglected roofs, windows and doors with considerable seriousness.

"We'll go to the Army and Navy store next week and git you some proper winter clothes."

"Aunt Carrie, I've seen snow before. And I've been through winters too."

"Unless you been north a here, you ain't seen no winter yet. That nice breeze we so partial to in the summer will turn on us like a snake in a few more months. Mark my words."

Aunt Carrie's warning was more extreme than usual so Bibsy decided to play it safe and went shopping with her the following week and bought some thermal clothing, a heavy winter coat, wool hats, scarves and gloves and a pair of rugged winter boots. Just in case. She smiled to herself imagining what her mother would say seeing her purchase an entire wardrobe from the local Army and Navy store.

When Jake didn't return Bibsy's smile when she came in the house with all her new purchases, she knew something was wrong. "What's going on?" Bibsy dropped the packages on their bed, changed into more comfortable shoes and sat at the kitchen table with him. He looked beat. She thought all the extra work he'd been doing lately finally slowed him down to where he couldn't even smile.

"What's wrong with you? You been doin too much. Can't people call on somebody else to help them out sometimes? Why is it always you?"

Still no answer.

"How long you been sitting here Jake?"

Finally he said, "Mason T's leavin. Said this winter comin will be his last one on The Beach."

It was sadness that had Jake's body all slumped over. She knew the people on The Beach were like family to him, so it wasn't a surprise that he'd treat each move as a personal insult, if not injury.

"When'd he tell you that?" She asked without knowing the significance of the question.

"Today, while we was fixin his roof. Stayed over there talkin ta him a good while after we finished."

"Why's he leaving? I thought he liked livin down here."

"Said he saved enough ta buy a house...an wants ta move on it before the prices get too high. He said these farmers sellin their property jacked up the prices sky high an he won't be able to buy after awhile if he don't do it soon." Jake stretched his legs and leaned his shoulders against the back of the kitchen chair.

Junior and Robert burst through the door playfully punching each other and Bibsy told them to go next door for a little while so she and Jake could finish talking.

Junior did a double take at his father saying, "What's wrong with Pop?"

"Is he sick?" Robert asked.

"No. Now go on. Come back in a couple of hours."

Mason T wasn't just anybody on The Beach, but had become one of Jake's closest friends and his absence would place a big hole for Jake personally and among his support to stay there. He was younger than Jake but liked to fish and hunt, and he was at every poker game that Bibsy could remember. Even though he didn't put as much money on the table or stay as long as some of the other men, he was a regular. She remembered the day he introduced himself, and how odd it was that he lived there and walked so gingerly on the dirt road. Its significance now proved an indication this was intended to be a temporary stop for him all along, and Bibsy quickly concluded he hadn't been honest with Jake.

"Did you eat?"

"Naw, too tired. I'm heatin up some water ta wash up. That's all I got the strength for right now." They both looked at the basin on the stove at the same time. "He's a smart man." Jake shook his head pondering his friend, "Young guy. But smart. Works two jobs and saves his money." Jake continued looking straight ahead at the flame under the basin, shaking his head in affirmation of Mason T's character.

Putting a little money aside, or saving at all, was not something Jake was apt to do. He spent money like it was attached to a time bomb set to detonate at any moment, and living on The Beach allowed him that luxury, because there was no place in all of Langston County where you could rent a house for fifteen dollars a month. Of course there were obvious tradeoffs, like in addition to being responsible for maintaining their residence they were responsible for removing their own snow as well.

"That's what this place is good for I guess. Savin money. Said he wanted ta get married and raise a family."

"He could get married and raise his family here, like everybody else. You did."

Bibsy didn't understand why Jake wasn't angry at Mason T. She saw what he'd done as conning the others into thinking he was there to stay, and knew all along he wouldn't.

"Guess he wants more for his kids." They let a longer than usual silence linger between them, each recalling the numerous times the boys wished for a television and other modern conveniences. "I'd have some money too if I didn't like ta drink and gamble so much, huh?"

"You're taking care of your kids, Jake. And that's a lot to say for yourself. My mother didn't even do that. You could have walked off and left em after your wife died, but you didn't. My mother locked us up with nuns who beat the shit out of us. So what if you drink a little bit and play poker once in awhile. It's your money. And you ain't hurtin nobody. I'm sure not complaining."

"Come here woman," Jake said stretching out his arm for Bibsy and moving his knee from under the table so she could sit on his leg. "That's what I love about you. You know that?"

Bibsy straddled Jake's leg. "I love you too." She leaned over and kissed him, and the meeting of their lips sparked a well of pent up passion. With the fire between them building, Bibsy pulled away abruptly and said, "That Mason T ain't heard the last of me. I'ma get him."

"Shhhh. Hush." Silencing her lips with his own, and cupping her behind with his oversized hands, Jake scooped Bibsy up, her legs reflexively wrapping around his waist. After carrying her carefully to their bed, her packages tumbling to the floor with a wave of his arm, he said, "Wait jus one minute," then went over to the door and pulled the shade over the door's four window panes, his signal to the boys to stay a little longer at Gus and Carrie's house.

A moment of hesitation before unbuttoning his shirt, he said, "I should wash up first. I been sweatin up on that roof all day."

"It's too late." Bibsy pulled him toward her, "I been missing you a lot lately, and besides, we'll be sweaty together in another little while."

Given how coarse Jake was in other ways, it continually amazed Bibsy how gentle a lover he was. His touch was especially tender this evening, delicately placing a trail of kisses from her lips to her navel.

When the boys came back in, Jake and Bibsy were in the back room sponge bathing each other, their kisses and sweet talk easily overheard.

"We brought y'all some food back from Aunt Carrie's, Pop." Robert shouted through the closed door.

Jake and Bibsy heard their stifled laughter in the background.

Once the ground got too hard for a shovel to penetrate, all the men were laid off road construction until the spring. Oldtimers like Jake and Gus were able to pick up winter work in the practically dead ice-harvesting business on Langston Lake. Electric refrigeration had cut their work crew down to just a handful compared to the booming business it had been. But it would take a string of sub-freezing days to turn the lake into a solid mass for what little work was available to officially begin. In the meantime, for several weeks between Thanksgiving and the New Year, he was out of work.

Pleased with seeing more of Jake during those in-between weeks than she had throughout the fall, Bibsy hardly noticed the colder weather at first. It simply became a reason for them to draw closer at night, as the wood stove and kerosene lamp cast a reflection of their lovemaking on the walls of the front room.

During the day Jake was antsy with the down time. With Bibsy heading out to work everyday and the boys going off to school, he'd leave too, trying to pick up an odd job here and there. Usually somebody needed an extra hand for the day, and that supplied enough pocket change to get by.

Jake wasn't in the habit of getting a tree for Christmas, so Bibsy bought a small fake one at Woolworths, only because it didn't feel like Christmas without it. There was always a Christmas tree at St. Cecelia's and each of the students got a present from the nuns, usually socks or such. When Letty visited during Christmas she'd bring her girls a gift of a nice head scarf for Mass or underwear in a perfumed package from a high-class store. The mandatory uniforms limited her impulse to purchase more, however when they needed coats or hats, she supplied the latest and the best.

The only gifts under their tree this Christmas were the two sweaters Bibsy bought at discount from her job for the boys, because Jake didn't believe in all that stuff. He said people tended to lose their minds at Christmas and refused to go along with it. But the real truth was Christmas came at the poorest time of the year for him.

For New Year's Eve Bibsy wanted to go to the Haverton Bar and Grille but Jake didn't want to because he was broke and refused to let Bibsy pay for their drinks. When she suggested treating, it almost started a fight, so they settled on going next door. They brought in 1954 with a toast of Jack Daniels and Gus's usual stash of moonshine. Carrie had fixed fried chicken, black eyed peas and collards that she'd picked that day from her garden, saying greens were most tender when pulled after the first frost. They were sitting around laughing and talking, while listening to Ella Fitzgerald's "A Tisket a Tasket" on the radio in the background, when there was a knock at the front door.

"Come in." Gus yelled out. "It's open, as usual."

Mason T walked in, "Happy New Year," he said, handing Gus and Jake each a six-pack of Rheingold beer. No one noticed at first that he'd brought a woman in with him. She hung back by the front door, shy and draped in obvious discomfort. "Oh, I'm sorry," he ambled over to the young woman and grabbed her by the hand. "Sarah, this is Gus, Carrie, Jake and Bibsy. Y'all, this is Sarah."

After saying hello, she took a few slow paces back out of the center of attention. Gus got up, took their coats and hats and brought out two wooden chairs. "What you drinkin? You know we got the usual."

"I think I'll try a littla that moon you got, just to take the nip off right quick." Mason T leaned over to Sarah, "You want a drink, baby?"

She shook her head no. "Any water?" Her request was barely audible and her hands were clasped in her lap.

"Sure." Gus said and poured water from a glass jar in the ice box and handed it to her. Sarah said thanks, took a sip and held the glass in her lap, her brown fingers intertwined around it.

"Glad you came by T," Jake smiled. "Thought you mighta got so high on your horse that we wouldn't be good enough company for ya anymore."

"Aw, come on Jake. You should know me better than that by now. Only way I was able ta save enough to move is causa livin down here."

Bibsy waited for him to admit it was his plan all along to leave, but he didn't. It had been about a month since Mason T first dropped the news that he was moving, and he'd been scarce on The Beach up until now, although Jake and Gus had seen him from time to time. Bibsy watched their movements with such scrutiny you could tell it made Sarah more uncomfortable than she already was; as her courteous smiles in Bibsy's direction were being reciprocated with an angry scowl.

"Thought I'd drop by, this bein my last New Year's down here." Mason T looked mostly at Jake. I'm gonna miss this. I had some good times livin here."

Started off lying right away, Bibsy thought. Right there. If they were such good times, then why was he leaving? She wondered why the others didn't catch on to him.

Gus handed Mason T his drink. "Sure am sorry ta see you go. Won't be the same here, that's for sure."

"Me too."

"This the woman you talkin bout marryin?" Jake said, then added, "I hope so, or you in some hot water now." They all laughed.

"Yeah, we're gonna tie the knot." They looked lovingly at each other. "It's time for me ta settle down."

"Where you from, Sarah?"

"Kancy. My mother works over at Kancy Hospital. In housekeeping. Connie Carlson, you know her?"

"I think so. You got any other family in Langston?"

"Got an uncle who works at the paper mill in Pierpoint, Uncle Charlie. Charlie Carlson. You might know him."

"Yeah, I think I know him," Jake said, nodding his head. "See him sometimes when I play poker over at Skunk Hollow. Good guy. I remember when he came up here from the south. They brought up a lotta colored guys from down south ta break that white union at the paper mill there. I forgot, where's your family from again?'

"South Carolina. Charleston."

"Yeah, that's right. Now I remember."

Carrie said, "That's where y'all plannin on movin to, Pierpoint?"

"Well, we ain't decided that yet. But almost." He looked again into Sarah's eyes. "We might be headed back down south."

Jake looked surprised. "South? Why would you wanna do that?"

"All that mess goin on down there right now with the schools, an the buses in Montgomery?"

"We jus had the same mess up here not too long ago, don't forget." Sarah said. Her addition to the conversation interrupted the familiar banter they'd grown accustomed to among each other.

"That's the truth." Carrie said, quick as ever.

"They givin Sarah's grandparents a hard time wit some property they own down there. You know white folks can git some funny record-keepin when your land is paid up. Suddenly their books don't match wit yours, or the property line somehow changes after a bunch a years."

"So, you thinkin bout movin to South Carolina, T?" Jake studied his friend. "That's a long ways from Langston."

"Yeah, we're thinkin bout it." Mason T nodded. "Sorta leanin in that direction too."

"Lawd." Gus and Carrie said simultaneously. "You gonna have a time on your hands."

"After we're married we might buy a plot from her grandparents, then we can build our own place right there near em. They own such a big parcel we wouldn't even be within yellin distance to em. I'll sit on my porch wit my rifle across my lap if that's what I gotta do to keep them crackers at bay."

"Might haveta do jus that. And it could git ya killed, boy." Gus said. "You talkin bout sure nuf lynchin country down there in Carolina."

"Gus, tell im bout what your brother seen." Carrie put down her glass and pulled out her familiar tin. "Your brother Edward. You know the story I mean."

"I know. I know." Obviously annoyed, he began with, "It ain't a easy story ta tell. It's the main reason we moved from down there." Respectful silence waited for him to continue. "My brother Edward, we all called him Eddie, was comin home from fishin one day. He took a short cut through the woods and he heard some voices when he came across a clearin. Not knowin who it was he commenced ta creepin up slow til he got ta where he could see a group a white folks, men, women and even chilren gathered round laughin an talkin." Gus visibly shrank into a deep place inside which was completely out of his usual spirited character. "They was all lookin up in this tree, so he looked up too and saw a colored man tied to a limb up there wit a rope around his neck, his legs kickin wild like in the air. Said he froze dead in his tracks at the sight of it."

Carrie said, "Humph," followed by a ping into her spit can.

"He was scared. Crouchin down in the tall reeds an bushes makin sure nobody seen im, now he became afraid for his own life too. He stayed there quiet and still. Kept watchin em. Every now an again he'd peek up ta see what they was doin and he said once the man stopped movin, they commence ta cutting up on his body while it was still hung up there. Laughin and drinkin the whole time. Even fought over his private parts. When they finished takin what they wanted ta keep, they put some dried sticks up under im, got a fire goin an burnt im up. He eventually fell inta the flames. After they finished eatin and drinkin and havin a good time an all, them white folks pulled off in their trucks and jalopies an went on. Laughin an all like they'd jus been ta the county fair.

"Eddie stayed in the woods all night. We didn't know where he was. My daddy got a buncha us ta go out searchin for im an we found im still crouched down in the woods. In the same position he been since the day before. He'd been like that so long till he couldn't stand up right away and we had ta carry him home. His eyes was all wild. The boy had crapped all over hisself. We brought Eddie home and tended to him. Nobody even recognized the man in the ashes. Burnt to a crisp."

Carrie added, "Poor Eddie. The boy ain't never been the same after that neither."

Jake watched Mason T's reaction to the story, but the young man's face was expressionless and hard.

"It takes a particular type a person ta mix sport and family outings wit torture," Gus continued, "and then collect human body parts for keepsakes."

"I don't believe God gave white folks a conscience," Carrie added. "That's how they can do all the evil they do and not ever be bothered by it."

"Looka what you all did. I come over here ta celebrate the New Year an you got my baby all scared."

"Unh, unh, I ain't scared." Contrary to her outward shyness, Sarah's face matched Mason T's toughness. "My family worked too hard and too long for that land."

Mason T grabbed Sarah's hand and said, "You know we can't keep livin scareda white folks. If we do, we won't never have nothin. If anybody look like they comin toward me with a rope, they better have some bullets as a back up, cause I'm takin a bunch of em down wit me. An you know I'm a good shot. Right Jake?"

"Yeah, you a damn good shot T," Jake said. "But I don't know bout venturing down there. Not jus now. From what I hear, they stirrin things up quite a bit down there now."

"We know there's a lot to consider." The young couple looked at each other again. "Or we can buy somewhere in Langston. Won't be as much property though, and her folks still won't have nobody lookin out for em. Mosta her uncles and stuff left from down there an don't wanna go back."

"Where you gonna work? You know they ain't gonna let you make no money in the south. If you plannin on workin for white folks, they got you man, cause they don't wanna pay you more'n enough ta barely git by on. An if ya do make a little money without needin em, then ya gotta watch your back. White folks get pissed off when you're doin better'n them."

"That's the part we workin out now. Only way we kin manage it is if we open our own business," Mason T said. "Jake you gotta come down and visit us. All a y'all. But I'm warnin you, ya might not wanna come back up here. I'm tellin you the truth."

"Truth be told," Carrie said looking directly at Jake while rubbing her knees, "don't know how much longer my legs kin take these winters up here."

"Oh no, don't tell me I'm gonna lose you two. Please don't tell me that. Please. I don't know what'd I'd do if that happened."

Although Jake was being playful, it was clear there was a lot of seriousness behind his words. Mason T and Jake were close friends, but Gus and Carrie were considered family, and he'd be lost without them.

"Ain't nobody talkin bout movin, Jake, so don't get yourself all riled up." Gus said.

"Oh. Jus checkin. Cause I can't take too much more of this here." He nodded in Mason T's direction.

"But, we ain't no spring chickens, Jake." Gus said. "One day we gonna haveta think about where ta live in our old age. We ain't gettin no younger. An like Carrie says, the winters are gettin harder ta take."

"How old are the two of you? If you don't mind me askin." Mason T said. "I always wondered."

"You know it ain't polite ta ask a woman her age, young man." Carrie joked.

"I'm sorry. I didn't mean no disrespect. You know, you can never tell wit colored folks."

"I'll be seventy-seven my next birthday, October 12th." The shock was evident on every face in the room as Gus looked at Carrie, "an I got sense enough not to offer her age. She kin do that herself."

"I'll be seventy-four, the eleventh of November." Carrie said. "God willin."

"Gus, long as I've known you, I don't think I ever knew that." Jake said.

"Yep. We're gettin up there, man."

"You'd never know it Gus. The way you work. Put soma these young men ta shame." Mason T turned to Sarah, "You should see him cut wood, or handle a jack hammer or whatever work's being done." Then he turned back to Gus, "I see why you don't go round tellin your age."

"You all ain't never had ta work like we did comin up."

"From sun up ta sun down." Carrie added. "But can't expect ta do that forever. I tell Gus that every dern year but he don't listen."

"You got a piece of paper, Gus?" Mason T felt all his pockets until finally pulling out a pencil stub from his shirt pocket and Gus handed him a torn piece of paper bag. "Whenever you two get ready ta go south again, look us up. This is Sarah's mother's phone number. We'll be stayin there till we get settled. I'm tellin ya there's room for alla us down there. You too, Jake."

"Thank you son." Gus said as he took the information Mason T had written. "But we got plenty of family down south. Virginia mostly. We figure at our age we'll be safe from them crackers. It's you youngins that's more a threat."

Carrie, Gus, Jake and Mason T spent the remainder of the evening reminiscing about the good times they'd shared on The Beach over the years. They all laughed at how green Mason T was when he first came to The Beach seven years ago. He thanked Jake for taking him under his wing and showing him the ropes and asked him to seriously think about joining him. Jake thanked him for the offer but said it wasn't likely because he didn't plan to ever leave The Beach. Said he was born here and planned on staying for good. Mason T and Sarah left wishing everybody Happy New Year, and Jake and Bibsy soon followed, both of them a little tipsy.

As they walked across the yard toward home, Jake said, "I guess I shoulda seen it comin wit Mason T. The man been hoardin his money since he got here. Workin two jobs. Givin rent parties. Plain ta see he had a plan for somethin else one day.

By the next weekend, Jake was hard at work with Gus and Mason T on Langston Lake harvesting ice with the last remaining company doing so. The skeleton crew that was left of the industry passed around a whiskey bottle all day to keep warm as they used hand saws to cut twelve-inch-thick chunks of ice from the lake. Because the work had slowed to a crawl, once in awhile they'd even get in a little ice fishing during the day to kill time. Occasionally Jake would come home drunk.

It wasn't long before Jake sealed the two windows facing the river in the spare room with plywood he bought from the lumber yard. Even though it darkened the house considerably, Jake said it was the only way to block the wind off the river. He purchased extra kerosene for the heaters he brought out of storage too.

For Bibsy, it was difficult listening to the wind howl outside in the dead of night. She now considered the structure of the house, and was fearful the wind could blow the rickety frame dwelling completely off its foundation and they'd be left unprotected from the bitter cold. Those nights, she'd wrap herself more snugly around Jake, confident in his ability to protect her.

The first time it snowed that winter, four-foot drifts had fallen stealthily through the night, covering half of all the windows. Even Rain and Tiger who slept indoors with them in the winter began barking as though understanding the predicament as they all watched Jake struggle unsuccessfully to push open the screen door. With the raucous barking accenting her own panic, Bibsy was glad Jake found homes for the rest of Rain's litter.

Frowning at the few logs left stacked in the corner of the kitchen across from the stove, Jake put on a pot of coffee and yelled, "Junior! Robert! Come on, we got work ta do."

Arming herself with her new thermal layers, Bibsy joined their efforts. They all had to use pots and brooms to make their way outside to where the shovels leaned against the house. By the time they cleared a path to the wood pile, the water pump and outhouse, they made their way to Gus and Carrie's house and helped shovel them out. Everybody else living on The Beach was similarly busy, and by the time Jake was satisfied the residents in the other six houses had clear access to the outside, it was nighttime again.

The next day, the men used shovels and wooden boards strapped to their vehicles pushing snow from the road, then drove over it repeatedly until it was packed down enough to drive on. By the time Jake came down the road hauling a pile of spent coals to throw on the ground for traction, another day had passed and they were exhausted all over again.

It snowed three more times that winter, but fortunately, none as bad as that first snow. Each time, everybody pitched in and helped each other dig out. As the snow melted and refroze each night, Bibsy appreciated the insulated boots Carrie advised her to buy as she learned to navigate the treacherous ice on The Beach as well as the walkways and sidewalks in town. During the evenings, they listened to the radio and regularly found some of their favorite programs no longer being offered, as television was quickly and steadily replacing it.

The boys taught Bibsy to play card games like rummy, tonk and a memory game they'd made up. Jake tried to teach them all poker, but found it a lot less exciting without money on the table. Besides, Bibsy always gave away her hand, excitedly grinning whenever she got good cards.

As their boredom increased that winter, so did Jake and Bibsy's drinking, and they were sometimes short with each other and the boys for no real reason. Occasionally, Jake would go out without Bibsy and come back drunk, and that would start a fight between them that would last all through the night. Unlike previous fights where they made peace, usually in bed, their spats gradually began to stretch over days, with nighttime finding them lying back to back. Something about those nights felt so similar to her childhood punishments that she'd usually drink herself to sleep to get through to the morning.

Finally, the end of February came and brought with it the gift of more daylight hours and a new disposition for everybody. And on no particular day in March while on her way to work Bibsy saw daffodils in area flower beds emerge through the remnants of the last snowstorm, and was certain she could do this all over again next year.

Chapter Thirteen

Before leaving The Beach that spring, Mason T bought a used truck and sold his old Chevy to Jake for fifty dollars. Jake wanted to pay him a fair price for it but Mason T wouldn't have it, saying their friendship was worth more than the money. Jake gave Mason T twenty dollars and ten more each payday until he'd paid it off. After packing all that he wanted, Mason T allowed Jake and Gus to help themselves to whatever they wanted of the rest of his belongings. Everybody else, he charged a price. He said hauling it down south would be too costly and the furniture wasn't worth transporting. Jake took a couple of kitchen chairs for extra seating, a fishing rod and one of his shotguns.

The boys liked having graduated from the back of the truck to an inside cushioned seat, and Jake and Bibsy got a kick out of seeing them peer through the car windows and wave to their friends with an obvious measure of pride. Now that they didn't have to worry about their vehicle breaking down so often, they took more frequent road trips, and enjoyed the pleasant breeze that accompanied traveling at the speed limit.

Some evenings after supper they'd go for a drive and pick up sodas or ice cream with the boys. On those very hot late nights while most people were drifting off to sleep Jake and Bibsy stole away to the swimming hole, their favorite summer place. Because of Jake's fascination with his new car, they spent less time there, making their evening swims even more precious than they already were.

One Friday evening when they were riding nowhere special, Jake suggested they visit Martha and Kalvin. Bibsy called from Louie's store to see if they'd be home and also check if Letty was there.

"Hi, Sis. How's everything?" Bibsy's voice exploded with excitement.

"Oh, we're fine. Why do you sound so tickled? What's going on?"

"Is Mom there?"

"No. She's visiting Cora in Baltimore this weekend. Why? What's going on?"

"Well, are you all gonna be home tonight?"

"Um....yeah. Why? You visiting?"

"We sure are! Jake and the boys are in the car now." Bibsy laughed at her own excitement.

"Oh." There was a noticeable delay that Bibsy ignored. "Well, come on then, I guess...since you're all ready to go. I'd love to see you. And everybody."

After another delay where Bibsy could hear a muffled discussion in the background, Kalvin finally got on the phone to give Bibsy directions to their apartment in case Jake had forgotten. A little more than an hour later, they arrived at her sister's Harlem apartment with smiles as wide as the Hudson.

"How was the ride?" Kalvin asked Jake as they shook hands. "Did you have any trouble getting here?"

"Just fine. Just fine." Jake answered following Kalvin down the hallway. "Thought we'd take a little ride this evenin." Seeing a small group of people in the living room, he added, "Oh, are we interruptin somethin?"

"No, not at all." Kalvin said. "Just a little gathering. We closed on our house today and we'll be moving to Queens next month. A few of our friends came by to help us celebrate. Come on in and join us." Once they were comfortable Kalvin handed Bibsy an index card with their new Queens address in Kalvin's elaborate script, and Bibsy was reminded how unusual it was to see his name spelled with a K instead of a C. "This'll be the next place you visit us."

Jake looked at Bibsy, "Seems everybody's talkin about buyin a house lately, don't it?"

"Are you all moving, too?" A hopeful tone framed Martha's words.

"No we're not." Bibsy answered flatly. "We're fine right where we are."

Kalvin introduced them to their guests.

"Where are the kids?" Junior asked, and upon hearing his voice the children raced from their bedrooms to greet them, wearing their pajamas.

"Y'all gettin ready for bed already?" Robert asked. "This early? It just got dark outside."

Kalvin looked at Martha before saying, "We'll let you stay up a little longer, since Bibsy's here."

Martha turned to her sister explaining, "Usually, after their bath it's lights out, but since their auntie's here we'll make an exception tonight."

"I remember those house rules. I guess I forgot."

"Would you like something to eat?" Martha offered.

"I'm starving," Junior and Robert said at the same time.

Bibsy said, "How can you all be starving when you had supper and even ice cream before we left?"

Martha laughed, "You know how children are."

They went into the kitchen with the children and Jake followed Kalvin into the living room.

"Come on and sit down, Jake. We've been listening to Sarah Vaughan's new record, *They Can't Take That Away From Me*, you heard that one yet?" Kalvin handed Jake the jacket to his latest seventy-eight record.

"Naw, can't say that I have." Seeing Kalvin's extensive record collection, he added. "Man, you must be really inta music."

"Oh yeah. Jazz mostly."

At that moment Robert burst into the living room excitedly with, "Can we see television? Can we see Amos n Andy?"

Their guests all looked at each other before Kalvin said, "We're listening to music right now, son." Seeing Robert's dejected face he added, "Maybe later." A slight change in Kalvin's facial expression was the single hint of his annoyance.

One of his guests asked, "Does that come on tonight?"

"I don't think so," said another.

"They should take that mess off the air," Kalvin said finally.

"Nobody likes Amos n Andy?" Jake's surprise was genuine.

"Well," Kalvin began cautiously, "That kind of humor is beginning to be a little over done if you know what I mean."

"No," Jake was clearly puzzled. "I don't know what you mean."

One of their guests interjected, "I think what Kalvin's trying to say is that white folks are too quick to put those shuffling, grinning, rolling-eyes-kind-of-colored folks on television and the movies. And it makes us all look bad."

"I don't know nothin bout that. I jus think they're funny." Jake thought a moment then added, "Kalvin, I didn't know you didn't like Amos n Andy. Didn't we listen to it at my house together on the radio?"

"No offense, Jake, but I can't dictate what a man listens to in his own home. You know what I mean?"

"Yeah. But if youda said somethin, I'da changed the station." Apparently still considering the humor issue, he said, "Hmmm. I always thought they were funny."

In the kitchen Bibsy and Martha were trying to handle the chaos unfolding after Junior and Robert having spotted a box of Cheerios in the cupboard, asked for some. Martha dismissed Bibsy's objection telling Junior to get two bowls from the second shelf of their kitchen cupboard and when he pulled down two of her cake-mixing bowls instead of cereal bowls and emptied the entire contents of the box into them, the other children began snickering.

"Mind your manners or you three will be saying goodnight," was enough to stop the rude behavior.

"Looks like we caught you at a bad time, Sis. I'm sorry. Why didn't you tell me on the phone that you had company? And you're buying a house? That's big news! Why didn't you tell me?"

"Well, I was going to wait until we signed the papers and it was final." That they found it appropriate to celebrate with friends made that an awkward response so she hastily added, "We're always glad to see family, Bibsy. You're always welcome here. You know that."

Once the children were done with the cereal spectacle, Buster said, "Wanna see my new erector set?"

"Yeah!" Robert and Junior both answered with more enthusiasm than she expected. Bibsy thought Junior and Robert were too old for such toys, but realized she didn't remember seeing any real toys in the house. Robert and Junior entertained themselves with fishing, reading, card playing and tinkering with cars, the same as any adult would. Still contemplating their recreational activities, she watched them rush off into the boys' bedroom.

Cheryl hung back and asked, "Can I stay in here with you and Bibsy, Mom?"

"Honey you know you're not supposed to be around grown folks when we're talking. You can go on in there with the boys if you want to. Tell them I said so."

"I don't want to play with their construction set, Ma. I'll read my book in my room."

Bibsy was sad for Cheryl, and remembered in that moment how the two of them would play together when she stayed there. Of course the child never knew that Bibsy was indulging a luxury she hadn't had as a child.

"Okay, honey. Maybe you can start that new book you got from the library."

Martha smiled at her daughter before directing her attention back to Bibsy. "That child loves to read."

"So does Junior." Bibsy said even though she didn't know what the boy was reading most of the time, only that he was most content when buried in reading material. Watching Martha busy in the kitchen reminded Bibsy of another familiar scene from her time living there. "Sit down a minute, Martha, and visit with me," she said. "We didn't get to talk much when you came up to visit with Mom."

"Yeah, you're right," Martha sat down putting a clean ashtray on the table between them and lit a cigarette. "Sometimes I forget to come up for air," she laughed at herself. "The kids sure enjoyed themselves at your place that day." After striking a match and lighting her cigarette, she paused after taking the first drag and her demeanor became more relaxed after exhaling.

"Heard about the argument you and Mom had. I don't understand why the two of you never could get along."

"You don't understand it because you didn't grow up in St. Cecelia's, that's why. Sis, the place was like a prison. And we kept tellin Mom what it was like and she kept us there anyhow."

"How come Mary and Cora didn't leave there feeling the way you do?"

"I can't speak for them. I know they used to complain about it, but somewhere along the way they stopped and just accepted things. Maybe they decided that was best after seeing me get into trouble all the time. Sometimes I swear it felt like they went after me and this other girl, just to keep everybody else in line."

It baffled Bibsy how they always got to this place, but it was a familiar dance between them; Bibsy attempting to justify the anger St. Cecelia's left her with and Martha minimizing it. She would never be able to articulate the deep sense of inferiority she felt, because that reality was wrapped in too much scar tissue to reach. Despite the flattery often extolled upon her, especially by men, she would never truly believe that she was pretty, because all the images of those who were considered beautiful, pure and deserving of God's love, never looked like her.

Martha expressed her frustration by slowly shaking her head from side to side. "It's over now, Bibsy. Been over a long time now."

"They hid their meanness behind those robes, Sister. That should be sinful. Not the little stuff we was doin."

"It was, Bibsy. And one day they're gonna have to answer for that. That's all. You stay too angry all the time." Martha flicked her cigarette in the ashtray and paused before taking another long drag from it. "Mom said she told you about her mother and grandmother." Martha appeared even more pensive with the shift of topic. "That was something else. I knew her mother. But the story she said she told you about her grandmother was news to me. Never heard that one before."

"Oh, so she finally told you, huh?" Bibsy sighed. "Finally we get to know something about us and our family."

"Yeah, she said she might as well let all of us know since she told you. I don't think I'll be handing that story down to my kids though. That's too much for them to handle. Shoot, it's too much for me to handle."

"What about when they get older?"

"I don't see any point in holding onto something like that, Bibsy. What would be the point?"

"The truth, Sis." Bibsy couldn't understand her sister's reasoning. "The truth is the point. People should know their past. It's important. Part of who you are."

Martha shook her head in disagreement as she blew a round of smoke into the air. "It's too much. I'll let God handle that. White folks got a lot to atone for. Believe you me."

"So does Mom."

"Look Bibsy, you got to get past this. Otherwise, it'll eat you alive. Let it go. You're happy now with Jake, right?"

"Yeah, but..."

"But nothing. That's enough. Right there. I'm telling you, you gotta stop this. Hey!" A wide smile brightened Martha's face. "You all can come visit us when we move into our house. We'll even have enough room so you can sleep over if you want to."

"I forgot to say congratulations, Sis. Sorry. That's really good news. What's the house look like?" Bibsy was actually glad to change the subject. Talking to Martha could be exhausting sometimes because she always had to be right.

"Well, it's got…"

Just then Kalvin poked his head through the kitchen door, "Tell the kids they can come watch the television now. *I Love Lucy* is on. You all want to watch?"

"Yeah, that's a good idea," Martha said while getting up from the kitchen table. "We could all use a laugh right about now. Come on Bibsy."

Kalvin brought kitchen chairs into the living room for Martha and Bibsy while the children filled in empty spaces on the area rug to watch the program.

In spite of their ongoing disagreement about whether their mother was justified in putting most of her children St. Cecelia's, Bibsy liked Martha and appreciated her upbeat personality, and the fact that the closest Martha got to going to church was listening to Mahalia Jackson's records on Sunday mornings. She remembered the laughs they shared. Like the time Martha burnt the previous year's palm in an old pot on Palm Sunday morning and had the entire top two floors of their apartment building smelling like a Catholic church. The scent brought Bibsy into the kitchen to see what was going on, and as a gag she stopped to genuflect before entering. They laughed an entire morning over that. Even the memory brought a smile to her face as she began to redirect her attention to the conversation the boys were having in the back seat on the drive home from The City.

"That was *My Favorite Husband,* when it was on the radio." Junior said on the ride home. "All they're doin is takin the same shows off the radio and puttin em on the television."

"But that was a white guy playing her husband on the radio. You could tell cause he didn't have that accent."

"The Spanish guy is her real husband too."

"I know. I seen it in the paper before."

"It's funnier on the TV," Junior added. "Her in that clown outfit cracked me up."

Their *I Love Lucy* chatter continued nonstop until they were well out of The City. They even compared the commercials on the radio to those on television. But by the time they pulled into the yard, the boys were snoring in the back seat and Jake had to wake them. Bibsy was struck by the boyish expressions on their faces as they slept, as it contrasted their near grown up image she was accustomed to seeing.

"Seems like they had a good time," Bibsy said of the boys when she and Jake were in bed that night. "How about you, Jake? Did you enjoy yourself tonight?"

"It was alright, I guess. Kalvin's a good enough guy. You can tell he thinks long and hard about things. Guess there's a need for that too in this world." He stroked her arm gently. "But I'm about to enjoy myself a whole lot more right about now." Jake lightly kissed Bibsy's shoulder, then her lips, before his hands tenderly explored other parts of her body.

Their evening at Martha and Kalvin's provided the exact change of pace Bibsy felt they all needed. Everyone talked about it for days afterward. The boys especially. Bibsy thought it was great to get Jake's mind off of Gus and Carrie's news of moving which now seemed to preoccupy most of his time. She was hoping their visit would bring him back to his old self because recently he'd become moody and the least little thing irritated him. She'd seen him snap at the boys to do their chores, even as they were in the midst of doing them.

Clusters of new houses sprung up in some part of every village or hamlet in Langston that summer, placing ranch-style rectangles where hundreds of acres of fertile farmland had been. As the bridge and thruway were near completion, the men began to speculate among themselves that there was roughly one more season of work left before the vision of the nation's longest highway system, connecting Buffalo to New York City, would be realized. No one knew of another long-term construction job on the horizon, and that prospect had many of them openly worried.

Some with political connections were being pulled into the burgeoning local communities' infrastructure throughout the county, obtaining work in various public works departments or other employment using hard labor. Much of it was needed to maintain the actual highways and bridge they were building. However, there were no colored men being selected for those positions, and the few who were offered lowly laborer positions anywhere were considered lucky. Jake was not one of them, likely because his fondness for drinking was local legend.

Gus, Carrie, Jake and Bibsy were sitting on the porch one evening after dinner one day when Gus said, "You heard about Louie's brother-in-law Jimmy gettin a job with the county? Hired as part of the steady maintenance crew they're hirin for the highways."

"The man ain't worked a good month his whole life, to hear Louie tell it." Jake shook his head in disbelief. "Thought ya had ta pass some kinda test ta get them jobs."

"Louie's brother's in politics, so you know he's gonna make a way for him ta get in."

"Figures. Guess he'll be the next ta leave The Beach."

"Never expected him ta stay no how. He was jus livin down here ta get outta havin ta work too much."

Later that week Jake went by Louie's store to hear the news firsthand.

"Howya doin, Jake?" Louie said when he saw Jake come into the store. "What you been up to?"

"Nothin much." Jake dug through the ice chest, selecting a beer from the bottom where it was coldest. "What's new with you? I heard Jimmy's got a new job."

"Yeah." Louie was busy stacking corn meal onto shelves. "My brother Frank took care of the bum. You know my sister's pregnant again?"

"Whew! How many's that now?"

"Six." Louie said. "It's time for him to earn a regular paycheck of his own. The family can't afford to keep carryin him."

"You're right. A half-dozen mouths to feed is no joke."

"Is it true what I heard, that Gus and Carrie is leavin?" Louie came over to the counter wiping cornmeal residue from his hands onto a towel he kept tucked inside his belt.

Jake nodded yes as he shoved a quarter across the counter to pay for the beer. "Won't be the same around here without them. I know your families have been close for years."

"Yep. I'm sure not lookin forward ta that day."

"I'll tell you what else is gonna happen." Louie leaned in closer even though there were no other customers in the store to hear him. "I'm sellin the business."

"No shit! Why? Thought you were doin good over here. You own the whole buildin and you got tenants upstairs. How much money you need, Louie?"

"It's nothin like the old days, Jake. Besides," Louie continued at a whisper. "My brother's gettin me a county job, too. He says I won't haveta work as hard anymore."

"Your brother's takin care of the whole damn family. Sheeez! He got any more jobs layin around? We could pretend I'm family, can't we? I'm light enough."

Louie laughed, as Jake put his forearm against his and compared their skin tone. "He told me to please not ask for anybody else. You know how it goes. We're lookin at a house in Stone Point now."

"How much longer you gonna be open?"

"I dunno. Soon's I get a buyer. I'll haveta tell my customers to settle up their bills now, but you're not one of the ones I'm worried about."

"Well, if that don't beat all. Guess we'll need to find someplace else to make phone calls."

"Woolworth's has a phone booth, Jake."

"Yeah, but they won't get messages to people on The Beach like you do. Won't be the same, not after all these years. There's too damn many changes goin on for me."

"I know. It's just a matter of time before The Beach is history, Jake. Hope you're ready for it. There's a lotta movement in the county now. You shouldn't have any problem finding a place to rent. It's time to come from down there anyway, Jake. Life is hard enough without havin to live like that."

"To tell you the truth, it ain't hard for me cause I'm used to it. But the way it looks now, I'm gonna be the only one livin down there, cause I ain't leavin." He let out what sounded like a forced laugh. "But, I'ma miss you man."

"And I'll miss you too, Jake." Louie extended his hand and the men shook. "I've had this place for so long I don't know if I can work for somebody else now. But I need more money, and a bigger place to live." With his thumb, he pointed to the curtained doorway behind him. "You know how it is."

"I guess so."

When Jake came home he told the family that Louie was selling his store and they'd have to make other arrangements for their phone calls, but didn't share anything else of their conversation. Knowing there were other phone booths in downtown Haverton, Bibsy wasn't worried. She kept her family phone numbers safely in her suitcase under the bed with other important papers. She had appreciated Louie getting messages to them, but also knew she could do without it.

She was more concerned about Jake than the phone at Louie's. Lately Bibsy found him at home drinking by himself when she'd come home from work instead of busy getting supper started like usual. Besides that, there was a certain infectious high energy about Jake that was fading. His usual good spirits were too often being replaced with a moody irritable disposition that had a particular tendency of surfacing whenever he drank too much, and even that was becoming more frequent.

"Comin ta terms with Mason T leavin was hard enough," he said to Bibsy one night. "But I wasn't ready ta hear Gus and Carrie say they been thinkin bout it too. I knew they was gettin along in age. But I really thought they'd be by my side to the end."

It was just another version of the same thing he'd been saying over the last few months. At first, Bibsy tried to ease his mind by saying, "Maybe they were just talking and it didn't mean nothin."

"It's not like them to bring up something like that before discussin it among themselves." He had said that night. "I could tell by the way Gus put it that they likely talked it through already."

Since Jake knew them his whole life Bibsy didn't question him further, but it dashed any hope of imagining otherwise for herself. It was hard for her to fathom The Beach without Carrie. Although they had a similar straight way of speaking to people, their friendship wasn't immediate, but grew gradually, allowing their bond to take hold on its own. She remembered Carrie telling her that usually time revealed everything in the end if people were patient enough to wait on it; but most people didn't respect time that way. Actually, Bibsy had taken much of Carrie's wisdom for granted all along, until the realization set in that one day, fairly soon, she'd be left without it. Now those adages were a reminder of the void she could expect.

"They raised me when my daddy died, then helped me to raise my two boys when my wife died." Jake said on another occasion. "They're the kinda people who jus step in and do what needs doin without bein asked. Never heard em complain. You don't find people like that every day."

"You think they'll move nearby?" Bibsy's question sounded more hopeful than she realized.

"I asked him that already." Jake let out a weary sigh. "He said for years his sister been writin him ta come back south and live. Funny thing is I believe Mason T movin back there helped them ta see the south different. He said him and Carrie were too old now ta be seen as a threat by white folks down there."

"Carrie been complainin about her knees since I've known her, and that ain't been long I know. But I think the winters are really gettin to her."

"Yeah." Jake said, then looked off.

The boys were back in school and the adults busy preparing for another winter. Bibsy and Carrie were enjoying a rest on the porch after having finished their canning. Jake and Gus had their heads under his truck, taking care of any necessary repairs before winter expressed its full potential.

"There's the leak, right there." Gus held the flashlight with one hand and pointed with the wrench in the other.

"Thought it might be the carburetor. We kin look for one over at the junkyard."

"Yeah. If we don't find one there, we'll haveta take it over ta Ray's. We should be able ta fix it at least good enough ta get it over there."

"Yeah, we haveta. Don't wanna take no chances and get stranded in the snow this winter."

They heard a commotion and pulled their heads from under the truck's hood and peered down the road. At first, from the distance it looked like a white blur. Eventually four black women wearing white from head to toe came into focus, each clutching something in their hands as they made their way down Beach Road stopping briefly at each house.

"Damn. Here come the Holy Rollers," Jake said as the women steadily approached going from house to house.

When the group from the local storefront Pentecostal church made their way to Jake's house the spokesperson for the group said, "Praise the Lord, ladies and gentlemen. We came by to pray for you today. We come by every now and again to give you the opportunity to be saved. Make your life right with God."

"I don't need no prayers." Jake grumbled. "You got some money? I could use that." He and Gus were the only ones who laughed at his joke.

"Yes you do need praying for Jake Tucker," said one of the women in the group who'd grown up in Haverton and knew Jake a lifetime, as was the nature of very small communities.

Carrie piped in, "I know you not talkin bout needin nothin, Elsie."

The spokesperson shut her eyes, pressed her Bible to her breast and shot her other hand into the air, "Heavenly Father," she began and the sanctified women stopped in their tracks and closed their eyes. "We love you and honor you. Jesus, we praise your holy name."

"Yes Lord."

"Hallelujiah!"

"Please Father God, open the hearts and minds of this family, so that they can see you and know your perfect work."

"Yes, Lord, yes." The woman who had spoken to Jake previously now began to jump up and down with her hand reaching for the sky and eventually they all began to praise dance, their steps kicking up dust in the yard.

"Help them to know you Father and come into the fold. Help them to learn to follow your light, Lord."

"Yes, Jesus."

"Do your perfect work Father, in Jesus' name. Amen."

There was a resounding chorus of amens from the group and the leader now resumed her conversation, walking over to Carrie and Bibsy handing out their type-written church literature. “Here, this is a prayer booklet and a schedule of our services. We worship over on Hudson Street Wednesday evenings and Sundays at ten. Stop by sometime. You all have a nice day now,” and the women in white headed back down Beach Road.

They left humming *His Eye Is On The Sparrow*, but Bibsy didn’t recognize the song.

“Well, I guess we had church today.” Carrie said. “That’s the way church ought to be, short, sweet and to the point.”

“And no collection,” Jake added before slamming shut the truck’s hood.

“I’d come to church all the time if it was like that,” Bibsy said. Privately, she wondered how those women were able to have such direct access to God without having to go through a whole string of folks all claiming to be closer to Him than everybody else.

Chapter Fourteen

Bibsy and the boys were in the living room half listening for the Lucky Strikes commercial preceding the Jack Benny radio show, which was their cue to stop whatever they were doing and prepare to give the program their undivided attention. Jake was visiting friends somewhere in the county and Bibsy knew if he came across a poker game, he'd be late coming home. So the three of them looked forward to this being a cold cuts night, the boys' favorite.

Listening carefully as Junior and Robert talked about their back-to-school plans, Bibsy was fully aware they'd only recently started speaking freely in her presence as well as including her in their discussions, a development that just happened one day out of the blue. The boys had sold bait to fishermen all summer. Whenever they went fishing and lucked up on a larger than usual haul, they sold their catch to a local market in town minus what they needed for supper that night. That, along with maintaining several lawns in the area, doing odd jobs and running errands, provided them with decent enough spending money.

Jake fully expected the boys to carry their weight. He said giving children too much would make them not know how to fend for themselves when they got grown and needed to. Bibsy thought Jake expected too much of the kids and they deserved a break from time to time, so she'd slip them money now and again to see a movie or hang out at the soda fountain with friends and play the jukebox.

The boys knew if they wanted any new outfits or supplies for school, they'd have to buy it themselves. Jake didn't put much stock into school. He said more than once that what he was teaching the boys was more useful in life, and keeping kids in school past learning how to read and count was a waste of time when they could be earning good money during the day.

Junior and Robert sat at the kitchen table spilling out jars of saved money onto the porcelain kitchen tabletop when Junior said, "How much are the dungarees we saw at the Army and Navy store the other day?"

"I don't remember. Four dollars?" Robert was arranging stacks from the sizeable mound of loose change.

"We haveta see if they're cheaper at Woolworth's."

"Yeah, betcha Woolworth's is cheaper."

"We should check Robert Hall's too. We can hitchhike there if Pop or Uncle Gus can't take us. Sometimes they got good sales just when school starts." Junior placed the paper money in like piles.

"Gimme a coupla them nickel wrappers," Robert said, and Junior slid him the handful of paper coin wrappers they picked up from the bank recently. Bibsy was on the couch smoking a cigarette and stroking Tiger despite Jake's warnings that she'd make him into a good for nothing lap dog if she continued doing so. To Jake, Trap was the model dog on The Beach. Most everyone else considered Trap a dog to steer clear of, but Jake maintained that once he knew you and knew you were connected to someone on The Beach, the dog left you alone. Only strangers needed to be fearful. He warned Bibsy that keeping Tiger on her lap would make him lazy and ruin his natural instincts to sniff out danger and protect them. Bibsy on the other hand thought Rain could make up for anything Tiger lacked, and didn't want to be party to creating a dog as mean as Trap anyhow.

"What are you all doing? Getting ready to go back to school?" Bibsy said while smiling at Tiger's contented expression.

"Yep." They each said without looking up.

"Oh, look at that. Something just ran across the room." She pointed with the Viceroy between her fingers.

"What was it?" They both looked in that general direction but saw nothing and went back to counting and tallying into a composition notebook.

"I don't hear nothin." Junior said. "Tiger woulda barked if somethin ran across the room, Miz Bibsy."

The boys were so engrossed in their money they went immediately back to what they were doing. She knew Junior was right, but she went and investigated anyway, and found nothing. "Well, I coulda swore I saw...oh well, it's probably nothing."

Junior said, "Miz Bibsy, I hear they got them soap operas on television now."

"Wish we had a television."

She'd grown used to hearing Robert wish out loud for a television. When televisions first came out, the most popular radio programs stayed on the air because everybody couldn't afford TVs and no one knew if the new medium would take hold. Bibsy experienced both and preferred the radio because most of the characters on television never lived up to the way she had imagined them.

"We ain't even got no lights, stupid. How we gonna have television?"

"I know that! I'm just sayin I wish we had both. I hate being from The Beach. We the only ones in school that don't have electric at home."

Bibsy felt sorry for them. At work, when some of her co-workers talked about something funny or interesting that they'd seen on television, she felt disconnected and excluded from those casual conversations at break time. Even though the absence of amenities didn't bother her that much, she knew how children could sometimes be mean spirited with teasing, making it more difficult for Robert and Junior to handle.

"I seen *Rin Tin Tin* over at my friend's house," Robert said excitedly, "Rain is good as that dog. Rain's a smart dog."

"Smarter."

"Junior, you think she's smarter than Lassie? I do?"

"Maybe."

"The best shows is on Sunday," Junior said.

"How do you know that?" Bibsy knew the answer but was curious how they'd respond.

They just laughed without answering. However, she'd suspected for awhile now that their absences from home in the early evenings after supper were spent at their friends' homes in town watching television. Robert was clearly more taken by it, as most of his conversations centered around not only the programming, but the mechanical specifics as well. Bibsy'd heard him speak about the inner workings of televisions with knowledge he could only have by taking one apart and hoped he'd gleaned that information from old sets he probably found at the nearby junk yard, and not from someone's living room. Although television interested Junior, it wasn't enough to wrest him away from the books and comics he was so fond of. He loved westerns, but was prone to read everything, even the small print on packaging.

"But the same programs is on the radio, too." Bibsy didn't expect that piece of information to satisfy them since it hadn't worked in their previous discussions. She just didn't know what else to say. It was always Jake's stock response so she simply repeated it. "I like the Jack Benny Show better on radio anyway."

"Why? Rochester is colored. And he's a funny guy. He always outsmarts Jack Benny."

"Every time." Robert added.

"Oh, I don't know." Bibsy said. "I don't like to see him roll his eyes when he talks. There's something about seein him do that...I don't know."

"Oh yeah?" Junior pondered Bibsy's comment a moment before saying, "I seen in a Jet Magazine where Rochester's got a big house in California. He's rich you know."

The long-awaited Lucky Strikes commercial came on and the boys put away their money and positioned themselves right next to the radio even though Junior already turned up the volume. By the time the program went off, they were all wiping their eyes from laughing so hard.

“Oh, that guy is so cheap,” Robert was still holding his sides.

After the program they fixed baloney sandwiches and sat at the table eating.

“Wish we can get mayonnaise once in awhile.” Robert whined. “I get sick of mustard on my sandwiches all the time.”

“Robert, you know why,” Bibsy said. “I know you do, because I’ve heard Jake tell you many times. Mayonnaise won’t keep that long in the ice box. You’ll be sick as a dog eatin that stuff after it goes bad.”

“Miz Bibsy,” Junior said, “you think we’ll haveta move from down here one day? Soma my friends say they gonna tear down The Beach one day and we’ll haveta move.”

Robert said, “I can’t wait till that happens. Wish it was tomorrow.”

“We’re always bein teased in school cause we live on The Beach. Everybody else in town got lights in their house....”

“And inside toilets.”

“There’s music we hear on the jukebox that other kids know all the words to cause they got record players at home and they can play the songs over and over till they get the words down pat.”

"Charlie's family got a television, record player and electric fans in his house!" Junior said, "And his family ain't even rich."

"Where's Charlie live? Around here?" Bibsy asked. "Is that where you all disappear to every night after supper?"

They looked at each other before Junior spoke, "How'd you know that?"

"Because I figured it out, eventually. You two been easin outta here almost every night right after we eat supper. And practically every Sunday evenin."

"Can't you talk Pop into movin, Miz Bibsy?" Robert was so much like his father, not wasting time getting to the heart of the matter. "We started usin the laundromat in town after you came, and not jus in the wintertime neither."

"Ooohhhh, no." Bibsy laughed at the notion. "It looks like your father is pretty set on staying down here. And I can't much blame him. I like it too. All this outdoor space."

"How can you say that, Miz Bibsy? Don't nobody live like us no more."

"Just because everybody else is doin something, don't make it right." She said.

In her heart she believed the boys were right and hated that they felt so much shame associated with their living conditions. Jake would never consider leaving on his own. Even though their pleadings tugged at her heart, she considered their plight a lot better than how she grew up.

Occasionally even she would wonder how much longer they'd live there, particularly whenever someone at work shared with her the latest rumor going around about The Beach being bulldozed or the county forcing them to move. But in the end, she always believed they had nothing to fear because Jake was the kind of person who took care of his family no matter what. If life offered any certainties, that was one.

That night Jake came home in an especially good mood because he was the big winner that night at a poker game that took place in The Hill section of nearby Springville.

"Y'all shoulda seen me," he said laughing as he pulled two fistfuls of paper money from his pants pockets and piled it onto the table. "Took all their money. They was beggin me ta leave."

"Wow." They all said at the same time.

Junior scanned the pile and picked through the bills, saying, "Must be almost two hundred dollars here, Pop. Wow."

"I cleaned em out." Jake laughed. "Cleaned em out." After sorting and tallying the money he said, "One hundred and sixty-five dollars! Hot damn!" He was beaming at his new fortune, "What y'all need?"

Bibsy was the first to speak. "The boys was puttin their little money together for things they need for school. Why don't you help em out."

"Okay." Jake gave them each a twenty dollar bill and said, "That should do you."

"Yes!" The boys blurted out and took their money to their bedroom where Bibsy imagined them retallying their totals in their notebook.

"What you need for yourself, baby?"

"Nothin, I got all I need already."

"Well here," he said handing her forty dollars. "Get yourself something nice. An don't buy nothin for the house with it like you usually do. I mean it now."

"Okay," she said, even though she was already thinking about what they could use. She always put something aside from her salary, just in case they needed it, despite knowing Jake would do without before taking her money. He had his funny ways like that. There wasn't much they needed to buy, and she wasn't big on shopping so about half of her salary every week went into an envelope in her old suitcase under the bed where she kept her birth certificate, diploma from St. Cecelia's, rosary beads, a tattered Baltimore Catechism and a Daily Missal that she didn't know why she kept.

After the boys retired and they were about to get ready for bed, she said to Jake, "What do you think about puttin some of that money aside?" Bibsy knew in a couple of days, Jake's winnings would be gone and this was the best time to approach him.

"Aside for what, Bibsy?"

"Aside for...I don't know. I keep hearin we're not goin to be able to stay here a whole lot longer. That's what I hear at work all the time."

"Pshhh. Just rumors. That's all." Jake waved his hand at her suggestion. "Folks been sayin that for years now. Years! An it ain't happened yet. All that talk for nothin. Who told you that, Evelyn at work?"

"No, Charlie, my boss. He says that's the latest talk goin round an we should start lookin now."

"Did he tell you that's been the talk for the last fifty years? Did he tell you that?"

"Um…no. But Jake," she said, "what do you think about movin? Just so the boys can be more like the other kids in their school." She knew once she got started to keep talking fast to sufficiently make her case before Jake interrupted, "And you wouldn't have to work so hard either." She figured focusing on him and not just the boys was a better tactic. "We could probably spend more time together if you didn't have so much to do around here." She knew that would catch his attention if all else failed.

But Jake surprised her with, "You shamed of livin here?"

"No, of course not. I love it here. Especially being here with you. It's the kids, Jake. They're...I don't think they're happy. Other kids tease em."

Bibsy could see he was weighing her response which made her hopeful, but she was very anxious about venturing into this unexplored and potentially explosive territory with him. The expressions on the boys' faces when they spoke about the house touched a chord that reminded her of her childhood, and she couldn't stand seeing them suffer.

"Would you like to know why I want to stay here?" Bibsy was appreciative of Jake's calm manner. "Do you?"

Bibsy shook her head yes.

"I give that white man fifteen dollars a month for this place. It ain't a lot, but it's what I can afford. The way we live puts us out a little bit, but I take care of my family. Put food on the table. From time ta time we enjoy ourselves, right?"

"Yeah, Jake. We do." Hearing Jake speak from the heart this way made Bibsy regret broaching the subject.

"Truth is, Bibsy, I know I'm free with money. Always have been. I like ta gamble, and when I win it feels good, like tonight. And when I lose, you never hear me complain or get in a foul mood. Right?"

"No you don't, Jake."

"That's the way I like ta live my life an I won't apologize for it. An I know if I live anywhere else I couldn't live carefree like this, cause I'd be jus gettin by. Nowhere else. So I'm sorry the boys don't have what other kids have, but they got a daddy who can walk around with his head up."

That was the first and last time they had any conversation about leaving The Beach. Bibsy knew from that point on, she'd be helping the boys cope with their situation any way she could. But they were going to stay put.

A couple of weeks later, on a payday, when Bibsy came home from work and pulled out her envelope to put money in it, she thought it was thinner than it should have been. That night after the boys went to bed she told Jake about it and she was convinced by his initial response that he hadn't taken money out. But he woke the boys and marched them into the front room, still half asleep.

"Who stole Bibsy's money?" Jake demanded, but neither of them answered.

The shocked goofy expression on Junior's face as he rubbed his eyes dismissed him as a possible suspect, but Robert's initial reaction was one of fear, shortly followed by an expression of absolute calm and innocence, which convinced Bibsy he did it. She'd figured out many a thief at St. Cecelia's and she was just as sure this time too.

Junior said, "Pop, I didn't take no money from Miz Bibsy, or nobody else. I swear I didn't."

"Me neither, Pop. I swear."

Bibsy and Jake must have been of the same mind because Jake said, "Junior, you go back to bed. Robert you come sit a minute."

The three of them sat around the kitchen table where Bibsy could see Robert's calm exterior begin to crumble. He watched his father with eyes that anxiously darted around the room trying to anticipate the unknown.

Bibsy was getting nervous and began to wonder if there really was money missing or if she'd misjudged the thickness of the envelope. Struggling with the situation, in the end she concluded the envelope was definitely lighter than it should have been and she'd been right after all.

"I didn't do it, Pop. I swear. Miz Bibsy, I didn't take your money."

"There's only one thing I hate worse than a thief. You know what that is?"

Robert looked at his father without answering.

"Only thing worse than a thief is when the thief is family. Makes it ten times worse."

"I didn't do it, Pop."

"This is what we're gonna do. I'ma go over ta Louie's place tomorra an ask him if he'd do me a favor an take you on workin all day Saturdays for a month. And whatever he says he can pay you, you gonna hand all of it over ta Bibsy, you hear?"

"Pop, that ain't fair. I didn't take her money." Robert's eyes began to tear up. "I didn't do nothin."

The next four Saturdays Robert got up early and helped Louie around the store with whatever he needed. The first two weeks he helped stock shelves and clean up. The last two Saturdays he helped Louie pack up to move because he'd found a buyer for the store.

At the end of eight hours work, Louie paid Robert four dollars and he came home and handed the money over to Bibsy each week without saying a word. The boy carried a grudge against her from that point and their relationship was never the same. However, he would always maintain he didn't steal her money.

Chapter Fifteen

Around Christmastime that year they were sitting around listening to an episode of *The Shadow,* but this time, when the program ended the announcer said that was their last radio broadcast, and he thanked the listening audience for their support over the years. His chipper delivery was in complete contrast to the sadness his announcement brought into the house. The boys reacted by leaving and not coming home until nighttime.

"Everything's changin round here but us, Miz Bibsy." Junior was the first to say when they returned. "Pretty soon there ain't gonna be no more shows on the radio. What are we supposed to do then?"

"Not only that, everybody's sayin we gonna haveta move from here. And they say Pop can't stop it either."

"Yeah, things are changing but we'll be alright," was Bibsy's reply. "Your father's got a lot on his mind right now, but you know he always works things out." She knew they were more worried than angry and her words couldn't satisfy them, but she was running out of ideas and wouldn't admit she was beginning to feel uncertainty about their future as well.

Jake thought Bibsy's suggestion that they spend even more time with Gus and Carrie was a good one since it was their last winter on The Beach. They'd have a good time eating, laughing and drinking, but every time they got home Bibsy noticed Jake would brood the rest of the evening and drink himself into a drunken stupor.

The boys saw his change and tried to engage him in a game of cards or other activities. One time Junior even suggested going hunting.

"Since when do you ask to go huntin," was Jake's response.

"Come on Pop, you always said we oughta keep practicin our aim," Junior replied.

"Aw," he waved him away, "there ain't nowhere else ta hunt round here now. They buildin on every damn square incha this place. I know what they tryin ta do. They tryin ta crowd us out, but I ain't goin. Tell ya what I am gonna do. Gonna git my shotgun and hold em off if they come in here. I swear. That's what I'ma do."

By the time he finished he was shouting, "Goddamn triflin muthafuckas. The Beach was fine for years, but now outsiders is movin in they wanna act all sididdy an shit. Who helped build this muthafucka? Who, goddammit?" With veins bulging from his forehead and a grimace across his face, Jake slipped into someone Bibsy and the boys began backing away from.

The boys had certainly seen their father drink and even cuss before, but that winter he was always either drunk or on his way there, with no space in between. The boys responded by spending more time at Gus and Carrie's house.

The ice harvesting business was officially over, even for the stragglers who held on when business was slow, and that gave Jake even more time at home that winter. But since Jake was so well known in the area, he could still pick up odd jobs here and there that provided him with pocket money. Unfortunately, he used it mostly to buy more liquor, or beer if his cash was short.

Hoping to avoid getting him riled up everybody in the house found themselves being mindful not to wake him when he slept during the daytime, or ask anything of him even if they needed it, or say anything that might upset him. Bibsy didn't know what to do. She was worried for Jake, but also for the boys and herself, as Jake was steadily becoming someone unrecognizable. Her inability to come up with something that would comfort him and bring his old self back pained her. She didn't know how much longer she could tolerate Jake's behavior without getting into an all out fight with him and risk losing him altogether.

Fortunately she didn't have to find out. Gus just marched over there one day and asked if Bibsy could please give him and Jake some privacy so they could talk and she put on her coat and went next door. The boys were already there, as they'd gotten to the place where they only slept and changed clothes at the house now.

"Hey, man," Gus said when he came in and pulled up a chair across from Jake.

Jake was lying on the couch and sat up when he saw Gus. "When'd you get here, man?" Jake looked around and didn't see anyone. "I musta fell asleep."

Gus put a couple of logs into the wood stove. "It's chilly in here. Ain't you cold?"

"No, I ain't." Jake shook his head. "How long you been here? Where's Bibsy?"

"Everybody's over ta my house."

"Oh. What's going on?"

"Look Jake," Gus said, "we need ta talk. You need some coffee? I'll make you some cause I wanna make sure you don't misread none of what I got ta say."

"No," Jake said, sitting up now. "I don't need no coffee. What's wrong? Somethin goin on at the house?"

"No." Gus said, "Ain't nothin goin wrong at my house, but it is over here."

"What're you talkin bout, Gus?"

"Jake, man...you're close as I ever came to havin my very own son. An you know Carrie feels the same way."

"I know Gus. As far as I'm concerned, y'all is like my momma and daddy. You always been around."

"But how you actin here lately, Jake. Drinkin till you pass out, an stayin drunk all the damn time. It's jus plain shameful."

"It ain't that bad, Gus. I'm jus havin a little taste from time ta time. This is the wintertime, an you know work is hard ta come by this time a year. I'm jus havin a drink now an again."

"You can't bullshit me boy, you know I can drink with the best of em."

Jake blinked a couple of times and sat up even taller.

"Ain't useta hearin me cuss, huh?"

"I don't believe I ever heard you talk like this, Gus."

"Well, now that I got your attention, listen to me real good." Gus scooted his chair even closer to Jake. "You know I know the difference tween a drunk and havin a drink now and again, don't you?"

Jake got up and began fixing a pot of coffee and Gus followed him to the kitchen and sat at the table. Once he got the coffee pot on the fire, Jake took a seat and joined him.

"Never seen you so serious before, Gus. This ain't that big of a deal."

"The hell it ain't. Your father started out jus like this and see where it got him."

"What? Come on Gus, my daddy died when a horse reared up and caught him in the chest. You know that. Damn near everybody does." He'd heard the story so often Jake could recite it as if he was there. His father loved horses and groomed them for extra money at a local horse farm on his days off from the brickyard.

"Yeah, damn it I was there!" Gus shouted. "If he wasn't drinkin so much he'd a taken that horse out for some exercise regular like he shoulda, steada passin out drunk in the stable, an it wouldna come boltin outta that stall like it did. He knew better, but his mind was too tangled up with that likka."

The men sat staring at each other it seemed like forever, and in that space of time neither of them so much as batted an eye. Then Jake quietly got up and poured himself a cup of coffee. "You want some?" He said over his shoulder while at the stove.

"Yeah, I'll join you in a cup."

Jake poured Gus' coffee. "How come you never told me this part til now?"

"Wasn't no need to, til now. Your daddy was a good man. But you're bringin shame to his name and ta me an Carrie with the way you carryin on here lately." Gus sipped his steaming coffee. "You're family, boy. I ain't gonna stand by an watch you take your own self down. You gotta family that needs ya. And the boys is watchin you everyday like this. It ain't right."

"You sayin my daddy was a drunk?"

"I'm sayin he started drinkin too much toward the end there, specially after losin your mother when she was tryin ta have that second baby. And they'd waited so long ta have another one. You know alla that part, but his drinkin is what cost im his life. Don't wanna see the same thing happen to you, Jake. That's all I'm sayin."

"That ain't gonna happen to me. Jus got a few things on my mind is all."

"What's got you in such a state? Don't tell me causa we're leavin neither. Cause that's some bullshit."

"No…well, yeah…I don't know. I tell you, man, hearin you cussin got me all confused." The two men laughed. "It ain't jus that." Jake was clearly uncomfortable with the discussion. "Ain't nothin the same Gus. Things is changin too fast."

"That's the way life is. Always been. Ain't gonna stop now."

"But things are really, really, changin now."

"You think this is the first time things have changed? I've seen a whole lot more changes since I was your age. That ain't no good excuse, Jake." Gus paused to take another sip of his coffee, then continued. "We might as well accept it, The Beach gonna go one day too. Look at the way the farms is cashin in now. They hit pay dirt, sho nuf."

"What about us? Where we sposed ta go?"

"Why don't you come south with us? You'd love it down there. We could hunt an fish as much as we want. An mosta the year too, cause the weather's so nice."

"Ha! With all them crackers down there? Gus, you know that won't work with somebody like me. Big as I am and the way I speak my mind, I'd stand out everywhere and be strung up from a tree before I could even unpack my bags. Ta tell the truth, I'm kinda surprised you goin."

"Nah, I'ma ole man with not a whole lotta time left. They won't fear me."

"I wouldn't be so sure of that."

At that moment Bibsy and the boys came through the door, cautiously looking around as they entered.

"Y'all finished talkin?" Bibsy said. "We gotta get up in the mornin."

The boys walked quietly to their room with their heads hung.

"Yeah, we're jus about done here," Gus said, as he and Jake stood up and hugged. "Guess I needed that. Thanks, man."

Jake never discussed his and Gus' private conversation with Bibsy, and she didn't ask. She was just thankful that the old Jake had come back to his former self. He went out to find odd jobs every day the rest of that winter and in the evenings he was his familiar charismatic self. No one questioned why but knew Gus had a big hand in it.

Every now and again he would take a drink and she and the boys would hold their breath, but Jake would have one or two and no more. Bibsy was happy, especially as they made love more frequently. Things were back to normal. By the time March came, she and Jake were on a short trip to a local farm where he picked up his usual crate of chicks and a rooster for the summer and she spotted a half-empty pint bottle of Jack Daniels under the seat; but she didn't say anything since things were so much better now.

Emotions began to peek through when Carrie and Gus began preparations to move. Unable to watch them pack, Junior and Robert stayed away as much as possible and visited their friends in town. During this time Bibsy noticed the boys' usual playful punching each other took a more serious turn as if each was intending to inflict harm on the other.

Carrie gave Bibsy all of her canning paraphernalia and had her write down each step of the process as she recited the instructions. Bibsy graciously attended to every detail in the written directions to appease Carrie even as she doubted she'd ever do it alone. For Bibsy, it was more about the pleasure of the time they spent together laughing and talking than it was about the food.

She had a strong hunch next year she'd be purchasing canned fruits and vegetables at the local A&P.

Jake expected that he and Bibsy would take the ride down south with them, but for the first time they were faced with the dilemma of the boys being home by themselves for an extended period of time and no one to rely on as a back up, so she offered to stay back with them. It was funny how she and Jake were already missing Carrie and Gus when they hadn't even gone yet.

Months before Jake made arrangements to drive with Gus and Carrie to Virginia, and said he'd stay a couple of nights to make sure they were settled in properly. Using the extra car allowed them to take more of their belongings. Everything was planned out perfectly. Jake would drive down on a Friday, stay with them a couple of nights and be back by Sunday, in time to report for his first day of work on Monday where he would work as a laborer at a construction site for the final phase of the thruway connecting to the bridge that planned to open that year.

Realizing it was the first time they spent a night without each other since she arrived on The Beach two years ago, Bibsy had some anxiety about the separation, but figured it'd give them a reason to celebrate when he got back home. But she was bored in his absence. She played cards with the boys, but they'd fight among themselves practically every hand.

She sat at the river with her coffee in the mornings as usual, but knowing Jake wasn't inside the house made her restless out there. She began talking to herself.

"Wonder where he is now," she said checking her Timex. "Hope he gets a good night's sleep before he comes home. He might be looking for a place for us while he's down there. Maybe Carrie and Gus convinced him to. That'd be nice. I'm gonna say welcome home, as soon as he comes through the door."

Finally Sunday morning came and Bibsy was up before daylight, excitedly anticipating Jake's return. She got a basin of water from the pump, heated it on the stove and was finished washing up just as day broke. As she was getting dressed she heard a popping sound in the distance and momentarily wondered what it was but didn't dwell on it. Not knowing when Jake would arrive, she kept finding busy work to do, just to waste time until he came home, then she heard a loud commotion on The Beach. From the front door window she had the vantage point of the entire Beach Road, and saw people coming out of their homes in their robes and night clothes. She came outside and walked toward them wondering what the fuss was all about.

When she came up on the nearest group of people she approached a woman wearing a bathrobe with curlers in her hair, and said, "What happened?"

"Somebody shot Trap. Killed em." She said, "Left him sprawled out right up under the mailboxes with a bullet in his throat. Blood everywhere. Nobody even heard him bark."

Bibsy looked around at the many worried faces milling around discussing the possible ways in which the dog was killed and she turned and walked back to the house saying to herself, "Jake you better come on home. We need you."

Chapter Sixteen

Jake already knew what happened when he walked through the door late that evening. He said he would have been home a couple of hours earlier if it wasn't for all the people along The Beach needing to fill him in. They tried to keep the dog out in the open until Jake came home to see for himself, but as it got dark Ida feared animals would gnaw at him through the night, so she and a few neighbors buried Trap behind the house.

"Somebody said he had a big piece of meat in his mouth. Like steak or somethin," Junior said to his father.

"Probably coaxed him with it," Jake said. "I bet that's how they got him ta quiet down, cause people said he never barked." Jake took off his shoes and rested his neck on the back of the couch and closed his eyes. "I need some rest right now. Been on the road all day. We can talk about this in the mornin," he said as though answering an unspoken call for direction from Bibsy, Junior and Robert seated around him.

The next morning Jake got up early and dug under the bed for his shotgun and a box of shells. When Bibsy woke, she saw him cleaning the barrels of the weapon with a long-handled brush that had bristles circling its opposite end.

“What you doin?” Bibsy strained to see in the early dawn, rubbing her eyes. “What you got there?”

“A shotgun, baby. If they wanna play cowboys, I’ll play right along with em.”

“Who’s they?”

“Whoever shot Trap. That wasn’t no accident, Bibsy. Somebody tryin ta send a message.” He held up his shotgun. “This here is my answer.”

“Wait a minute Jake.” Bibsy sat up and drew the covers around her shoulders. “You can’t be serious.” The whole business about Trap being shot made her nervous enough, but Jake’s response made her outright fearful of the tragic consequences a shootout on The Beach might bring. She worried privately who was the enemy Jake seemed so certain of, but kept to himself. Could it be someone they all knew?

“I’m more’n serious.” He put down the brush and picked up a rag and began rubbing the metal until Bibsy could see it glint in the predawn light. “That was a damn good dog, that Trap. Watched this whole area down here for years."

Once he was satisfied the shotgun was clean enough, he washed and prepared for work as usual. Except, he made sure to take Rain with him, and took the dog with him everywhere from then on.

"I useta take Rain with me everywhere but got lax with it lately," he explained at first. "Whoever killed Trap might think about takin out all the dogs down here. An if that's what they got a mind ta do, they gonna haveta come through me first."

Whether going to work or on a short errand, Rain was in the car with him. When they went somewhere as a family, Rain sat between Robert and Junior. On those occasions, Bibsy rode with Tiger on her lap as well because Bibsy felt the pup would be better protected with them.

A couple of nights later Ida came by to say she was leaving. "Ain't the same down here no more." She said. "It ain't like it useta be. Nobody bothered us in the old days, right Jake?"

Jake shook his head in agreement. "But if everybody leaves, won't nothin stop em from doin whatever they want down here."

"Jake, I ain't slept since they killed my dog. I keep listenin for his bark, and it's gone. I even fixed im a bowl a scraps a coupla times outta habit." They'd always known Ida to be a tough lady but the loss of Trap was too much even for her. "He was like family ta me. I can't stay. Sorry, but I gotta go. I already got family comin ta help me move." The next day they saw some people helping her move out.

After that Junior and Robert joined Jake and a few of the men and their sons taking turns patrolling The Beach with their own shotguns in the evenings. Jake said making their presence felt more would put people's mind at ease. However, the extra security made Bibsy feel more anxious than safer. Never having weapons as part of her world, Bibsy reluctantly accepted their use as a means of putting food on the table, especially since the shotguns were out of sight most of the time. But now, seeing them daily in the hands of so many, even young boys, kept her uneasy.

Junior usually started his rounds first and Robert would join him after he got home from football practice. Bibsy noticed how much like Jake Robert was becoming, even copying his father's gait.

If Jake wasn't patrolling the area in the evenings after supper he, Robert and Junior went out back in the woods and practiced shooting beer cans and empty bottles they set up on a wide stump. Bang, bang, bang, could be heard until it got too dark for them to see their target. Even when the boys went to bed Jake would sit on the porch in the dark with his weapon across his lap as if waiting for an excuse to use it.

Bibsy couldn't believe that the death of one dog could create so much tension in the house. She couldn't engage Jake in conversation anymore because the only thing he wanted to talk about was being prepared to retaliate and nobody knew who against. He began drinking hard again. At first it was just a drink after he got home, but it didn't take long before he was drinking all the time and finding fault with everybody.

"Why didn't somebody tell me we was out of chicken feed?" He'd say to no one in particular.

"Junior told you last week, Jake." Bibsy said.

"Well he shoulda reminded me again. I can't remember everything."

Junior gave up his part of patrolling the area and so did most of the others once it became obvious Jake had started back drinking heavily. Robert was the only one to keep it up with him. Junior began staying out as late as he could at Charlie's house and sometimes not coming home at all, even during the week. Bibsy worried about him, but she worried about Jake more.

She thought about calling Gus and Carrie but was so tense the only time she'd remember was after she'd come home and far from a telephone. She was forgetting about the cigarettes she was lighting as well, having two or three lit in different ashtrays in the house. Knowing she was the only smoker, it startled her to find a lit Viceroy in an ashtray on the porch, one near the bed, and one in her hand. She secretly suspected the boys were lighting them but didn't say so since Robert was now only barely speaking to her ever since she accused him of stealing her money.

Having occasionally seen Jake leave the house with his shotgun to join his friends, brimming with laughter and searching for adventure and a good time with his buddies as he took off to go hunting was one thing. Watching him search for unknown human prey was quite another. Bibsy believed Jake was trying to secure protection for them, but with his drinking and evening target practice behind the house, she felt a sense of terror for the first time since moving to The Beach and had not been this frightened since she was a youngster trying to avoid the daily acts of the nuns' meanness. Although Bibsy deeply believed Jake would never harm her, she was equally sure he had also become a very different man recently.

"Let's go for a ride for a change," she said one night trying to get him off the porch and hoping to entice him with something he previously enjoyed.

"Nah. What if somebody comes here while we're gone? You know whoever timed that thing, you notice they came when I wasn't here. Only time I'm leavin is to go to work, Bibsy."

Although she and Junior had been tiptoeing around Jake for the two weeks since Trap was shot, Robert stepped right in line with his father as though he'd been waiting for an opportunity to prove himself. Bibsy could swear the boy had actually grown taller as a result.

Then one day Bibsy came home and noticed an envelope from the landlord in the mailbox before realizing there was one in all the mailboxes. Seeing it wasn't the usual rent envelope, Bibsy's stomach started quivering. Catching sight of an orange marker out of the corner of her eye, and more of them every few feet around the perimeter of The Beach property, she knew the markers could not be good news for them.

"I see you got your notice," Big Mabel said when Bibsy walked past her house.

"Says we gotta leave in six weeks. They sellin the land to a power company. See all them orange surveyor marks they put all around every so many feet? Wouldna never happened if Trap was alive. They the ones who shot him. I'd bet my life on it."

The information Big Mabel shared made Bibsy outright terrified. When she got home there was a note on the table from the boys saying they'd done their chores and were spending the night at Charlie's house, so she sat on the porch and waited for Jake to come home. Unable to tolerate her nervous stomach any longer, she plopped two Alka-Seltzer tablets into a glass of water and returned to her seat on the porch feeling the fizz from the medicine spray the back of her hand as she held the glass.

"I don't know what he's gonna do behind this," she said to herself while sitting there. "It's gonna make Jake mad for sure. This is a mess. He's gonna be real mad now." Bibsy downed the medicinal liquid and licked the salty residue from her lips.

She went in the house and fixed a drink and came back on the porch with a lit cigarette, only realizing there was one already lit in the ashtray which she stamped out. Finally, she saw Jake's car headed down the road, stopping every now and then as he came. She knew he'd have all the details by the time he got to the house. Her heart raced as he walked up the porch steps.

"So it finally happened, huh?" He said flatly.

It was painful to see Jake with deep disappointment and fear lining his face. Bibsy wanted to wipe it away. Push time back to when she first came to The Beach and see his presence light up a room again. She was sure she could retrieve it somehow and thought again about contacting Gus and Carrie and made a mental note to go by Woolworth's on her way home from work the next day and make the call. Their address and phone number was put away in her suitcase under the bed. I'll call them tomorrow she thought, and hoped she'd remember.

He opened the letter and read, "Due to the sale of what is known as The Beach Property to Langston Power and Electric, all residents must vacate the premises by October fifteenth nineteen fifty-five. Anyone not in compliance with this order to vacate will be subject to an eviction. Sincerely, Maxwell Pulaski, Owner." An uncharacteristic and sinister half smile swept across Jake's face. "Humph." He looked at the paper in his hand, crumbled it and threw it to the ground. "Langston Power and Electric, huh? Wish they would try an put me out. I wish they would."

Bibsy said, "I hear there's plenty apartments in Kancy, Jake. People at work say so all the time. Or I'm sure we can get something in Haverton if you want to stay here. Wherever you want to go is fine with me.

Don't matter at all." Bibsy wished she had the right words that would get through to Jake so they could move peacefully. But she knew what The Beach meant to him and he'd feel its loss for a long time after it was gone. Maybe forever.

She watched Jake as he went to the car and rummaged under the front seat and retrieved his pint bottle and took a swig and returned the bottle where he'd gotten it then went inside and came back with his shotgun. Throwing the empty box of shells on the ground once he went back outside, Jake headed toward the car and threw his shotgun inside once he got there.

"Come on Rain," he said, opening the door and folding down the front seat for the dog to jump in.

"Where you going, Jake?" Seeing him get in the car with his shotgun made her more nervous.

"Goin ta Casey's. Gotta get more shells for my shotgun. I'll be right back."

Knowing his friend's general store was on the outskirts of town, Bibsy thought it'd be a long enough drive for Jake to think things through before doing something they'd all regret. Maybe Casey would talk some sense into him while he was there. This might be the answer, Bibsy thought.

By the time Jake turned down the long driveway to Casey's place the first thing he saw was the store windows boarded up with plywood. He drove up on the grass and faced the store to get a better view, then turned off the engine and sat there staring at the faded General Store sign in front of the building.

"Damn, Casey," he said, "not you too." Repeatedly pounding his fist on the car seat upholstery set off Rain to alternately bark and cower in the corner of the back seat. Realizing the dog's fear, he got out and held the door open. "Go ahead and run awhile. You got fifty acres here and there ain't no tellin how much longer you'll be able ta run through it." Rain lept from the car and tore through the wooded property.

Jake took out his pint bottle and took a sip. "Wonder what he got for alla this," he said to himself while glancing over the property.

After getting back in the car and rolling down the windows, Jake leaned his head against the cushion of the bench seat and closed his eyes. After awhile Rain's barking woke him and he peered in the rearview mirror and saw a car approaching.

Observing it was a police car Jake made sure his liquor bottle was safely under the seat before saying, "Hush, Rain. It's alright."

The cruiser pulled alongside Jake's car and the officer said, "Oh, it's just you, Jake. Whatcha doin sittin out here?"

Five men made up the Haverton Police Department and most people knew all the officers by name, and they all knew Jake. "Hey Charlie," Jake said to the man he attended grade school with. "Thought I was gonna buy some shells for my shotgun today. When'd all this happen?"

"About a week ago. Casey got fed up with the way things're goin around here and said he was gonna move upstate or to Vermont, where people appreciated land like he did."

"Yeah." Jake sighed. "I guess we better get useta the way things is gonna be, or else do what Casey did, huh. Things is changin awfully fast around here."

"Yep. Sure is. There's even talk about addin a couple more men ta the force. Causa all the buildin goin on. Gonna be a lot more people comin this way."

"Is that right?"

"Sure is different from when we was in school, huh? Who woulda thought that would be the good ole days so soon?"

"You're right. I was just sittin here rememberin when my daddy brought me my first fishin pole. Now we gotta move off The Beach."

"Yeah, I heard. Well I guess that had ta come one day." Charlie began backing up his squad car. "You know how fast night can fall out here in these woods. Better head back home soon."

"Yeah, I will." Jake waved.

Noticing the sky was getting gradually darker he called Rain and once he got the dog situated in the back seat, started up his engine and left. He took the unpaved back roads home, a route only locals knew, just to see if there was any other new developments that slipped by him. Jake knew his way around Langston so well he used to joke that he could drive anywhere blindfolded and get to where he wanted to. Short cuts were always through the mountains in Langston, and to get back home on this route meant taking a series of steep narrow curves downhill along a crude mountainside road that started out as an Indian path long ago.

Navigating his new Chevy was a different experience on this road, but Jake was pleased with the car's extra power. With his new ability to take the sharp turns on the mountain faster than he used to with his old truck, he drove the vehicle as if he had more experience driving it than he actually did.

Despite Rain's barking, Jake smiled broadly enjoying the roller coaster ride. Quickly looking back at Rain he said, "Quiet down girl. Quiet down." As he turned back around and faced the road he came upon a series of sharp turns just as the sky went suddenly black, and he veered off the road. Realizing his mistake Jake swerved back cutting the wheel too sharply and the weight of the car on the steep decline tipped it over onto the embankment and it rolled over a few times crashing into several sturdy oaks along the way. The car finally rested at an angle wedged between trees at the bottom of the steeply pitched hill. It wasn't long before steam spewed from under the hood making a low hissing noise and the driver's side door popped open and Jake's limp upper body slumped out. Blood covered his head.

Chapter Seventeen

Bibsy sat on the porch until late into the night waiting for Jake to return and finally went to bed when he didn't show up. She lay in bed tossing all night as her stomach started up again, and she wished the boys were in the house. Getting up in the middle of the night taking Alka-Seltzers quieted her upset stomach but did nothing for her increasing nervousness, especially as she unconsciously felt for Jake throughout the night, only to find a blank cold space where warmth and comfort should have been. She went to the window often, thinking she saw someone looking through the glass at her, but each time she looked nothing was there. Bibsy gave up trying to sleep and again wished the boys were home so the house wouldn't feel as empty.

She fixed a pot of coffee, bathed, dressed and was sitting on the porch sipping from her favorite Mason jar as the sun rose the next morning. At this point she knew only the sight of Jake would erase the knot in her stomach and realized she had no choice but to live with it until he returned home. "All this worryin and Jake probably found a poker game somewhere," Bibsy said in an unsuccessful attempt to comfort herself. "But he knows he's gotta work this mornin. He wouldn't miss work for nothin."

Bibsy tried to put her worries of Jake aside and left for work hoping the job would absorb her thoughts, but before leaving she pulled out her suitcase from under the bed and retrieved her rosary beads and put them in her dress pocket. "He'll probably already be home when I get back, smilin all wide as usual," she said as she left the house. "Got me worryin for nothin."

When she came home from work and saw the boys she felt slightly better until Robert said, "Where's Pop?"

"I don't know." Bibsy said. "He didn't come home last night." She averted her eyes while answering, hoping not to reveal her growing panic. "He probably found a poker game that went on all night and decided to go right to work from there. And there's no way to let us know because of no telephone. That's probably what happened." She said attempting to quell her own fear as much as theirs.

Junior said, "He ain't never did that before."

"There's a first time for everything, Junior!" It was the first time Bibsy shouted at him and regretted it immediately. "He's got to come home eventually," she tried saying more calmly.

When she got back from work the second day and Jake still wasn't home, Bibsy went house to house on The Beach asking the few residents left if they'd seen Jake during the last two days, but no one said they'd seen him. When he didn't show up after a second night passed, Bibsy began to wonder if something awful had happened to him. Everybody busied themselves with their usual morning chores until they heard Tiger yelping in the yard. Hearing the dog reminded her that Rain was also gone.

Robert pulled back the doorway curtain and said, "The police is comin. Betcha it's about Pop."

"Don't even say that, boy." Bibsy yelled as she and Junior both peered through the window to see for themselves.

Watching the police cruiser slowly making its way down the road, the trembling sensation she'd been feeling the last couple of nights increased as the squad car passed each house and continued in their direction. Bibsy's lips quivered as she said in a whisper, "No, God. Please, no."

The three of them hurried outside and met the two officers in the yard. The one behind the wheel said, "Is this the Jake Tucker residence?"

Junior was the first to say, "Yeah. What's wrong?"

The policeman turned off the engine, and the two officers got out of the car and walked toward them. "Can we come inside, please?"

"Yes." Bibsy said. "What happened?"

"What's going on?" Junior said.

"Something happened to Pop?" Robert added as they all went into the house.

When they got inside, they stood by the door. One officer was looking around and the other one who'd been driving took out a pad from his shirt pocket and began talking. "You did confirm that this is the Jake Tucker residence. Are you his wife, ma'am?"

"No. But we been living together." Bibsy pointed to Junior and Robert. "These are his kids."

The officer shook his head. "Ma'am, are you the only adult here?"

"Yes. What happened to Jake? Where is he?"

"We have some bad news," the policeman with the pad began as he looked at each of them. "Maybe we should sit down." They moved to the kitchen table and the other officer continued standing nearby. "There's been an accident." He said once they were all seated. Tears began welling up in Bibsy's eyes as she stared at the officer's lips as if reading them to verify every word. "His car was found this morning at the bottom of an embankment on North Mountain Road. We're sorry to inform you that he was found dead at the scene."

Robert threw his head back and wailed, "Iiiiieeeeee...." His chilling cry felt strong enough to lift the rickety house off its foundation. "No," he said slamming his fist against the porcelain tabletop before pushing himself away, turning over his chair and a milk crate along the way saying, "no, no, no, no," over and over.

Junior was eerily quiet, his eyes becoming bloodshot from the strain of holding back tears desperately needing release, while Bibsy sat still silently staring at the officer with tears streaming down her face.

"His car dropped a good hundred feet."

Gasping, Bibsy's hand sprung up covering her mouth. Her other hand reached for Junior's and they sat holding hands.

"There was no way he could have survived it. He had a dog with him that also died in the accident."

"Rain," Junior said.

"We're gonna need somebody to identify the body," the officer said looking from Bibsy to Junior and back again, obviously mistaking Junior for much older than he was.

The boy shook his head no and pointed to Bibsy. "She can do it. I can't do that," he said, still shaking his head no.

"It really should be a spouse or a blood relative. Ma'am you stated you two were not married?" The officer said looking at the notes on his pad.

“No, we’re not.” Bibsy said. “But he’s only fifteen and his brother is thirteen.”

“Oh.” The officer looked again at Junior. “You’re both mighty tall for your age,” he said. “Are there any other family members locally?”

“No, I don’t think so.” Bibsy looked at Junior who shook his head no. “We’re it,” she said and watched Junior leave the table to join his brother.

“Well, ma’am, looks like you’re gonna haveta identify the body. Can you come with us? We’ll take you over to the morgue.”

“Do I have to? You must know already. How’d you know to come here?”

“Actually, we recognized him. Plus the identification he had on him and the license plate confirmed it, ma’am. But the official protocol is he has to be identified by family. It’s the law.”

“I don’t see why, if you already know.” Instincts told her she needed to be alone with the boys right now. The last thing she wanted was to see Jake in any other condition than laughing and talking at her side or with his arms wrapped around her.

“That’s the procedure. Sorry. You can take a minute to get ready if you need to. We’ll be in the car waiting.” He stood up. “We’re very sorry for your loss. I knew Jake for years and he was always a decent man.”

After the officers let themselves out Bibsy went to the bedroom to see about the boys and stood in the doorway watching Junior comfort Robert in his arms a moment before approaching them. They opened their arms to include her as they huddled together and sobbed in each others arms unleashing the kind of wrenching sounds only severely wounded spirits make.

"We should call Cousin Gus and Aunt Carrie." Junior said eventually.

"Yeah." Bibsy said. "We need them now."

Sitting in the back seat of the police car Bibsy barely heard the policeman say, "You know I saw Jake just yesterday evening sittin outside of Casey's old General Store. You know, we were in elementary school together. That Jake was even popular back then."

"Said he was headed there to get some shells for his shotgun." Bibsy answered automatically but at the same time wondering what was the last thing she and Jake said to each other. She couldn't remember.

"Was he plannin on doin some huntin?" Said the officer who'd stood by the door while at the house.

"He just ran out, that's all." She said, annoyed with his probing questions.

Before they accompanied her to the hospital morgue, Charlie said, "Better brace yourself, cause he's pretty banged up."

In the morgue, they pulled back the white sheet draped over Jake's body revealing dried blood mingled through his hair as well as splattered and streaked across his face. The image was too grotesque and Bibsy's eyes traveled the length of his arm before settling on his hand which she cradled in hers. Surprised at its stiffness, she recognized every detail of his beefy hand from the exact roundness of his fingertips, to his split cuticles, to the calluses that peppered his palms, and she quietly said, "That's him. I'm certain of it." Bibsy left before her knees buckled and each officer grabbed her by an arm and directed her to a bench just outside the room where she wailed uncontrollably.

The officers took her to the local funeral home to make arrangements and she talked to herself in the back seat of the squad car all the way there repeating herself many times.

"Jake, why? Why, why, why? You said you wouldn't leave me. You promised. Why'd you have to go looking for more bullets for that shotgun? We coulda moved somewhere else. All of us together. Why?"

Charlie kept an eye on her through his rearview mirror, and the two officers occasionally glanced at each other throughout the ride as Bibsy wept in between fussing at Jake.

"It didn't matter to me where we lived. Long as we was together. I didn't care. Never did. Damn you, Jake!"

"Uh, Miss," Charlie interrupted, "the funeral home is right over there, on the corner."

Bibsy was surprised the car had stopped but looked in the direction he was pointing.

"Tell McGregor Jake's over at the hospital morgue. He'll handle things for you from there. We're really sorry about Jake. He'll sure be missed around here."

Bibsy thanked them and got out.

After quickly establishing there wasn't any insurance money or church affiliation, the funeral director laid out Bibsy's options for the service and burial saying, "The cheapest funeral we can provide would be a few hundred dollars using our least expensive casket and having the service right here. Of course we can lower that considerably if we used a pine box if you prefer. Then again, some people like to have their loved ones close to them and cremate the body and keep the ashes either in the house with them or sprinkle the remains at a favorite place of the deceased. I know Jake loved fishing, for instance. You could sprinkle his ashes in the Hudson if you'd like."

"Or I can keep him home with me, right? Didn't you just say that?" Bibsy was sure she had at least a several hundred dollars in her suitcase so the price didn't matter.

However, Bibsy's heart began to race just imagining Jake would always be with her. "I like that idea. Why don't we do that? What'd you call it? Cre-what?"

"Cremation,"

"Yeah, let's do that."

The funeral director wrote something on a paper in front of him. "Now I have to tell you, most people prefer to bury their deceased in the ground. To have some place to go and pay homage to them from time to time." Then he began to whisper as if the rest of his presentation was a secret. "Most colored don't cremate their people."

"Why?" Bibsy looked perplexed.

"To tell you the truth I don't know." He hunched his shoulders. "That's just the way they always been."

Bibsy didn't think to talk it over with the boys since they'd already told her to handle everything however she wanted, saying they didn't want to have anything to do with making any of the arrangements. So she made the decision to have a small service at the funeral home in three days and cremate his remains afterward, which she intended to bring home.

Walking home from the funeral parlor Bibsy kept reminding herself to get her phone book from the suitcase and come back out and call Martha and Carrie later that day. As she got to Beach Road, she was grateful it was in the middle of the day and most people were at work so she and the boys could have some time alone. However, that notion disappeared when she saw a car in the yard that she didn't recognize.

When she opened the door of the house Manny and his son Josh were sitting in the living room with Junior and Robert.

"I came as soon as I heard," Manny said as he got up to greet Bibsy with a kiss on the cheek. "Can't believe it."

"Won't be the same around here without Jake," Josh said.

"It already ain't the same." Bibsy said. Unprepared and unwilling to entertain, she wished they weren't there quite so soon. The events of the last two days were swirling in her head like a cyclone and she needed time to adjust. The image and feel of Jake's stiffened hand was still fresh.

"Katherine sent some food. I put it on the table over there," Manny said. "And there's some money in the jar over there."

Bibsy didn't even look to see where he was pointing. "How'd you find out so fast?" She asked. "I just looked at the body this mornin and I'm just now gettin back from the funeral parlor."

"I know everything that's goin on in this county. Jake must not have told you."

Manny forced a laughed. "When's the arrangements?"

"Thursday."

"Where? McGregor's?"

"Yeah."

"Well, I guess you're right to get it behind you quick as possible." Anybody call Gus and Carrie? And Mason T?"

The boys looked at each other both saying they forgot, and they all agreed they should be contacted as soon as possible. Manny and his son were the first of a procession of people that streamed through the house that day and all night. Some people Bibsy had been introduced to by Jake, but most of them she didn't know. It got too much for the boys and they spent most of the evening in their room with the door closed. That night there was food everywhere and a pile of money stuffed into a quart size Mason jar, and by the next day two Mason jars would be filled with cash and even coins. She emptied the money into her suitcase without counting it and clamped it shut then fell into bed.

The bottle of Alka-Seltzer tablets on the milk crate reminded Bibsy that this time yesterday she was sitting on the porch waiting for Jake to come home. Even though her stomach was a quivering mess, she never allowed herself to imagine today's outcome was a possibility.

Bibsy woke up early as usual the next morning but struggled to get out of bed. The only way she could respond to the morning silence created by Jake's now permanent absence was to linger under the covers much longer than usual. When she finally did greet the day the boys were already making breakfast from some of the food Jake's friends brought by the night before.

It was Junior's, "You want some of this meatloaf, Miz Bibsy?" that prompted her to get out of the bed. Robert and Junior had never found Bibsy still in bed once they were up.

"No. I just want some coffee this mornin, that's all." Bibsy put on her robe and ambled over to the table and sat down heavily as if the few steps exhausted her.

"Well, coffee's already made," Junior said and placed a steaming cup in front of her along with the sugar bowl and milk bottle.

"Hope the milk's still good. Hardly any ice left, and this tray in the ice box ain't been emptied in a long time." Robert said while removing the tray and taking it outside and dumping the water in the yard. "We need another block of ice. How we gonna get more ice? How we gonna get around now?"

"I don't know, Robert, but we'll find a way to manage. Give me a little time," Bibsy said.

Understanding his anger, Bibsy ignored Robert's hostility. She felt if she wasn't so sad she'd be angry too, but that took more energy than she presently had. Getting dressed was all she could manage before flopping down on the couch. Bibsy didn't know what to do first or where to begin, but she knew there was probably a long list of things she ought to be doing. Some of the details she knew would get lost, but tried desperately to focus on the larger issues. Already, Robert reminded her of the ice box which she'd totally lost track of. When the dogs barked to alert them of somebody coming, she was hopeful it would be someone willing to offer assistance.

"How y'all doin this mornin?" Sweet Lou said when he came through the door.

"Fine." Junior and Bibsy both said.

Robert said, "We need some ice, Mr. Lou."

"Alright, alright. I can take you ta get some," Lou said walking over to Robert extending his hand. "Glad ta see you're stepping up bein the man of the house. That's good. Your daddy would be proud."

"How'd he get ta be the man of the house when I'm the oldest?" Junior said.

Sweet Lou went over to Junior extending his hand again saying, "This house can have more'n one man, can't it? It's gonna take more'n one a y'all to fill Jake's shoes anyway. Your daddy was a mighty big man. Mighty big."

"That's funny, I thought I was the only grownup here." Bibsy said.

"Oh Bibsy, you know I was just…."

"Never mind Lou." Bibsy cut him off not wanting to hear his flimsy excuse for disrespecting her. "We need to go to Robert Hall's and get something presentable to wear to the funeral. Can you take us? And McGregor asked me to get a suit over there for Jake today. If Jake has a suit I wouldn't know where to begin to look for it so I'd rather buy him a new one."

"Can't say that I'd ever seen him wear one. But anyway, that's why I came by. To offer my services. Since I had the day off I figured you'd need a way to get around. We can go now if you're ready."

Bibsy remembered when Jake introduced her to the only department store in Langston County was when they bought her first bathing suit. The recollection incited memories of the swimming hole and how Jake so easily boosted her confidence in the water. Those remembrances drew Bibsy into a quiet place lasting the entire ten-mile ride.

When they got to the store Bibsy went with Sweet Lou and the boys to pick out a suit for Jake. Searching through the endless rows they all finally settled on a navy blue one, complementing it with a white shirt and pale blue tie and gold-tone cuff links.

"Looka that," Sweet Lou said holding up the ensemble. "He'll be lookin sharp tomorra."

"And lookin like somebody else altogether," Bibsy said acknowledging the fantasy they were creating.

After agreeing on the selection, their whole purpose of being there suddenly hit her with such intense sadness that she held back tears and became tired and weak. Handing Sweet Lou enough money to cover the boys' purchases, she left Junior and Robert in his hands to buy their clothes and headed to the ladies' department where she sat in the dressing room and allowed herself a good cry. Afterwards she selected a navy blue size ten dress, a size larger than she wore since she planned to purchase it without trying it on; she couldn't summon enough strength for that.

Later that day when Katherine came by and delicately suggested Bibsy might want to make an appointment at Emma's, she went to the beauty salon even though she thought Jake would probably prefer she show up with her hair braided, but she was too distraught to challenge the charade that was in full swing.

"Honey, I'm so sorry to hear about Jake." Emma said when Bibsy entered the shop. "What a shock that was. How are the boys handling it?"

When Bibsy didn't answer but sat meekly in a folding chair with the two other women waiting their turn, Emma said to them, "Y'all don't mind if I take her first do you? She's Jake's woman and she been through a lot." The women nodded in agreement and also expressed their condolences. Bibsy maintained the same unresponsive demeanor throughout the hair-grooming ritual and pushed away the mirror Emma handed her when she was through.

"No, I can't take your money today, Bibsy," Emma said when Bibsy attempted to pay. "Let this be my small contribution to the family."

Bibsy said thanks and left.

On the walk home she found herself constantly preoccupied with thoughts of Jake. She'd remember his smile, his caress or how the sight of him was enough to put a smile on her face. And now he was gone. Poof. So fast she couldn't adjust. Bibsy tried to remember to call Martha, Aunt Carrie and Mason T, but when she thought about it she was already walking down Beach Road where she'd have to turn around and walk at least a mile in the opposite direction to the nearest pay phone.

When she returned from Emma's there were so many people in the house that Bibsy slipped out and sat by the river alone for relief. Soon the boys joined her and she welcomed their company. Remembering Robert's coolness toward her since she accused him of stealing her money, she was hoping his softened features extended to his heart as well.

"Can't wait til this is over and we can get the house back," he said.

"Me too," Bibsy agreed.

"Yeah." Junior said. "People is everywhere. Can't even think straight."

"It'll be over after tomorrow." She sighed. "Then we can figure out what we're gonna do."

The boys looked at each other but said nothing until Junior said, "I'ma quit school next year when I'm sixteen. I wanna go into the service. That's what I'ma do. I don't wanna stay around here no more."

"Me neither." Robert said.

"Robert, you can't quit for another three years." Junior said.

Bibsy vaguely recalled Junior saying something about not liking school and his teacher always making him sit in the back row due to his height, even though he couldn't see the board from that distance. Now she thought maybe she or Jake should have gone to the school to talk to the teacher, but neither of them thought it was important at the time.

"The service is a good idea," she said, knowing what it was like being stuck somewhere that was hurtful. She never discussed St. Cecelia's with them and didn't plan to.

Manny, Katherine and Josh came by early the next morning to take them to McGregor's Funeral Parlor. Their movements that morning were so slow and quiet it was as if the funeral procession had already begun.

Seeing Jake in the casket looking very unfamiliar, wearing a suit with his hair all slicked back, Bibsy thought it amusing how nobody looked themselves that day. Midway through the service Bibsy looked around and saw people had spilled into the lobby of the small establishment. Jake's regular poker buddies, Sweet Lou, Big Mabel and Plunkett sat together along with the Weaver brothers. She got a glimpse of Emma and Evelyn sitting with another woman she recognized from her job. In the front row seated between the boys clutching each by the arm for the first time, reminded her of the time she and Jake walked down the street together in Harlem the morning after they'd met, and Bibsy sobbed quietly, soaking the Peter Pan collar of her new navy blue dress. She ignored the rumble through the crowd when the funeral director announced that the family requested Jake's body be cremated and his ashes would be presented to them the following day.

On the ride back to the house Manny asked her about the cremation and Bibsy told him, "Jake is never leaving me again, and that's all I got to say about it."

The boys glanced at each other but remained quiet.

As news of Jake's death filtered throughout the county, people continued to stream through the house over the next several days extending their condolences to Bibsy and the boys. They came to pay homage to a friend and neighbor many described as someone they could rely on to lend a hand whenever and wherever needed, smiling all the while.

"He never held a grudge that I knew of," Plunkett said when he came by one evening with Big Mabel.

"But he wouldn't tolerate cheatin at cards neither. No, no, no," Big Mabel said. "That's for sure."

"Jake knew how to keep people honest, too." Bibsy said after exhaling cigarette smoke. Even as she spoke those words she wondered whether or not Robert really took her money or if she'd imagined it. Since Jake died, the boy came around a little, but she knew their relationship would never be what it was.

"Remember the time that fella came up here from The City. A real slickster at the card table. Don't know how he even got inta one of our games."

"I think he was related to Ida." Plunkett said.

"Oh yeah." They both doubled over laughing so much at the memory it forced Bibsy to laugh along with them. Mabel went on, "This fella kept gettin the best hands all night long. We couldn't get shit."

"We was sittin right here at this table. I'll never forget it." Plunket's laughter kept interrupting the story. "Finally, Jake got up from the table in between hands, cool as you please. And went over to the bed and commenced ta fishin under there for somethin.

"Then he pulled out his shotgun from under the bed..." Plunkett paused for effect. "....and came back and leaned it against the table, and picked up his hand again like he'd gone ta get a glass of water or somethin."

Plunkett managed to say while still laughing. “You know Jake had him a few tastes by then.”

Mabel said, “The fella asked Jake what was he gonna do with that shotgun, and Jake said the guy had been pullin aces all night long, and said I’ma just rest this right here and see if I can change your luck any.”

“That guy folded his hand right then and there and said goodnight.” Plunkett said. “I don’t believe he ever came back up this way again. Thought cause we lived in the country, that he was dealin with some country bumpkins or somethin.”

“Jake showed him though. We laughed on that for months. Months. I swear, I don’t think I ever laughed that hard.” Mabel said.

There were so many similar stories shared that they effectively extended Jake’s presence in the house for Bibsy and the boys, and it temporarily helped cushion the shock of him dying so suddenly. But after visitors left, it was as if they’d left an even bigger void because the memories of their stories were more poignant reminders of his absence.

After a couple of days of mourning Junior said, “I’m goin back to school tomorrow. Or I’ma have too much work ta make up.”

“Yeah.” Robert said. “I have a football game comin up. I gotta be in school or I won’t get ta play.”

Bibsy couldn't blame them and actually thought it was a good idea to get away from the house and all the memories it held. She never told them that she'd begun to hear creaking noises at night she never heard before. She placed Jake's ashes in the middle of the kitchen table, assuming the prominent placement held more protection for them, but at night she brought the pewter urn to a crate at her bedside so Jake could be near her throughout the night. As soon as she brought the urn home Bibsy began the habit of stroking it before drifting off to sleep. In the morning it was the first thing she looked for when she opened her eyes and began her day with, "Morning, Jake."

Dave seemed surprised yet pleased that she'd returned to work so soon.

"Welcome back," he said her first day back. "Sorry to hear about your... uh...husband. Did you get the flowers we sent over?"

"Yes," she lied. The day of the funeral had been a twenty-four hour haze. "They were nice. Thanks," she said before quickly heading toward the employee lockers.

"Sometimes work is the best healer when you experience a loss." Dave said before she got too far away. "Evelyn will sure be glad to see you, Bibsy."

Bibsy continued walking to the lockers where she would put away her purse, put on a smock and tie up her hair. She smiled at Evelyn whose surprise and enthusiasm was evident by the way her face lit up at the sight of her. Bibsy realized then that her absence probably slowed down the production line considerably since no one was as fast as she and Evelyn with button holes. After a few sweaters, the job was back to being as routine and automatic as before, and by the lunch break Bibsy was preoccupied with thoughts of Jake once again. Preferring to sit alone during breaks, Bibsy sat outside gazing at the river rather than being cooped up in the small cafeteria with everyone either engaging in small talk or staring at her.

On her way home from work she saw Louie's brother Jimmy and his family moving out which put a smile on his wife's face for the first time that Bibsy remembered. His wife and older children occupied the younger ones while Frank and a few men made multiple trips to a truck parked in front of their house.

"Sorry to hear about Jake," Jimmy stopped to say to Bibsy after depositing a cardboard box into the truck. "It won't be the same down here without him."

"No indeed." Bibsy nodded and continued walking.

Jimmy said, "How are the boys?"

"They're doin okay," she answered even though she didn't know. She was afraid to mention Jake to them for fear of falling apart herself and she suspected they sensed her fragility and steered clear of the topic as well.

The closest conversation they had about Jake was one day when Robert was about to sit down to dinner and complained about the urn on the table, "Why's this thing gotta sit on the table? Can't we put it somewhere else?"

"How can you say that, Robert? That's your father in there." Bibsy said.

"That ain't Pop. He's gone. And there ain't nothin left of im. Nothin," he shouted at her and left the house and didn't come home until late at night after she and Junior were already asleep. That's when she moved Jake's ashes from the table to her bedside permanently. Bibsy thought Robert was getting out of hand but she didn't know what to do.

She didn't know what to do about moving either. Lately, it seemed like every day somebody else was moving out. But rather than face it, Bibsy came home and fixed herself a drink from one of the several liquor bottles left behind by the stream of recent visitors. She hated coming home to an empty house and the drinks dulled that reality.

One drink led to two and in no time Bibsy dozed off and was startled awake by the slam of the screen door and Robert saying, "I'm starving." It wasn't long before she saw the long shadow of the lamp being moved and Robert was bent looking into the ice box. "Ain't nothin here to eat. This stuff is old. Probably ain't even good no more."

"Where you been?" Bibsy said rubbing her eyes. "I know school musta let out a long time ago."

"Football practice. Bibsy, there ain't no food here. What we gonna eat for dinner?"

"What?" Bibsy sat straight up. "What'd you call me?"

"What I always call you, Miz Bibsy."

"Just make sure you remember to put a handle on that name," she said. "Shit. Don't think you're grown because your daddy's gone."

Junior came in. "What's all the commotion?"

"There ain't no food in here," Robert answered.

"There's food. You just don't want to eat what's here. Make a peanut butter and jelly sandwich then. I'll bring something in with me tomorrow. It's too late to go out now," she said. "Junior where you been all this time?"

"The library. I had a book report due. Did y'all see Jimmy and them movin out? Where we gonna move to, Miz Bibsy? I heard they gonna put us out if we don't move on our own. Is that true?"

Robert said, "They ain't puttin me out. I'll get my shotgun like Pop did. I know what to do."

"Robert that ain't gonna help." Junior said. "Max'll probably get the police to come do it."

"Ain't nobody doin nothin," Bibsy shouted. "Just stop alla that foolish talk. And ain't nobody gettin a shotgun neither."

"Then what we gonna do?" Junior said.

"I'll figure it out. We just had the funeral the other day." Bibsy prepared another drink. "We'll be alright."

The next day Bibsy brought a stack of luncheon meat home from the butcher and put it in the ice box. By the time the boys got home in the evening, she was passed out on the couch again. It was a routine she repeated for the next few days and she was satisfied that the evening drinks helped free her thoughts of Jake so she could sleep. The boys repeatedly came home late enough to avoid her and she used their absence as an excuse to drink even more. Every time she thought about moving from The Beach she'd fix a drink and in no time it was no longer a pressing issue.

About a week after Jake's funeral she had that dream again. A long slender white hand protruded from a billowy black sleeve. The bony fingers spread apart against the coarse gray uniform of the student and she knew she was back at St. Cecelia's. Again, that now familiar hand pushed the child down a flight of stairs. But this time, the dream didn't end with the girl falling, screaming through her descent. Bibsy saw her head hit the radiator at the bottom of the staircase and screamed out at the loud clang of her skull meeting iron followed by a pool of blood that slowly seeped from under her cheek as she lay in a heap on the floor. Bibsy recognized her as her childhood friend Helen.

"Miz Bibsy! Miz Bibsy!" The boys were screaming and jostling her as she heard dogs barking in the background. "What's the matter? Please wake up."

Seeing their darkened shadows in the night and feeling her gown stick to her perspiration drenched body, Bibsy wasn't sure if this was more of her dream until she saw Junior light the lamp with a wooden matchstick. His hand shook as he said, "What's the matter Miz Bibsy? You was screaming so loud you woke us up!"

The dream eclipsed the alcohol haze she laid down with, but it was the expression of terror on Junior and Robert's faces that registered with her enough that Bibsy struggled to regain her composure. However, her efforts were overpowered by the part of that horrible recurring dream presenting itself for the first time in its entirety. Bibsy's face was so wet it looked as if someone doused her with water.

"The blood!" She said grabbing each of them by a shoulder. "That was my friend Helen and she disappeared after that. They musta killed her. She was my friend." Bibsy shouted hysterically as her body shuddered. "Oh my God, how come I forgot that?"

"Who, Miz Bibsy? Who you talkin about?" Robert said then went to the ice box and got the water pitcher, poured some in a glass then handed it to her with his hand shaking so badly he spilled some on the bed covers.

Bibsy sipped from the glass taking in the boys' faces more fully and only realized her true state through their frightened reaction. She then made a conscious effort to try and calm herself. “I had a bad dream,” she managed, “that’s all. I’m sorry.” As she contemplated the crucial missing piece of her recurring dream, Bibsy now saw the complete story and held tightly to the boys’ arms as she felt droplets of sweat continue to pour off her body.

“What was the dream about?” Bibsy heard earnest concern in Junior’s voice.

Robert said, “You were screaming Helen! Helen! They killed her! Did somebody else die Miz Bibsy?”

“Who is Helen?” Junior added.

The words ‘somebody else’ jolted her back to her senses and Bibsy curled up into a fetal position on the bed. Knowing she had to come up with an explanation, she decided to concoct something. The truth was too frightening even for her. Bibsy lay there quietly even though her heart pounded so forcefully she thought they could hear it.

Making every effort to collect her thoughts and reclaim calm in the house, she finally said, “Helen is the name of somebody I saw killed in a scary movie years ago. And every now and again I have a dream about it. That’s why I don’t care for those scary programs you all tease me about. They give me bad dreams.” Seeing their faces relax she knew her lie worked because they’d already seen her discomfort with some of the scarier episodes of *The Shadow*. But it took the better part of an hour before she was able to convince them that it was safe to go back to sleep.

Bibsy sat up all night drinking coffee and smoking cigarettes as she remembered Helen, a young dark-skinned girl like herself who she befriended at St. Cecelia's after she and Mary were separated into different schools. Helen didn't have family that visited and she always thought that's why she tended to get more beatings than the rest of them. The nuns always said they could tell the whippings didn't hurt colored people as much because the belt didn't even leave bruises on their skin.

Chapter Eighteen

After the nightmare about Helen there were a few nights Bibsy was afraid to go to sleep, fearing something even worse that the liquor couldn't even hold back. Bibsy was sitting on the porch with Tiger as the sun came up one morning.

Stroking Tiger and watching her complacency on her lap, Bibsy doubted this dog had any chance of measuring up to Rain. However the boys had that expectation and convinced Bibsy to let her sleep outside under the porch during the night to get her better acquainted with the area so she could become more of a guard dog. It was obvious even to Bibsy that the dog lacked the natural instincts of its mother and her hearing was nowhere near as good, something that became evident with all the company they'd been having lately and Tiger's bark tended to present itself once people stepped onto the porch, whereas Rain's fierce bark used to bring their attention to anyone or anything approaching their yard. Jake used to joke that Rain would bark if anyone even thought about coming to their house. It was no small difference to a family suddenly vulnerable and unprotected, and another striking reminder how dramatically their lives changed.

Bibsy sat consumed with childhood memories that felt like open wounds and again faulted her mother. She wondered what else she had forgotten in addition to Helen's death. "Jake, this is bad. I don't know what to do first," she said to herself.

"How you doin, Miz Bibsy?" Junior said when he was up and about. "You feel better? Boy, you scared us last night."

"I wasn't scared," Robert said.

"You were too." Junior countered.

"I'm fine, Junior. Thanks. It was just a bad dream. That won't happen again, I'm sure of that." Bibsy said, with conviction.

"We're runnin low on kerosene. And we need more ice." Robert said. "We havin cold cuts for supper, again?"

"Boy, you need to remember your manners and change your tone." Bibsy felt the tension between them mount daily and didn't know how to handle it other than taking a strap to him. She had to admit she was intimidated by his size, but if he kept pushing her she knew she was apt to haul off on him and forget his height, or worse, that he was still a child. "We'll get what we need in here eventually. Let me worry about that."

At work that day, Bibsy kept making mistakes and she knew it was due to her recent lack of sleep and preoccupation. When Dave called her into his office after the button holes weren't aligned on the third cardigan she'd worked on, she expected it. She'd seen women fired for consistent sloppy work, but this was the first time he ever called her in.

"Elizabeth, I know you been through a lot," he began, "and I'm sorry about that, but this is my business and it can't continue like this."

"I know. It won't happen again. I just got a lot on my mind."

"Three sweaters? It's a good thing you wasn't workin on the cashmeres today. And I can usually trust you with them. Whew! Why don't you take a smoke break before you go back to your machine?"

Bibsy knew she had to pay closer attention because she couldn't afford to lose her job on top of everything else. Before she left work Evelyn slipped her a piece of paper with an address and phone number.

"There's an empty apartment over on Clinton Street. You gotta call him quick though cause places don't stay empty very long around here. That's the landlord's number. His name is Mr. Greene. I don't know how many rooms it is, but if it's too small, maybe it'll do for awhile until you all get on your feet."

"Thank you." Bibsy said to her co-worker. "I didn't know which way to turn to tell you the truth." She looked at the slip of paper containing the address. "But I guess it's clear I can't handle that place without Jake... and we gotta move anyway. Thanks a lot Evelyn."

"It'll all be ok. Just give it time. Losing my man would be rough for me too."

"I'll see you tomorrow."

It was interesting how she and Evelyn communicated mostly through eye contact because they rarely had a chance to talk during work hours with all the background noise of the industrial looms.

"Call him right away. My sister lives in his building."

"Okay. I'll call him on my way home. Thanks again, Evelyn."

Bibsy put the phone number in her dress pocket and for the first time since Jake passed she felt slightly upbeat. She figured once they moved into a new place Robert's attitude would change for the better. Things were finally looking more positive. She imagined them living in a place with running water, radiators and electric lights. That alone would make the kids happy she thought. The first thing she wanted to purchase when they moved was a television. That, she was sure would cheer up the boys. She kept fingering the slip of paper as she walked to Woolworths, staying focused, even mentally rehearsing what she'd say. As she dialed the number, Bibsy double checked the letters and digits as her index finger completed each turn of the phone dial, it dawned on her that she still hadn't called Martha or Carrie. When I get home I'll write it down on this same piece of paper to remind myself, she thought.

"Hello?" A man answered on the other end.

"Hello. Is this Mr. Greene?"

"Yes. Who's this?"

"I'm calling about the apartment you have for rent."

"Oh, that. Sorry, it's taken already. Rented it just this morning."

Bibsy hung up without saying goodbye. Having put all her hopes into that one call, she didn't think she could muster up enough energy to do it again. The mere thought of the effort made her sad. She needed Jake. This would be so easy for him. These were the kind of moments where Jake's absence loomed even larger, and intensified with each passing day. A few days after the nightmare, she began sleeping in the bed again, simply because she was too exhausted not to. But even a couple of nightcaps didn't keep her from absentmindedly reaching for him, especially after a familiar dream she had of their lovemaking. She missed his scent. The comfort of his arms. The rush she felt just from the sight of him. How easily he made her laugh. The sense of protection around him. All gone.

Approaching the mailbox on her way home after that disappointing phone call, it occurred to her that she hadn't checked the mail in quite awhile and retrieved a fistful that afternoon. When she got inside and saw a letter from Carrie and Gus she tore open the envelope immediately. It read: Dear Bibsy, we heard from Mason T that Jake passed. Plunkett called him. And Mason T called us. It breaks my heart that you never called us so we could be there. We were like family to Jake. I heard you all got notices to move, so I guess you had your hands full with that and the arrangements and all. We're not mad. Jake wouldn't have wanted that, and besides The Good Lord allowed us to spend time with him a few weeks before he left this world. Kiss the boys for me and please call whenever you get time. Sincerely, Carrie and Gus. P.S. We got our niece Judy to write this for us because her handwriting is so much better than ours.

"I keep forgetting stuff," Bibsy said out loud. "Now I got them mad at me."

When the boys came home that evening Bibsy was in the midst of pouring her second drink. "How come you all didn't remind me to call Carrie and Gus about your father?" She scolded them.

"We kept remindin you, Miz Bibsy. But then we forgot too." Junior said. "You heard from them?"

"Yeah. The letter's over near the couch."

They both read the letter, Junior looking over Robert's shoulder.

"I figured somebody woulda called em." Junior said. "It was too much goin on, you can't blame us, Miz Bibsy."

"Aw, never mind." Bibsy said obviously annoyed, she waved her hand at them.

"Maybe we can visit em down there this summer." Junior said.

"Everybody's gone practically but us. We should move down there with em. Be better than living here like this, without Pop." Robert said.

She didn't tell them about the apartment they almost had. The disappointment was still too fresh. Bibsy had two more drinks before turning in that evening, saying to herself, "I'll write Carrie tomorrow. No, better than that, I'll call them from Woolworth's on my way from work. I never even called Martha to tell her and Kalvin about Jake either. I'll call all of them tomorrow." Bibsy rubbed Jake's urn and blew out the kerosene lamp.

She went to sleep thinking maybe her sister could tell her what she should do next. Martha was always full of ideas. "She's going to be surprised about Jake though. I don't even know how to tell her. Maybe I'll call Manny and see if he can help us find a place. That's what I'll do. I can't do this by myself. I don't even know Langston County all that good."

With help from all the whiskey she consumed Bibsy drifted off into a deep sleep fairly quickly. Again she dreamed of Jake. It was a hot night and they were in the swimming hole cooling off, playing in the water, splashing and caressing one another. Bibsy was laughing loudly expressing her delight at Jake's friskiness. She began shivering when she got out of the water and Jake enveloped her in his massive frame until she warmed up. His touch was warm and sensual, gradually warming her thoroughly. Basking in their glow she got warmer still, eventually sweating. Hearing Rain bark in the distance and wiping the sweat from her brow, Bibsy held tightly to Jake's arms as he caressed her. But she began to sweat profusely from the heat and became faint.

Instinct coupled with a crackling sound opened her eyes and Bibsy saw a bright light shining on the edge of the bed illuminating the crate at her bedside where her ashtray and romance magazines were. It took a moment to realize the light was a full-blown fire and she yanked the covers off and jumped out of bed. The jerking movement of the blanket fanned the flame and the fire jumped to the nearby window curtain. She ran back and forth in a panic a few times before running into the boys' room, shaking them awake.

"Get out. Get out of the house. It's on fire. The house is on fire."

The boys jumped up still groggy, grabbing their pants and putting them on while running through the house haphazardly. In that short amount of time, the flame had taken hold of half the mattress and was steadily making its way across the bed to where the kerosene lamp and Jake's urn was. Bibsy grabbed the urn and ran from the house behind the boys. Opening the door created enough draft to fuel the fire further and she heard a loud poof sound, then shattering glass as they stepped off the porch.

Once outside, Junior picked up Tiger who was in the yard yelping louder than she ever had. Robert ran to the water pump and looked around for something large enough to carry a sufficient quantity of water but before he could find anything they heard a series explosions and more shattering glass inside and they ran from the yard onto Beach Road. At a distance they looked back and saw bright orange and yellow flames light up all the windows. The three of them stood in the cool night air in absolute shock watching the flames claim their home. They stood watching, Junior holding Tiger, Robert with an empty basin in his hand and Bibsy holding Jake's urn.

By the time the fire truck came the house was already destroyed, leaving their efforts more to keep the woods from catching fire than saving anything. The extra kerosene Jake stored in the spare room for winter created a series of explosions that lit up The Beach sky like July Fourth and brought out people from everywhere.

"Anybody know who lived here?" One of the firemen asked the crowd now assembled.

"I live here." Robert said.

"We all do," Bibsy said, pointing to herself and Junior.

The fireman walked toward them. "You have any idea how this started?" He said looking at each of them.

"Cigarettes, probably." Robert said then pointed to Bibsy. "Hers. Kept leavin em lit in ashtrays everywhere."

"Well, it's usually that or wood stoves or kerosene heaters or lamps down here," he said. "You can expect everything's lost. You might be able to look through the rubble in the morning, not til then though cause it's gonna be pretty hot for awhile. But I don't think anything is gonna be salvaged from this one. Sorry." He turned and walked back to the smoldering house that other firemen continued to douse with their hoses.

Bibsy was hurt by Robert's accusation. She didn't remember leaving a lit cigarette anywhere. But truthfully, of late everything had become foggy. The boys might have brought her attention to a burning cigarette that she'd forgotten from time to time, so it seemed a likely scenario, but even if it was she could never have anticipated such a catastrophe due to sheer absentmindedness. The thought of being responsible for the devastation crushed Bibsy. The craving for a cigarette at that moment was so strong she couldn't fight it and asked if anyone in the crowd had one. A stranger stepped forward with one, lit it for her and gave her another for later. With shaking hands she took a drag and it did calm her momentarily. She nodded thanks to the stranger.

"It wasn't bad enough that Pop died," Robert said. "Now this."

“We ain’t got nothin now.” Junior said.

“You got your life, boy.” Big Mabel said. “Coulda been you all burnt up in there.”

“Thank God it wasn’t,” Bibsy said. “Thank God we made it out.”

That night they slept on pallets in Mabel’s living room between her moving boxes, and once again they were reminded that everybody was leaving The Beach.

The next morning Pastor Daniels and a couple of church ladies from Holy Mount Baptist Church arrived offering their assistance. That was all he’d gotten a chance to say before Manny drove up with Katherine and Josh. They all rushed over to the boys and Bibsy as soon as Manny parked the car.

“You all are a sight for sore eyes.” Manny said, embracing Junior and Robert as one. “I held my breath when I heard about it, hoping everybody got out safe.”

Katherine came over to Bibsy and hugged her. “Thank God you’re all safe.”

“And that’s just the one you need ta thank...God.” Pastor said to an accompaniment of amens behind him. “It was God that saved you. Don’t ever forget that.”

“How did it start?” Josh asked no one in particular.

“Cigarette, I guess.” Bibsy repeated what she heard Robert say. “I musta went to sleep with one lit. I can’t believe it. I'm so sorry." Bibsy faced the boys with her apology. "I don't even remember it."

"You don't havta apologize, Miz Bibsy. It was an accident." Junior said. "I'm sorry we lost our stuff, but I'm glad that house is gone. Hated livin there anyway."

"At least nobody got hurt. Everybody's safe. That's the main thing." Josh said, shaking hands with Pastor Daniels and acknowledging the few church ladies with him.

"Now, the one thing we have to do is find you all someplace to live. But now you need everything." Josh looked down the road at the charred remains of the house. "What a shame. I need ta take a look at this." He began walking toward their burnt home and the others followed.

The church group and Manny's family walked over to where their home once stood to get a closer look. Junior, Robert and Bibsy stayed back but watched their reactions carefully, even how they covered their noses as they got near. Watching them point at the heap that was once their home forced her to look away.

When they returned Pastor said, "You all got a whole lot to be thankful for. Yessiree. A whole lot. God spared your lives."

"Now we gotta find y'all someplace to stay, quick." Manny said. "Pastor told me him and his wife have an extra room, but y'all might haveta split up. We got an extra bed at home. Gimme a coupla days and I know I can find you all an apartment somewhere." Manny was animated as his plan took shape. "How about letting the boys go with Pastor, and Bibsy you can stay with us until we can find a place for alla y'all?"

"Bibsy, I know of a place in Kancy that might still be available, but it might not be big enough for all of you together," Mabel said. "It's over a diner on South Broadway. I can take you over there to see it. It might be big enough, but I don't think so."

"That's a good lead... "Katherine began before Robert cut in.

"I don't want to go to Kancy," he said. "Why can't we go stay with Uncle Gus and Aunt Carrie down south? I wanna get far away from here."

"No son." Josh said. "The south ain't a safe place for colored boys right now."

He looked around at the others. "Y'all heard about that Emmett Till boy? It was in the Jet a coupla weeks ago."

Bibsy and the boys were the only ones who hadn't heard about it.

"He wasn't but ten-years-old." Katherine added.

"Said he whistled at a white woman. Pshhh...I don't believe it." Mabel added.

"Even if he did he didn't deserve what he got," came from one of the churchwomen.

"I don't wanna live with her no more." Robert said without looking at Bibsy. "She might burn us up next."

Big Mabel stood up from the porch steps and the sudden movement further magnified her large size. "You hush up bein so ornery, Robert. You know better. Don't think you're too big ta be knocked down ta size. And you're really disrespectin your father talkin like that."

"We don't haveta find a place together." Bibsy said, making a courageous effort to hide her embarrassment and guilt. "Maybe it's best if we go our separate ways. If that'll make them happy," she said unconsciously rubbing the urn cradled in her arms.

"And the way she carries on about that thing." Robert pointed to the urn. "Our daddy ain't in there. Ain't nothin in there but some dust. Me and Junior already looked in it."

Manny stepped forward and grabbed Robert by the collar and pulled him aside. He took him far enough away so they were out of earshot of everyone. Pastor Daniels and Josh joined them. The men stood scolding him. Then Robert could be seen talking, and it went back and forth like that for awhile before they came back to the group and Robert walked over to Bibsy.

"Sorry for bein disrespectful, Miz Bibsy," he said and walked away.

Except for his anger, the boy had a striking resemblance to Jake. Bibsy was so struck by the likeness at that moment she hesitated before answering. "That's alright Robert. I know you're just upset. Me too."

Manny, Josh and Pastor Daniels asked Bibsy to step away from the group with them so they could now talk privately. Pastor Daniels began, "This is a mighty delicate situation right here. Yes it is, Miz Bibsy."

"What's going on?" Bibsy said. "It's alright if they don't wanna live with me no more. Especially if they're not gonna be happy. I grew up not happy where I lived so I wouldn't force that on em."

"Okay. Okay." Manny said. "It's a little complicated but we'll work it out. The other problem is the boys ain't got no people left around here. Jake's folks is gone an Gertie wasn't from around here an she didn't keep up with her people no way. Gus and Carrie's down south. We'll get it straight, though."

As soon as Manny stopped talking, Pastor Daniels piped in. "Miz Bibsy, I'd like ta have your blessing to keep the boys with me for awhile. My wife and me have taken in some foster kids in the past. I might be able to turn that Robert around. Right now he's too mad ta think straight. He wants to quit school and go inta the service. I think I can work on that. Good Lord willing. The older boy I see is more too himself. And somethin like this is likely ta put him even deeper in a shell."

They all looked at Junior who stood off from everybody aimlessly peeling the bark from a stick he'd found. Bibsy was grateful for his calm demeanor throughout this chaos and so appreciated him saying the fire wasn't her fault. As much as she tried to hold onto that thought, a single glimpse of Robert in his full blown anger erased it.

"If that's where they wanna be, it's fine with me." Bibsy was so deeply hurt by Robert's anger and the enormity of the situation that she struggled staying focused on their conversation. "I wanna look for a place, but, I don't have any money now. All the money I put aside got burnt up in the fire."

"Don't worry about that. We'll help you with that." The three men dug in their pockets and between them handed Bibsy fifteen dollars. "This should hold you for a bit. Tomorrow's Sunday. I'll take up a special offering for you." Pastor Daniels said.

"We got an extra bed so you can come stay with us until we find you a place," Manny said.

"I think I'd rather stay here with Mabel for awhile, if she'll have me. Then I can keep my job and save enough to move."

"Oh yeah." Manny said. "That's true. Good idea."

"We'll keep an eye on the boys from time to time so you won't have ta worry." Josh added.

After that, everyone said their goodbyes.

Junior gave Bibsy a kiss on the cheek saying, "I'll stay in touch, Miz Bibsy."

Robert got into the car without saying a word. Bibsy and Mabel sat on the porch waving goodbye which Junior returned with a half smile. But Robert looked straight ahead, never even giving them eye contact as they pulled off.

Chapter Nineteen

It wasn't long before people, many of them total strangers to Bibsy, began stopping by Big Mabel's to drop off food, money, clothes and all kinds of household items. A couple she barely knew but remembered seeing on The Beach came over and donated towels and five dollars. A white woman she didn't know stuffed two dollars and rosary beads in Bibsy's hand and left without saying a word. Bibsy's job took a collection for her and some of her co-workers brought in used clothes for her and the boys. Her boss donated two sweaters for each of them and gave Bibsy twenty dollars.

Without ringing the bell, Bibsy dropped off a bundle of used clothes and the new cardigans at the parsonage of Holy Mount Baptist. Pausing first to inspect the button holes, she placed the sweaters within a neatly wrapped bundle with a note explaining they were for Junior and Robert, along with two five-dollar bills. Assured Junior would be glad to see her, and equally certain Robert wouldn't, Bibsy knew she couldn't handle his rejection so left without seeing either of them.

The first Sunday after the fire, Pastor Daniels came by and gave Bibsy an envelope with sixty dollars in it from the special collection taken at Holy Mount, saying he and his wife added to it to round off the total. The money was inside a bible he handed to her. He said the boys were doing well and they were good kids, but loved the television more than most. He also said their school took a collection and the kids brought in lots of clothes and even winter coats for them; and Robert's football team chipped in to replace the cleats he lost in the fire. The mention of the word fire in the same sentence with the boys initiated pain, but she was glad to hear they were getting along well and seemed to be in good hands.

On her way home from her first day back to work, Bibsy stopped off and purchased a pint of Jack Daniels and three packs of cigarettes before reaching Mabel's place. It irritated Bibsy that every time she lit a cigarette she could feel Big Mabel watching her every move, which only reminded her more of the fire, so Bibsy got in the habit of having an evening drink and smoking on the porch steps each night. When she came inside from the cool October air she'd lay down on her pallet hoping to fall asleep right away before another cigarette craving. The aid of a few drinks helped her to sleep but did nothing to cease her nightly dreams of a blinding bright fire. Mabel had already awakened her from one of those dreams, saying Bibsy was screaming in her sleep.

Given the amount of scolding the nuns doled out over the years, the most Bibsy ever aspired to in the hereafter was an extended stay in Purgatory where her tainted soul could be sufficiently purified until she merited entry into heaven. That had always been her expectation because the nuns convinced her heaven was out of the question. Until the fire, she was certain the few blemishes on her soul warranted no worse. However, feeling responsible for coming so close to killing the boys and herself, must surely be worthy of God's condemnation. And her soul, she was sure would now be destined to burn in hell eternally just as Sister Mary Margaret predicted.

Over the next few days and nights she couldn't shake the remembrance of Robert's disgust as the boys pulled off in Pastor Daniels' car. It wasn't even that Bibsy could recall the exact words Robert said, but the hostility he exuded was pure hatred, and painfully familiar. It reminded her of the contempt she lived with every day of her childhood.

Mabel and Bibsy were alike in that neither of them had much to say unless spoken to; and it created long stretches of silence between them broken only by the need to communicate necessary information. One evening Bibsy was on the porch having her now customary few drinks and cigarettes with Jake's urn by her side, and she began talking to herself, "I didn't do it on purpose. It was an accident. I see how some people are looking at me. Shoot...they act like I'd do something like that on purpose."

Mabel sat in the house listening to every word. The next evening she joined Bibsy on the porch with her own drink and said, "Bibsy, I think you need to get away from this place. Even this whole town. Too many bad memories for you here. You was already grieving Jake when this happened. The boys are in good hands, and Robert'll come around eventually. He's just too hurt right now. Pastor Daniels and his wife have taken in lots of youngsters for years and did well by em. You need ta try and live your life now."

Only occasionally aware she should have been looking for an apartment, but confused as to where to begin, Bibsy was grateful Mabel offered direction. Bibsy's confusion and lack of initiative lay in her belief that she'd done something so horrible the boys not only didn't need her in their lives, they obviously didn't want her around anymore, at least Robert certainly didn't. Because of his strong likeness to his father, it was as though she'd let Jake down. That was an acknowledgement too painful to endure without a few drinks to ease its sting. Everything wrong happened so fast she couldn't keep up with the many details. Maybe it wouldn't be as hard living somewhere else. Maybe a new town and living situation would help.

Wishing she had Martha's new phone number and address was a constant. But Bibsy was forced to accept that it was destroyed along with everything else in the suitcase, including her money, and the few pieces of her life worth saving. She and Mabel had even gone over to the charred remnants of the house nosing around for it, but found nothing. Only ashes atop a blackened brick foundation remained from the aged wood frame house that was home.

"You know what, you might be right." Bibsy said. "Maybe another town would do me good."

"Where's your people Bibsy? I heard you got family in The City. You know their phone number or address? We should call them too. We could look it up. I could ask around for a City phone book in town."

"No, I don't remember the number, and besides, my sister and them moved. They bought a house somewhere in The City. Probably not even in the phone book yet. She just gave me the address and phone number a little while ago." Bibsy didn't want to admit to Mabel that she couldn't even remember her sister's married name either. With the recent series of stressful situations there were a number of things slipping through spacious gaps in her memory, but attributed it to temporary lapses due to the recent stress.

"I'll make a few calls from Woolworth's tomorrow." Mabel looked around at the donated bags and boxes occupying most of the porch and said, "All you probably need is a bed for now."

After a few phone calls the following day Mabel came home with news that Bibsy could look at an apartment the next evening after work, which they did. On the drive to see it Mabel told Bibsy four times in the car not to mention anything about the fire and to tell the landlord she was new in town but had enough money to cover the rent for two months until she found a job.

Bibsy was glad to see the apartment was in the middle of downtown Kancy with a fair amount of people coming and going, and hoped being in the midst of so much action would help her escape the sour mood she was stuck in. However, listening to Mabel's voice reverberate against the empty shell of high ceilings, plaster walls and hardwood floors, Bibsy thought the three large rooms might be too much space for her. After asking if he had anything smaller, the landlord said it was the smallest place he had and she probably wouldn't find anything smaller anywhere in town.

Walking through the apartment Bibsy and Mabel peeked in the bathroom and smiled at each other just seeing it. Bibsy flushed the toilet simply because it was there. The large kitchen Bibsy didn't think would get much use, but she couldn't fight the urge to turn on the water at the kitchen sink and light the gas stove. Mabel reminded Bibsy of all the donations she had and assured her the echo would go away once she began to fill it with her things and got some furniture. Bibsy's head was spinning and her insides trembling from the thought of suddenly having sole responsibility for herself. Fortunately Mabel knew what questions to ask the landlord and guided her through.

With Mabel doing all of the brokering, Bibsy agreed to take the place, despite the landlord's no-pets policy.

"No pets." He was firm.

"Aw, he's just a lil pup." Bibsy used her hands to demonstrate how small. "He won't get into anything."

"If you're bringing the dog, you can't have the place. Sorry. Animals have ruined too many of my apartments over the years. And it's in the lease, so if you bring it in anyway, I can ask you to leave. You tell me what you want to do," he said, before stepping aside leaving Bibsy and Mabel to discuss it.

"Bibsy, you've gotta take it. The deadline ta leave The Beach is a week away, and I'm leavin in a few days myself. You don't have time ta look for another place. I'll take Tiger with me so you don't haveta worry. He'll be fine with me up on The Hill. Really. Come on, you can't say no now."

Bibsy reluctantly agreed to the rental terms and the other hitch was she had to forego the customary new coat of paint if she wanted the place that weekend. She didn't even notice the need for paint. She was more concerned about the echo in the apartment, but signed an agreement to pay thirty dollars a month and secured the keys to her first apartment.

Leaving The Beach was more emotional than Bibsy anticipated. Her co-workers were sorry to find out she was going but understood how much hurt was associated with Haverton and wished her well. She hesitated at first, but ultimately decided to leave ten dollars and a note stuck in the parsonage door for Junior and Robert informing them that she was moving and left her new address in case they wanted to visit or even write.

When Mabel's cousin and nephew came to move her to Springville to live with her family, she arranged for them to move Bibsy to Kancy first and they refused to accept her money once Mabel told them about the fire. Mabel said, The Hill section of Springville was all colored and nothing like The Beach, but it was the closest resemblance around and that's where she wanted to settle.

Mabel's cousin was jabbering away at the wheel in a one-way conversation when they pulled off, Bibsy in deep thought. She looked down the road at the charred heap that was once her home and remembered the day Jake showed her how to prepare a chicken for dinner. They stood in the kitchen, his big hand swallowing hers as he guided her through every joint, around each bone, feeling for cartilage like a map until the bird was transformed into recognizable pieces. His touch, something that used to radiate its own current through her, was gone forever. She remembered her arrival two years ago when she and Jake laughed and joked their way down the rutted road and how she bounced all over the seat of Jake's truck. It seemed so long ago.

Mabel followed the truck in her car for the half-hour trip to Kancy and Bibsy was deeply grateful she was at the helm supervising the move because Mabel had the presence of mind to ask the men to stop at the second-hand store on Franklin Street where Bibsy bought a mattress and box spring on a bed frame and paid five dollars down on the matching dresser on which Bibsy agreed to make weekly payments. Although the purchase depleted most of the money she had left, she'd been sleeping on the floor since the fire and looked forward to a mattress again.

Once she'd moved in, Bibsy thanked Mabel and her family and gave Tiger a goodbye hug that brought tears to her eyes she hadn't expected. Because Bibsy had so little to move, they left in short order to return to Haverton and begin Mabel's move.

Bibsy placed Jake's urn by the bed and was so tired she slept until the next morning. Sorting through some of the boxes and bags of donations when she woke, Bibsy came across a stack of ashtrays with deep bowls which she promptly distributed two to a room, including the bathroom, and four in the living room. Her trauma from the fire wasn't enough to stop her from smoking, actually she smoked even more since, but she became vigilant about making certain her cigarettes were extinguished when she put them down. So fearful of using ashtrays to merely rest her lit cigarettes, she began the practice of holding onto them whenever she smoked, and became obsessive about discarding ashes and butts in the toilet every ten minutes, complete with flushing.

Trying to hold onto the little money she had, Bibsy ordered coffee and toast from the coffee shop beneath her apartment, then went back upstairs and slept through the next day as well until hunger pangs woke her in the middle of the night. The next day she sorted through the rest of the donated items and found an envelope with two dollars in it which she used along with the two she had and bought peanut butter and jelly along with a loaf of bread and two packs of cigarettes from the A&P down the street.

Rested, but feeling financial pressure and needing to find a job, Bibsy left the apartment in search of work.

Walking around town to get familiar with the area and keeping her eyes open for "Help Wanted" signs, Bibsy soon realized that Kancy was a riverfront village like Haverton, only larger. Haverton streets were narrow and more compact with houses built tightly together. It was obvious Kancy was a more prosperous community, evident by the number of thriving businesses and shops downtown.

When she walked along Broadway and the businesses started being replaced with increasingly larger homes with expansive lawns, and fewer people on the sidewalks, she instinctively turned around and headed back toward the more populated downtown area where she felt more comfortable. As she fingered the lone dollar in her dress pocket, she saw a colored woman leaving from the rear entrance of a Victorian home with pink and red roses beneath a wrap-around porch. Noticing two wooden chairs that had been set out on the sidewalk, she went over to inspect them and decided one was in decent enough condition to take home. Bibsy stood with the back of the chair under her arm, and waited until the colored woman exiting the house made her way down the long walkway of the property and asked, "Are there any factories around here?"

"You're on the wrong side of town for that," the woman smiled. "There's a pocketbook factory in the other direction. Turn right on Cedar Hill. You can't miss it. It's pretty big."

"Thanks," Bibsy said more loudly than she needed but hoping to drown out the sound of her stomach growling.

Bibsy followed the woman's directions, stopping by her apartment first to drop off her "new" chair and spruce up her hair; combing and pinning it down with bobby pins. Her clothes were spread out all over the kitchen counter, radiators and the bed in hopes of reducing the wrinkles in the fabric.

"Jake, I have to get an iron when I get a job. Remember that old-fashioned iron we had on The Beach that we had to heat on top of the wood stove? And I didn't mind it neither, Jake. Not at all." Grabbing the rosary beads she headed for the door. "Jake, I hope we can get this job cause we need money right now," Bibsy said to the urn as she left. "See you when I get back."

Fortunately the factory was in the midst of an added hiring cycle to fill Christmas orders, and she got the job. After expressing an eagerness to begin, she was able to start her new job the next day. Even though she'd never experienced a problem finding a job before, Bibsy felt relief and a needed sense of accomplishment once she got it and looked forward to expanding her choice of meals beyond peanut butter and jelly sandwiches as soon as she received her first paycheck.

There was so much activity on the street below her living room window on Broadway that people-watching became her new form of entertainment. A dry cleaners, Chinese hand laundry, bicycle shop, restaurant, a vintage car dealership and laundromat were visible from her front window. The businesses all had apartments above them like hers and sometimes she could see the families inside the large windows. An A&P and post office were in walking distance and a bus headed for New York City stopped right in front of the coffee shop downstairs. Her evenings were spent sitting in her newly acquired chair sipping a drink and smoking cigarettes watching the lives of others.

She wished she hadn't had to give Tiger away and wondered if Mabel would allow the dog to cuddle in her lap the way Bibsy did.

"Jake, I tried to keep him. Especially since it was Rain's puppy." There was a short silence before Bibsy continued. "I know you didn't ask me, but I'm tellin you anyway."

Over the next several weeks all of Bibsy's free time was spent in her front room window being a spectator on life, looking at the people below so frequently she soon felt the rhythm of the street. Watching the shopkeepers open their stores in the morning, aware of the hourly schedule of the bus to and from The City, becoming familiar with the flow of the residents on the streets and the regular patrons frequenting the various shops, Bibsy began to feel comfortable enough in her new surroundings to venture outside and explore the town of Kancy a little more thoroughly. Constantly hearing the echo of her footsteps every time she walked across the wood floors, or that of her own voice when she talked to Jake, encouraged Bibsy to explore outside as well.

One weekend she discovered Memorial Park on the water where she sat on the pier thinking about Jake and the life they shared so recently. The river didn't look or feel the same without him near and she decided to bring him with her on future explorations of the town. The next weekend she sat in the same spot admiring the river like old times.

"Now ain't this just like before?" She said to Jake's urn in the shopping bag sitting on the bench beside her. "Didn't I tell you?"

At the factory there was a bin of pocketbooks with slight imperfections for sale at a fraction of their wholesale cost which Bibsy looked in every week until she found a large leather bag with a shoulder strap that seemed more suitable as an overnight valise than a pocketbook. She thought it a perfect carrier for Jake.

Now that Bibsy was able to carry Jake's urn in the oversized pocketbook as she became acquainted with the village, as the weeks went by she began to point out various sights to him along the way, oblivious to how she might appear to anyone passing.

"Look at that dress," she said pointing at a store window on Main Street, "How do you think that would look on me?"

She secured Jake's ashes in the pocketbook one Friday evening, slipped the strap over her head so it hung diagonally across her chest, and walked through town enjoying the night sights.

"Look Jake, it's a full moon tonight. Remember how we used to swim by the moonlight and you'd get fresh in the water?" She said smiling at the memory.

Bibsy ventured inside a rowdy bar on a side street off Main; the music audible through its closed door.

"Two Jack Daniels and water, please."

"A double?"

"No. Two glasses." She said.

Bibsy sat listening to The Platters' song *Only You* on the jukebox while sipping her drink. "Come on Jake and drink up."

"Excuse me?" The bartender said. "Did you say something?"

"No. Not to you." She said. "Okay," she went on. "I'll drink it myself if you don't want it," she said and downed the second drink and left.

Bibsy returned the next Friday night repeating the same scenario. By the third visit, she ignored the bartender's suspicious glances and sat at the bar and ordered her usual drinks. He continued with his regular duties and talking with other patrons at the bar until a patron asked, "Did you go down to the opening of the bridge the other day?"

"No," he answered. "But I saw it in the paper. I'm a wait til it's safe. Once I see enough people get over and back a few times, I'll take my car across."

Bibsy laughed. “Jake, did you hear that? The Tappan Zee Bridge is opened.”

Although not as small as Haverton, Kancy was a small town, so it wasn’t long before people began to whisper about her and eventually her odd behavior in town came to the attention of her supervisor at work, who’d already caught her talking to herself more than once, and unbeknownst to her had begun to watch Bibsy more carefully. On her first day back to work after the nineteen-fifty-six New Year, she received a pink slip in her paycheck informing her that she had been fired.

“What’d I do?” She asked her supervisor.

“Oh, nothing. That was just temporary holiday work. We can go back to our regular work force now. Sorry. You got whatever vacation time that’s coming to you in your check.”

“You never said nothing about temporary work.”

Devastated and panicky, on her next visit to the bar she asked the bartender if he knew of any jobs available in town and he told her the housekeeping department at Kancy Hospital usually needed workers. Housekeeping never appealed to her but new circumstances forced her to reevaluate that rule. He told her how to get there and the next day she walked the mile uphill, with the pocketbook strapped across her as it had now become a permanent part of her attire.

After several inquiries, she found the person in charge of housekeeping and inquired of any openings. She was told there weren't any at the moment, but to call once a week because they frequently needed extra workers due to the high turnover.

Only after getting a reminder from the landlord did Bibsy remember to mail the money order for the next month's rent. She also bought enough food to last awhile and called the hospital from Kobin's Drug Store every few days to check on openings. In the meantime, she began to ask anybody, even strangers if they knew of anyone needing help anywhere, but there was nothing available so soon after the holiday season. As time passed she was willing to do anything and found a job as a dishwasher in a diner on Main Street but the job only lasted a day because she wasn't fast enough. But she did get a day's pay.

Finally, on one of her frequent calls to the hospital three weeks after she inquired, Bibsy found out there was an opening and she should come in and fill out an application at the end of the week. Bibsy was excited when she was told she could begin the following Monday morning.

She came home laughing and in a good mood, even ignoring her echo in the room. "See, I told you I was gonna find something. You didn't believe me." She said and positioned her ear as though listening for a reply, then said. "I know you had faith in me all along. I was just kiddin. Thank you, Jake."

On her start date in mid-January Bibsy was a half hour early for her 7 a.m. shift. Greeting her supervisor, Bibsy was bubbly with excitement about working again.

"Good morning!" Bibsy was vibrant and upbeat.

"Good morning, Elizabeth. You're going to work with Marilyn today. She'll show you the ropes. Do whatever she tells you until you get the hang of it and can work on your own. And you can put your pocketbook in your locker. Marilyn will show you where that is."

Her new co-worker showed her the row of metal lockers for the housekeeping staff and gave her a light blue uniform which she changed into. Bibsy put her clothes and pocketbook into the locker, patting the leather bag containing Jake's ashes before closing its door.

"I'll be back soon." She whispered to Jake, but Marilyn had walked away to smoke a cigarette so hadn't heard her.

Everyday she'd walk to work with her satchel strapped across her front, even on those days when the weather was icy cold and the wind whipping against her face and legs and other workers were arranging carpools or taking taxis to work. Bibsy had a routine to look forward to and loved that she was earning money again. But it wasn't long before the work began to gnaw at her. She began to resent being expected to scrub the long hospital corridors on her hands and knees which provided daily reminders of the humiliations she suffered at St. Cecelia's. Marilyn told her that the supervisor always said they could use mops to pick up the excess water after the floors were scrubbed, but the mops weren't to be used without scrubbing them by hand first.

"And she can tell the difference. I don't know how, but she knows," Marilyn said.

"There've been many who tried to get away with doing it differently and got fired. So you might as well do it her way."

With that statement, Bibsy kept her mouth shut but over the next several weeks she became increasingly resentful of the work. She noticed that other members of the hospital staff either treated her with disrespect or as though she were invisible, often bumping into her saying, "I'm sorry, I didn't see you." This happened at least once a week and she couldn't understand in the midst of so many white people, in white uniforms even, and surrounded by white walls, how she couldn't be seen, as dark as she was.

Then one day she was on her hands and knees scrubbing the corridor when out of the blue she saw the water on the floor turn red and she tried to scrub it away. The red liquid became darker and thicker and as her hand grazed the nearby radiator she immediately remembered the ending of those horrible dreams she used to have. She was made to scrub Helen's blood from the floor and now, just like years before, her tears mingled with the red liquid in front of her. Bibsy looked up, and instead of seeing the registered nurse in her crisply starched uniform, she saw Sister Mary Margaret in her familiar habit.

Bibsy stood up and looked her squarely in her eyes saying, "You all killed her. You killed Helen and made me clean up her blood. I never did nothin to deserve that."

Clearly stunned, the nurse merely blinked without saying anything.

"Don't act like you didn't do nothin. We all saw it." Bibsy went on. "You didn't think I'd ever see you again."

The nurse calmly walked over to the nearby nurses' station where she picked up a telephone, but when she turned back around after finishing that short conversation Bibsy was gone. She went to her locker and retrieved her pocketbook and clothes and left the hospital through the emergency staircase still wearing her uniform.

Finally remembering the end of that recurring nightmare rattled her so thoroughly when she got home Bibsy paced back and forth saying repeatedly, "They made me clean it up. They made me clean up her blood..."

After running out of cigarettes Bibsy grabbed her pocketbook and left the apartment and wound up at the bar she'd been frequenting. It was the middle of the week and not too many people were there but the jukebox was playing.

The bartender set up her usual two shot glasses and asked had she ever heard the song playing on the jukebox. "It's new. Just came in today."

Bibsy cocked her head and listened to the harmonizing of Frankie Lymon and The Teenagers singing *Why Do Fools Fall in Love,* and began rocking to the beat. Then she downed her drink and said, "Jake, let's dance," and went onto the small dance floor hugging her pocketbook, swaying suggestively to the music. After a few minutes she felt a tap on her shoulder.

A man was standing there saying, "Can I join you?"

He began dancing with Bibsy even though she was clearly ignoring him and enjoying being in her own world. When the record finished he joined her at the bar and asked the bartender to refill her drink. He looked quizzically at the two drinks the bartender set in front of Bibsy. "That's her usual, man." The bartender said. "Take it up with her."

Bibsy thanked the stranger and downed the two drinks, still moving to the music while sitting on the stool.

"What's your name?" He said.

"Bibsy," she said.

The man doubled over laughing at her name and Bibsy packed up her things and left the bar. He followed her outside and apologized for laughing, but Bibsy kept walking. When they were almost a block away he grabbed her by the arm and forcefully slammed her against a parked car.

"I said I was sorry. Where you goin?" He shouted.

Bibsy maneuvered away and ran toward the corner with the stranger chasing her, his fist now raised in the air. She spied an empty liquor bottle in a garbage can, grabbed it by the neck and cracked it against the metal rim of the can breaking off the bottom half leaving her with a jagged glass weapon that she wielded as if she meant to use it, and her quick maneuver stopped him on a dime.

"You touch me again and see what happens." She shouted at him, the moisture from her breath visible in the cold February air.

He paced back and forth awhile looking into her wild vacant eyes seeming to reassess the situation and walked back to the bar cursing her.

After that incident, Bibsy decided to stay at home for awhile. Ever since the experience at Kancy Hospital and the bar she was convinced Sister Mary Margaret was after her. She even thought she saw her in the apartment from time to time, catching the fabric from her long flowing habit swish by late at night. Fortunately, after being home several days she received a final check from the hospital along with a dismissal letter formally letting her go. Again, Bibsy paid the rent only after she received a notice to do so, and ventured out only for food, cigarettes and liquor. Then Bibsy contentedly positioned herself at her favorite spot at the front window for the next several weeks.

Watching people from the front window became her new job. Sitting there until she became acquainted with her neighbors, sometimes watching them in their apartments across the street above the stores, she'd pretend to be part of their family gatherings. And sometimes gaining a sense of familiarity with the commuters who waited each morning together in front of the coffee shop she imagined herself returning with them in the evenings.

Bibsy put the March rent notice on the kitchen counter and forgot about it until she got a knock on the door one day from the landlord on the tenth of the month. She'd been responsive to his reminders previously and now that more time had lapsed he paid her a personal visit. By this time she subsisted on a diet of only peanut butter.

"I didn't receive your rent this month Miss Randolph. Did you forget?"

"No. I lost my job. But I'll get another one and make it up." Bibsy was sitting at the living room window with a coat on and a cigarette in her hand. "You don't have to worry."

"Can you give me anything towards it, something?"

"I don't have it right now." She said flatly.

"Okay. I'll work with you a little while but don't let another month go by without catching up or you'll force me to take legal action. I wouldn't want to do that because you seem like a nice lady," he said looking around at the sheets tacked to the windows and the sparse furniture in the apartment and the dense smell of cigarette smoke. "I'll give you two more weeks, then I'll be back to collect the rent you owe. Do you have a phone in here? A call would save me the trouble of coming all the way over here."

"Nope. Don't need one."

"Okay then. I'll see you in two weeks. Good luck finding a job. Did you try over to the pocketbook factory?"

"Yeah. Been there...that didn't work out. I'll find somethin, don't worry."

Bibsy was nervous after the landlord left. Throughout his visit their voices were echoing through the apartment and his loud voice invoked an even greater fear than she had before. Her mind raced through a blank inventory of possibilities to get money. She was afraid to go out and look for another job. After receiving a threatening cut-off notice from the power company she'd already gone out and bought a kerosene lamp from the hardware store for each room. Bibsy never missed the loss of the stove when the power was shut off because she never used it.

When she brought them home and lit a lamp in each room she said, "Jake, don't this remind you of The Beach? I thought you'd like it." A contented smile brightened her face.

Resuming her daily position at her living room window, Bibsy began to imagine the adventure people waiting at the commuter bus stop were having going into New York City every day and coming home almost in group fashion. They seemed to be pleasant enough people who all treated each other in such a congenial fashion, always smiling at one another and engaging in what appeared from a distance to be polite conversation. Eventually she began to mistake their pleasantries as a deeper bond and imagined them going as a group to the same place of work; keeping each other company throughout the day and coming back home together. Then she imagined Martha would be at the other end of the bus stop to welcome her and take her to her sister's new home. Maybe she'd have the children with her. One day she woke up in a panic because she couldn't find Junior and Robert in the apartment and apologized to Jake for having lost the boys.

Continually watching the same group of people commute to The City in the morning, then arriving back safely in the evening made the possibility of joining them seem more real every day. She thought what a nice outing it would be to go into The City for the day.

Not much more time passed when very early one morning she said, "Jake, maybe we'll see Martha and visit like we used to."

She got up from the chair, went into the bathroom to wash and get dressed, took out her last five dollars, made two peanut butter sandwiches and went downstairs and stood with the commuters she'd seen daily, smiling at each of them as though they were all old acquaintances. When the bus came she paid her seventy-five-cent fare and sat down in the cushioned seat, smiling at herself anticipating another visit into New York City like she'd had with Jake in the past.

Chapter Twenty

Like the rest of the commuters on the bus Bibsy got off at the last stop, the George Washington Bridge Port of Authority Bus Terminal, and was drawn along with the rush of the crowd through the bus station depot along winding corridors and descending steps. She mimicked the person in front of her who bought ten tokens for a dollar and fifty cents, placed one in the slot and went through the turnstile. Eventually she found herself on the subway platform at 175th Street waiting for the express A Train. She smiled to herself at the feeling of competence and determination so evident among the throng she believed to be a part of.

As the express train approached and people began to make their way on, she filed in with them and sat on one of the rattan bench seats and began amusing herself with the local train stations whizzing by in a blur. Lulled by the train's steady rocking motion she soon nodded off. When she woke, Bibsy was at Times Square and panicked momentarily because she didn't remember why she was on the train or how she got there, and none of the people looked familiar anymore. Dismissing her initial unease and opting instead for the potential adventure ahead, Bibsy soon settled down to explore the massive station that held many more people enroute to their destinations or other connecting trains. Constantly being nudged or bumped, as she walked much slower than the commuting public, she held tightly to her pocketbook containing Jake's ashes strapped across her chest.

Eventually finding comfort in the company of so many other people who didn't seem to pose any threat, Bibsy was thrilled at magically being thrust into the swirl of what was the essence of The City. She saw herself taking part in an audacious outing even as she was unsure how she became an active participant.

"Jake, we ain't been down here before. This is exciting, right?" Bibsy said unaware that people gave her a wide berth when she passed while in the midst of her dialogue with Jake.

Quickly tiring of the walk she got back on the A Train then got off at Hoyt-Schermerhorn simply because she liked the name of the train station. Getting in with another group of people, she found herself on the GG Train and unknowingly headed into Brooklyn. Her random movements from one train to another went on for hours. As schools let out and the trains began filling with students heading for home, she was reminded of the boys.

"Where's Junior and Robert, Jake? How come they're not with us?" Bibsy looked closely through the crowd of children hoping to spot them. "They mighta started playin with these kids already," she said completely unfazed by the children moving away into the next car.

Thoughts of the boys had a short lifespan once she took out a peanut butter sandwich and began to eat. That finished, Bibsy got on and off trains randomly. When she found herself on a train that began its ascent above ground and eventually elevated above street level, she thought it was thrilling as she gazed excitedly through the dirty glass pane of the subway window at the bustle of so many below.

"Isn't this great Jake? Look at all of these people!" Bibsy said as the woman seated next to her moved to sit elsewhere.

Once the Number 7 Train stopped at the last station in Flushing she sat still as before and waited for the train to begin its reverse course. As the engines revved up to repeat its run Bibsy felt as though she'd figured out a new game and her excitement matched that of children on an amusement park ride, even clapping once the train headed back underground.

She ambled from one train to another the rest of the day. When the evening rush hour started, she fell in with that group and this time wound up back in Queens in an elevated train along Jamaica Avenue, and once outside was surprised to see night had fallen. Briefly thinking there was something familiar sounding about the name “Queens” she couldn’t remember what, and the thought, like others before it, soon vanished.

She got on and off a few more trains before finding herself at Grand Central Station where she exited and sat on a nearby platform bench and pulled out the last peanut butter sandwich she’d made for the outing. Topping off her meal with a cigarette, Bibsy found a public restroom, then got on the D Train headed uptown to the last stop and waited until it went back downtown. As time passed and noticing there were fewer people riding on the trains with her, she kept going. As the number of people on the subway cars diminished from standing room only, to half full, to several people, to just herself and maybe one or two other people, to often being the only person on the subway car, she only then became concerned and it was no longer a game.

Reacting to boredom, she tried doing what she’d seen others do and walk through one subway car to the next. However seeing the train speed across the rails was too frightening and she sat back down. Tiring of the trains and needing sleep, she looked at her Timex for the first time since she waited at the bus stop and was alarmed to see it was one o’clock.

“We should be heading home now, Jake. It’s late.”

Being underground all day and unaware whether it was one o’clock in the afternoon or early morning, Bibsy decided it was now time to go home, yet only then determined she didn’t remember how to get there. All she could remember of home was The Beach and asked the few passersby where it was, but when she couldn’t distinguish which beach she meant they all left unable to assist her. Bibsy's panic increased as she searched all the signs around her for direction, but found none directing her to anywhere sounding familiar. Finally, she spotted a token booth and crossed the turnstile to approach the operator seated inside.

"How many?" He said without looking up from counting. When no money was shoved through the small opening, his eyes met hers. "Can I help you?"

"I'm trying to get to The Beach. I need to get home."

"Where, Coney Island?"

"No."

"Orchard Beach? Rockaway Beach?"

"No." She said, then more loudly, "Just The Beach!"

"Lady, I don't know what you're talkin about. Are you sure it's in New York City? I need more information than that."

"Why don't these people know where The Beach is, Jake?" She said. "They know but they just don't wanna tell me."

The token booth operator now inspected her more closely, leaning forward to get a better glimpse of her below the neckline which was the only thing visible from his vantage point. The bobby pins in Bibsy's hair had loosened and her dress was wrinkled. The sweater she wore had become slightly soiled from her day of riding the trains, and of course she carried Jake in her usual fashion.

"Looks like you need help, miss. Maybe I should signal a police officer to help you. I don't know where you're talkin about."

Associating the words "police officer" with some vague unknown horror, not even realizing it was because the policemen delivered news of Jake's death, she bolted away from the token booth and quickly took out one of her tokens and hurriedly moved through the turnstile and down the length of the platform out of his sight and waited for the next train.

Unaware that due to late hour the trains were on an infrequent schedule, after waiting several minutes Bibsy went to the very end of the platform to hide. Sitting with her back against the cold porcelain tiled wall she took out one of her five remaining cigarettes and smoked it before dozing off. The sound of the train woke her and she got on. After finding a newer rattan seat with no loose stems to prick her legs through her dress Bibsy lay across it and the train's steady rocking motion lulled her to sleep while holding tight to her pocketbook, saying goodnight to Jake before dozing off. Bibsy was awakened in an hour by a subway conductor who told her she'd have to get up and move because the train was going out of service for the night. She got up and found a bench on the subway platform and curled up on it and went to sleep until she heard a train approaching the platform in front of her.

The next day she repeated her wanderings through the subway system, minus the fun game it had been initially. Confused and becoming increasingly afraid, she desperately wanted to go home. She was out of sandwiches and bought candy bars at a newsstand inside the 59th Street-Columbus Circle station.

Riding the subways all day and eventually finding herself on the LL line through Brooklyn, she was surprised to find another night had fallen once the train meandered out of the tunnel. Boarding and disembarking trains at random from one subway line to another, Bibsy stowed away in the corner of a subway and found herself in a rail yard all night where she slept on a train until the next morning when she was awakened by daylight pouring through the grimy windows.

Making her way through another day of riding the subways, she used the last of her money to purchase more candy. She hazily remembered she got there with a group of people and told Jake, "Maybe if we follow them we'll get home," she said trailing another group of commuters in hopes of getting home. Not realizing they weren't following a group pattern, but getting on and off to their individual destinations, Bibsy was further confused and continued her wandering journey underground. When she came across a man with no legs in a wheelchair begging with a tin cup she gave him one of her candy bars since she didn't have anymore money to offer and he nodded a thanks.

During the daytime rush hours she'd ask people if they knew where The Beach was but by now she was so dirty and disheveled that people ignored her or looked at her in disgust without answering. On her fourth night underground she fell asleep on the A Train and panicked when she woke in total darkness and all the other passengers were gone. The conductors and train personnel were gone. And the train wasn't moving, nor did she hear or feel the engine revving as if it was preparing to move. Since she'd left Kancy it was rare to get several hours sleep at one time, but the added rest didn't decrease her anxiety about her situation or fill her stomach which began regularly cramping from hunger.

However, the satchel around her neck provided needed comfort. "Jake, I don't know what happened, but we're gonna get outta here."

"Don't ask me where we are. I don't know."

Bibsy felt for the urn and sensed his protection as she'd always had when he was near. "I'm just glad you're here with me. We just gotta stay here til daylight then figure it out."

Searching in the bag for her candy bars and finding she had two left, Bibsy ate one and went back to sleep. Intense sunlight woke her. Looking out the window, Bibsy could see she was someplace where hundreds of subway cars were parked. Contemplating her next move Bibsy felt the rumble of the train's engine then soon after, heavy steps going from car to car heading in her direction.

When the uniformed conductor got to her car he said, "What are you doing here? You're not supposed to stay on these trains all night." He talked as he continued walking through inspecting the windows and seating areas. "I wanna see you get off at the first station we pull into."

Bibsy whispered to Jake, "I don't know where we are but we'll get off this train soon."

True to his word the conductor returned just as the train pulled into the next stop and ordered her off at Union Square where she began walking aimlessly up and down the platform. Approaching people arbitrarily while trying to find her way home, they all shunned her. By now her money and candy bars had run out and she felt severe hunger pangs that reminded her of those times at St. Cecelia's when, as punishment for the most minor infraction, she went to bed without supper. The memory prompted her to look around for Sister Mary Margaret and Bibsy became fearful and got up unexpectedly from her seat and ran on and off trains as though she were trying to lose someone chasing her.

By the middle of the fifth day her hunger pangs had gotten so intense that she began to ask strangers for money, and now she scanned the subway and platform floor for loose change. Bibsy wound her way through the underground world for a few more days begging and scrounging for food, hoping to quell the hunger pangs that had become more relentless than anything she'd ever experienced. Becoming weak from the constant state of hunger she moved even slower, carrying Jake's ashes guarded against her heart.

Her existence became that of hiding from conductors and Sister Mary Margaret, whom Bibsy became convinced was following her. Now she became desperate to find anyone she knew, and searched faces for familiarity, but found none and was now one of the people with their hand constantly held out begging for anything. However, their instincts convinced people this strange unkempt woman with a large pocketbook who talked to herself was someone to avoid.

Again Bibsy found herself at the Times Square station but this time stumbled onto the uptown Number 2 Train exhausted, and fell asleep. This time, she awoke at 125th Street surrounded by a subway car entirely of black passengers. Again disoriented, but this time examining faces for any hint of familiarity, she said to Jake, "Maybe we're finally headed home to The Beach, Jake. It sure is about time."

At the next stop, 135th Street, so many people exited the train she left with them hoping not to lose the first thread of connection she imagined to have with anyone since her odyssey had begun. Getting pulled out of the train with the rush of commuters she unsuccessfully tried to separate herself from them to get her bearings once on the subway platform. She lumbered along looking about but still headed in the same direction as the group toward the exit where she saw others gravitating, but a figure of a nun seated nearby caught her eye and she stopped cold, nearly creating a human pile up.

So stricken with fear Bibsy couldn't move until she observed brown-skinned hands extend from a dark gray habit clutching rosary beads and a cup. Bibsy stood watching her every move. Whenever anyone offered a donation into her cup she simply nodded acknowledgement, no words, maintaining silent prayer.

"Mary!" Bibsy said after several minutes passed and almost everyone had exited the train platform.

The nun remained still, her head cast slightly downward as she focused on her rosary-entwined hands holding a simple paper cup.

Before taking a timid step forward, Bibsy said, "Jake, I think that's my sister. I told you about her."

Bibsy stepped closer saying, "Mary, is that you?"

No response.

Gradually moving closer by mere inches, taking a brief assessment as she went, continuing ever so cautiously, Bibsy finally stood directly in front of the nun and said, "Mary, it's me Bibsy. Elizabeth."

Behind wire-rimmed glasses, the nun's eyes met Bibsy's just for a moment, long enough to confirm mutually that there was no connection between them, and she resumed her prayers.

"Oh. I thought you were my sister. She…she's," Bibsy fought to remember her sister's order but couldn't.

No response.

Then from seemingly nowhere she spewed out, "Oblate…in Baltimore," came from her lips.

With that the nun interrupted her prayers to look up more closely at Bibsy, then reached in a satchel handing Bibsy a business card that read The Franciscan Handmaids of Mary in Harlem, with the address on 124th Street, still never uttering a word. Bibsy took the card and stuffed it in her dress pocket and headed toward the stairway disappointed.

"Jake, I was so sure that was Mary."

After existing ten days underground, the dirt of the subway system that was evident on her body and clothing now began to affect her throat. Dirt and metal became the consistent taste in her mouth, and together with years of smoking and factory work, Bibsy developed a constant hacking cough that wouldn't cease. In spite of it, she smoked the stub of her last remaining cigarette and ventured outside. A blinding sun met her as she leisurely made her way up the subway stairs forcing her to stop midway. Using her hand to shield her eyes, Bibsy peeked over the top of the landing, but having grown unaccustomed to direct daylight could not stand to look for long. Repeated blinking offered no aid to the light sensitivity she experienced.

Unconsciously scanning her surroundings to assess any threat, Bibsy looked into the many brown faces of the people hurrying past her hoping to find recognition, but no one materialized among the hurrying throng scattering in different directions. Thoughts of the nun in the subway continued as she forced herself to face the daylight, casting her head downward as she went.

Stretching as she made it to the top of the stairwell, there was a sense of something slightly familiar but didn't know what. She looked at the street and its cobble-stoned surface sensing faraway familiarity.

The evening sun began setting, casting a few final beams of light between brownstones while Bibsy looked up at the street sign, Lenox Avenue. She peered into a garbage can in front of a coffee shop and ruffled through searching for a morsel of sustenance. Finding a paper cup with a corner of coffee still at the bottom, she lifted it to her lips. After finishing and throwing the empty cup back in the can, she felt slight pressure on the small of her back and Bibsy turned to face the nun from the subway whose reassuring hand began to guide her, and they headed down the street together.

About the Author

Brenda Ross has honed her craft through years of writing workshops, a B.A. degree in creative writing from SUNY Empire State College, and finally completing "Bibsy" in The Novel writing course at Sarah Lawrence College.

The idea for "Bibsy" began decades ago with its first chapter entering onto the page at a writers' retreat at Skidmore College, August 1980.

She currently resides in Rockland County, New York and works part time as an editorial assistant for a daily newspaper in Westchester County. "Bibsy" is her first work of fiction.

CPSIA information can be obtained
at www.ICGtesting.com
Printed in the USA
FFOW02n1606080615
14035FF

9 781496 965899